The Trillionist

Sagan Jeffries

To Vanessa

Enjoy

Sagan Jeffries

EDGE

EDGE SCIENCE FICTION AND FANTASY PUBLISHING

AN IMPRINT OF HADES PUBLICATIONS, INC.

CALGARY

Edge Science Fiction and Fantasy Publishing
An Imprint of Hades Publications Inc.
P.O. Box 1714, Calgary, Alberta, T2P 2L7, Canada

In-house editing by Ella Baumont, Brian Hades,
Susan J. Forest and Matt Hughes
Interior design by Janice Blaine
Cover Illustration by Jeff Lee Johnson

ISBN: 978-1-894063-98-2

EDGE Science Fiction and Fantasy Publishing and Hades Publications, Inc.
acknowledges the ongoing support of the Alberta Foundation for the Arts and
the Canada Council for the Arts for our publishing programme.

Library and Archives Canada Cataloguing in Publication

Jeffries, Sagan
    The trillionist / Sagan Jeffries.

ISBN: 978-1-894063-98-2
(e-Book ISBN: 978-1-894063-99-9)

I. Title.

PS8619.E4447T75 2013   C813'.6   C2013-900451-3

FIRST EDITION
(M-20130820)
Printed in Canada
www.edgewebsite.com

Dedication

To the memory of Carl Sagan,
author of my favorite sci-fi book, *Contact*.

QR CODES

Within the pages of this novel you will find 17 QR codes. A QR code looks like a square block full of lines and smaller blocks. In many ways it is similar to a bar code and it can be scanned by a (free) QR reader app on any mobile device. Scanning the QR code brings up additional information relating to the story, making this book interactive and ever changing. The author can update the information at any time and make it relevant to new science discoveries, additional background information, characters, settings, technology, etc.

There is also a QR code on the back cover of this book. Scanning it will take you to a quick video introduction by the author.

Enjoy.

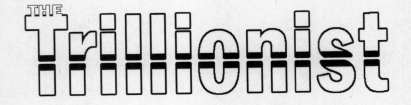

Prolog

GRAVITY SQUEEZED him into his seat and a deep throated growl filled his ears. He could barely breathe.

A voice crackled over the communicator, smooth, professional. Inside his helmet the amplified sound of his own breathing was offset by the steady rhythmic thumping of his heart.

"We have liftoff!"

The power of the massive three-stage rocket beneath him threatened to tear itself apart.

There was a moment of lessening roar and relative lightness as the first stage fell away. Then the rumble and shake of the second stage ignition, thrust, and eventual jettison, leaving the third stage to begin its slow burn, boosting Sage Rojan to where no Tidonese had gone before.

His home planet was miles below and the sight of the arching horizon and the star-splashed blackness beyond caused Sage to catch his breath. Memories flashed: his mother's teary final goodbye, his father's proud smile, and a lingering kiss from Tamara, who, as corny as it sounded, was always in his orbit and seldom showed any fear of the unknown.

He squeezed his eyes shut; waiting for the moment when the supreme Artisan noticed his presence in a place he had no right to be.

Chapter 1

NINETEEN YEARS EARLIER...

GENOSA ROJAN LEANED OVER the wooden bassinette that held her son and tucked the newborn's soft blue blanket tighter around him. The hairs on the back of her neck pricked.

The doctors had told her that an infant couldn't focus; would only see a blur of motion until the neurons in the vision center finished making all the necessary connections. But she was sure his emerald green eyes followed her every move, and had done so right from the moment the doctor had placed him on her deflating belly, even before his umbilical cord was cut.

"You're doing it again." Thaddeus leaned over to get a better look at their son, Sage. "Shrinking from him." The child's eyes shifted focus to his father. "He's just a fast-developer. Takes after his old man. I could read when I was three, you know."

Genosa turned the knob on the new Sound Box radio, something she didn't have when she was a child. Like so many other things, which, even if radio had been invented years earlier, her mother wouldn't have allowed in their house — dismissing such things as frivolous.

Genosa Rojan was doggedly determined that her son would have every possible convenience, from the soothing sounds of the radio to his warm woolly covers.

The baby watched her intently. "Three years, you mean. He's only three days old. Watch this." She picked up a plastic rattle from the bottom corner of the bassinette and shook it a few inches from the infant's eyes. Immediately, Sage's gaze locked onto the toy. His pudgy arms stirred under the blanket and he abruptly and unerringly reached out to seize the handle. When Genosa didn't let go, the baby's grip tightened — she could see his tiny knuckles whiten — and he tugged at it with surprising strength.

"That's some kid," Thaddeus beamed. "I got him a welcome-home present." He produced a tiny knitted cap, with a stitched-in design of a spinning atom on its front. "When he's old enough he can be my assistant at the physics lab."

"That might be sooner than you think," Genosa said. "Glad I know diddly-squat about your new spinners. It's absurd that things are made up of invisible particles going 'round and 'round each other. All of them held together by some magic force. Speaking of which, just try to take the rattle away from him."

As she spoke, the baby's gaze left the rattle. His bright, deep-set green eyes went first to her, then to her husband. His little knuckles turned pale again.

"Did you see that?" she said. "I think he understands what we're saying."

Thaddeus' arm went around Genosa's waist and pulled her to him. "You've just got new-mom heebie-jeebies," he said. "Come on. Let the kid sleep so he won't be worn out when your folks get here."

"Sleep?" she said. "I haven't seen him take more than a five-minute nap since he was born." But she let her husband draw her away from the bassinette. She knew it was wrong, but she preferred not to have to look at her son for too long.

From her baby's first kicks, Genosa felt her unborn child would be a boy. At birth they named him Sage Iden Cosimo Rojan, respectively meaning wisdom, wealth, and bringer of order to all. When the nurse slapped the baby's bottom to start the breathing reflex he let out a cry that made the doctor jump.

Genosa relaxed into her husband's embrace. *Maybe I am just a nervous first-time mother. I've got a healthy son. His bits and pieces seem to be where they ought to be. And if he's stronger and more focused than other babies, how is that a bad thing?*

· Ω ·

"They're here." Thaddeus had been peeking out through a split in the drapes. Now he closed them in a gesture of irritation.

"Thaddeus," Genosa sighed as she reached around him and fully opened the window coverings.

Her mother and father climbed down from the old family roadster. They were farm folk who had never quite warmed to the university physicist she'd married. Nor had Thaddeus grown to like them. She'd once overheard him at a faculty cocktail party refer to his in-laws as 'bumpkins.'

Though they struggled financially to make ends meet, Genosa never begrudged the love Thaddeus had for his collection of science books— or whenever he brought home new gadgets like the recent plug-in toaster. She didn't mind electricity making her life somewhat easier. She'd seen more than enough of the old times; hanging by one's fingertips to ancient ways and superstitions. As a youngster, she had tired of chores such as having to prime the pump to draw water from the family well. But mostly now she hated the way her parents disapproved of Thaddeus, making snide comments, seeing him as a dreamer who'd be better served to keep his head out of the clouds, as they put it.

Grandma Beth stepped briskly past her son-in-law, not even saying 'beya' to him and instead headed straight for the bassinette. "Gorgeous," she said, as she hoisted Sage into the air for an all-round looking-over.

"Careful, Momma!" Genosa cried. "He's easily stirred up."

"You always were a worry wart, daughter." Her mom smiled and put on a baby voice. "Grandma knows what she's doing." Beth went eye-to-eye with Sage, holding him right up to her face. "You're a tough little guy, aren't you?" Sage looked straight into his grandma's gaze. Again, a shiver went through Genosa. Beth handed the baby to his grandpa. "What do you think, Charlie?"

The old man took the infant in his work-hardened hands. The baby's eyes locked onto his. "He is sturdy, all right. He can help me on the farm when he's big enough to know which end of the mule gets hitched to the plow."

"Oh, Papa..." Genosa looked guiltily over her shoulder at Thaddeus, sitting back in his chair, fuming.

"Genosa, you know my stand on the matter. This city-slicking is best left to you jalopy lovers," her father went on, "Personally, I hate that noisy contraption of an invention. I still miss the old buggy. Never had to start a horse with a hand-crank. Ridiculous."

"It is inventions like that that keep Orlandia at bay," Thaddeus grumbled.

"Well they must not be doing a very good job, even us country folk heard about last week's raid. Another coastal town burned to the ground." Her father shook his head. Sage started squirming in his grip.

"Here, let me, Genosa why don't you serve us some tea," said Beth, taking the baby back into her arms and settling herself onto the couch next to her husband.

"Price of fuel's gone up thanks to them no good pirates. I've already paid more for that beast's fuel then I ever paid to buy a new horse." Her father hooked a thumb towards the roadster.

Thaddeus shrugged, "The Royal Navy's spread thin, the pirate raids are bound to slip through, but still they refuse to attack us outright. It's because they wouldn't stand a chance against us on open ground. Orlandia doesn't have automobiles or combustion engines. Even the King's talking about developing a landing party of war machines to stop them once and for all. It won't be long, you wait."

Sage's tiny fingers had been wrestling with the brooch on his grandma's blouse, and he managed to undo the clasp. The sharp pin dug into his hand and he started howling.

"Now look what you've done," Genosa bustled back into the room glaring at Thaddeus as if her husband's words had sparked the chaos, "Give him to me." Genosa took the baby. "Feeding him's the only way to calm him down when he gets like this."

As she said the words, the crying stopped and the baby turned his head towards her, reaching strategically for a button on her blouse.

"Is he eating well?" asked Grandpa Charlie.

"I can barely keep him satisfied." Genosa freed a breast and the baby latched on.

· Ω ·

"Have you been eating onions or too much garlic?" Thaddeus watched Sage toss and turn in the crib.

"He just doesn't want to sleep." How could Genosa be any more plain? "If I put him down he cries. If I pick him up he cries. If I leave him alone he cries."

"Let's just go to our room." Thaddeus looked as exhausted as she felt. "He'll eventually cry himself to sleep."

Genosa and Thaddeus lay awake until the crying subsided. Later, when it was time to nurse the baby, Genosa tip-toed over to Sage's bassinette and, instead of hearing the normal relaxed sounds of breathing, saw he was whispering to himself.

Her body trembled with relief as her milk flowed, and she softly sang a lullaby to the baby she wanted so much to love. But the song only seemed to enliven him. It would be another long night of walking him up and down, singing, talking — to wake exhausted at sunrise for more of the same.

No.

Tonight, she'd try a different strategy. She took him outside into the warm summer air. "See? That's our house, needs painting," she said, as much to keep herself awake as to soothe Sage. "There's the wooden fence your daddy built. Those are our saucer magnolia trees." She caught the fragrance of the pinkish blooms. "And next door, that's our neighbor's house. Pink, like our flowers. Crazy, don't you think?"

Sage's head swiveled and his eyes followed where she pointed.

She carried him, following the path to nearby Baxbury Bridge, traversing the slow-flowing waters of the Jalin Canal. The old bridge showed its age, weathered boards creaking as she crossed. "Porturn has hundreds of rickety old bridges above the canals. Did you know that? They're so beautiful. You're lucky to be born in such a subtropical city. See? I know one big word."

But the baby ignored her. Instead, he looked up into a sky filled with glowing stars. To Genosa, his gaze seemed millions of miles from her embrace. He pointed to the reflection of the moons in the canal waters and giggled.

Unbelievable. A happy moment.

Then, his little arm reached as if trying to touch the three crescent moons in the dark eastern sky and he screamed in frustration at his lack of success.

"Come little one," she said. "You can't touch a moon. Not any of them. They're too far away. Now, let's go home. It's time for sleep."

Sage wailed again, demanding to stay under the stars.

"Okay. Have it your way, my stubborn one," she said as she stepped softly on tiptoes down a few rungs to a gondola docked on the water's edge below the bridge. She knew the gondola's owner wouldn't mind. A swirled moustache of a man, she often saw him taking his wife to market days, poling his burgundy craft through the labyrinth of waterways.

In the gondola, she lay down on the bottom of the boat, allowing herself and Sage to feel the motion of the water beneath them. The inviting perfume of flowers floated over them as she

5

snuggled Sage close in beside her to keep him warm, making sure he stayed well wrapped. The rocking of the waters soothed the baby. Yet he was preoccupied, looking up as if trying to count the multitude of stars.

A light breeze touched her hair and slid across her skin. A soft murmur came from her baby, as if Sage whispered to the twinklers above, and she thought she saw one star pulsate. But, she was far too worn out to focus. She drifted, her thoughts troubled, as she wrestled with the desire to love her strange demanding child.

· Ω ·

It was getting late. The fingers of Thaddeus' hand pressed pen into paper. "Dackt," he said aloud. "I'm not getting anywhere with this." Without realizing it, he'd been outlining the same word, 'Bang', for quite some time. *Such a stupid way to describe the origin of our universe*, he thought. *I can't believe everything just flew out into space and then coalesced out of the cooling gasses. Still, the sun, Sintosy, blazes away, a hot fireball keeping us warm.* "Bang." he muttered. "Utter insanity."

Thaddeus knew he should have been heading home but the deadline for his Tidonese Science Journal article was looming, and he was fumbling with fitting the workings of Sintosy into the Bang Theory — to which he gave little credence. "It's as dumb as the Flat-Tidon Theory used to be," he said to himself. "I don't know why I agreed to write this article. If I had a larger telescope I'd probably disprove it."

The late hour demanded his conclusion: '...and Sintosy is millions of years old.' But no sooner he had written down the words then he scribbled out the word 'millions' and jotted 'billions' in its place. *I might just as well go out on a limb,* he thought, *heretics are no longer burned at the stake just because they have crazy notions. Maybe someday I'll be able to actually see light coming from stars billions of light-years away.* Thaddeus looked at his watch, "Dackt, I'd better call home."

· Ω ·

The phone rang ten times before Genosa had the energy to answer. Thaddeus asked if dinner was ruined.

She heard exhaustion in her own voice. "It's in the oven. Come home. I'm at the end of my rope."

She hung up. Today she felt as though she'd been through a war. She hadn't had more than a few hours of sleep in a row since the baby was born. She had planned, before Sage was born, to get back into shape as soon as he was settled, but the baby hadn't given her a break. The only blessing was that the constant stress had seen her post-partum weight drop.

· Ω ·

Thaddeus lugged his briefcase through the kitchen door, letting the screen door slam shut behind him. He removed his coat, and rubbed a thumb across her moist cheek. "Oh, Genosa. Is it that bad?" He spoke as if he was afraid to know. "I'm sorry. The faculty has me glued."

She knew what he thought. Sage was just going through some phase. *It's only been two months. Give it a chance. Sure.*

"I..." She didn't know how to say it. "I... locked Sage in the study."

"What?"

"It's just... you're not here!" she sobbed. "You don't know—"

"But we got him a jumper." He took her hands and sat with her at the chrome kitchen table. "I thought—"

They had bought Sage a standing jumper — a harness suspended by springs from a tubular frame — which was intended to help a young child strengthen his legs prior to walking. They hoped he could bounce away his over-abundance of energy.

"He used it for a while, even seemed to enjoy it. But, then he started to do twirls. He got the harness caught around his throat. He would have strangled to death—"

"Oh, Genosa..."

She almost laughed; a crazy laugh. "Weird thing is, he was smiling a devilish smirk as I tried to untangle him."

"You're saying he enjoyed nearly killing himself?"

"I don't know what I'm saying." She threw her hands up in the air. "I'm too tired to think. As soon as I had the harness straightened out he did it again. I had to put the jumper away. He had such a tantrum. It almost sounded as though he was screaming words."

"Genosa." Thaddeus frowned at his hands on the table. "I think you're under a lot of stress—"

"Don't patronize me. Listen. Sage grabbed a chair, stood and pushed it toward me. A two month-old standing and moving a

chair?" The tears welled up in her eye again, and she couldn't
hold them back.

Thaddeus put his arms around her and she sagged against
him. "It's all right," he said. "We'll do something. Sorry, I didn't
know how rotten it was getting. From now on I'll try to be here
more. Take the load off you."

She kissed him and wiped at her tears. "You want to help?"
she asked. "Lie awake tonight. Listen to him whisper in his sleep.
Then tell me I'm not crazy."

"I will," he said. "And you're not crazy, just tired."

$\cdot \Omega \cdot$

Thaddeus slipped from under his covers down to the floor, and
crawled, staying lower than the side of Sage's crib. There he lay
and listened, feeling somewhat idiotic, like a kid playing spies.

Faint sounds came from the crib. He peeked above the mattress.
Sage was grappling through some sort of dream; tossing and
turning in his crib, flexing and extending his arms and legs.
He made sounds like words; but Thaddeus could understand
none of them. One instant it sounded like a conversation, next it
resembled a rant of exclamations. It went on for an hour or more.

Thaddeus woke, lying on the floor beside the crib. In the dull
light before dawn he looked up to see his son's fixed gaze on
him. As though the baby studied him. Shaking off the unsettling
feeling, he crawled back into bed. Genosa was awake. "You're
right," he whispered. "There's something strangely odd about
our kid."

Chapter 2

AFTER SAGE'S SECOND birthday, Genosa and Thaddeus refitted his room by installing bars on the window and a lock on the door. And they repositioned the door handle to adult eye-level after Sage figured out that he could jump, grab, and pull the normal-height handle open.

Genosa looked through the newly installed peep-hole into his room. Sage should have been napping— he'd had a busy morning; much of it spent racing around the nearby park while Genosa struggled to keep up with him. He was like an athlete in training, running, jumping, climbing; even doing push-ups and sit-ups. Compared to the other children his age, the muscles in his little arms and legs were as hard as wood.

Genosa saw that Sage was sitting cross-legged on the floor near a pile of books. Spread across his thighs was a big book that his grandparents had given him for his birthday; designed to teach a child to read, every page full of colorful pictures accompanied by appropriate words.

Grandma Beth had tried to interest him in it, sitting him on her lap and pointing. But Sage had been restless and wouldn't focus. He'd pushed the book off Grandma's lap and wriggled free of her affectionate hold. Then he'd climbed on the couch to look out at the street through the big picture window. He'd rested his palms on the window sill and stared fixedly at everything that went by. The pose reminded Genosa of a famous painting of the deposed emperor, Balan, standing on the balcony of his island house where he eventually died in exile. The painter had caught the man looking out across the sea, to the islands he used to rule, every line in his rigid body exuding frustrated rage.

But now, as Genosa peeked through the peep-hole in the door, she saw her Sage, her beautiful little boy, bent over Grandma's book; one finger tracing the words on the pages while his lips formed their shape. A shock went through her as she realized how fast his finger was moving.

She must have made a small sound because he glanced at the door. A grin split his face and he spoke aloud, his finger still moving along the page. "Come in."

She opened the door and stepped into the room, closing it behind her. Sometimes, if she wasn't careful, he would slip through her legs and make a break for it. If a door or window was open, or even unlocked, he could be out on the street and running, paying no attention to traffic or any other danger. And she'd be hard pressed to catch him.

"You're reading," she said.

"Yes." He leafed through several pages, perusing them with adeptness beyond his years.

"You didn't like it when Grandma tried to show you."

He eyed her cautiously. "I didn't feel like it then. Grandma was treating me like a... child. Why should I read for her? You think I look like a baby. I'm not. I want you and dad to treat me... older. Your age."

Sage had never spoken baby-talk. At a year old, he had gone from forming his first words to speaking in complete sentences. And he'd sounded like an adult. She was almost used to it now. Almost.

"Well, that's quite the request. You're going to have to earn that with good behavior. Perhaps you should read something to me," she said.

"You think I'm lying?" There was an edge to his voice, as though he was testing her.

"No, I just want to hear you." The door handle rested beside her head, and she calculated whether she could flee and close the door before he could sprint across the room. But she sensed this was the more mature Sage today. "It's a special moment for a mother when her child first begins to read."

He cocked his head to one side, as if trying to determine if she was telling the truth. Then he shrugged and looked back at the book, reading off a string of words, rapid-fire. "How's that?" he said. "Nobody had to teach me to read. I did it all by myself."

She never lied to him. "Amazing."

He closed the book and pushed it off his legs. "This book is not about anything," he said. "You and dad have books. Are they about something?"

She let out a breath and unclenched her hands. "Yes. Some of them are about the world and things that have happened, and how things work. Some of them are about people."

"I want to read them."

"Which ones?"

"All of them."

She saw an opportunity. "I could bring you some," she said. "Or you could pick and choose on your own, from the bookshelves in the den."

"I want to choose my own."

"Then you'll have to make me a promise. And keep it."

His eyes lidded. "What promise?"

"That you won't leave the house without me or your father." He looked at her sharply, and she went on. "There are dangers out there: cars that could run you over; stray dogs that bite. We want to keep you safe."

She saw him thinking about it. After a moment, he said, "I want to be safe. All right, I promise."

Genosa nodded and eased herself away from the door. With cautious relief, she led him through the shell curtained doorway of their study where she turned on the standing floor lamp that lit the chair where Sage's father liked to sit and read. Sage pushed a footstool to the ceiling-high shelves and climbed up. He scanned the lower shelves— mostly novels and short-story collections.

"I like that one," she said, pointing to a thin green book that had seen younger days. She remembered reading it as a child.

Sage pulled it part way out of its place, "Vullantry. What's it about?" He glanced back at her.

"It's about a hero who flies to the sun on wings made of wax."

"That's foolish." But even as he dismissed it, his gaze lingered on its spine as he put it back.

Standing on tip-toe, he reached for a thick volume entitled 'A Concise History of Bella Yareo.' The book was heavy and the shelves tightly packed, but he pulled the book down, opened it and began to decipher its contents.

"What is Bella Yareo?" he said.

"It's the country where we live."

"Then that's where I'll start."

He carried the weighty book to the chair, set it on the cushion and climbed up beside it. He settled himself in, pulled the book onto his lap, and opened the cover; his eyes immediately began to move from left to right. She stayed beside the stringed curtains.

After a few moments, he looked up. "What's 'feudal' mean?"

She explained, as best she could. There was an abridged dictionary on the desk. She put it on the arm of the chair beside him. "This will tell you the meaning of any word you don't know."

His face brightened, and he smiled at her. "I know how to use it. You can leave me alone now."

"You won't try to get out?"

"I promise. Besides, I'll be busy here."

· Ω ·

When his father came home from work, Sage was still reading. Genosa caught Thaddeus as he came through the front door and told him, "I think you should go in there and give him some praise."

"I will," said her husband. He stuck his head through the dangly shells and waited for Sage to invite him in before entering.

Genosa eavesdropped from the corridor, silently forming a small space between the threads with her fingers so she could see in.

Thaddeus' back was to her. "Your mom tells me you've taken up serious reading."

There was a soft thump, as Sage set the heavy book aside. "I like it. It's showing me things I want to know. Beya— I already learned where our hello greeting comes from. It's the short form for Bella Yareo."

His father touched him lightly on the head. "Well, I'm proud of you." Thaddeus' voice came clearly through the divide. "I was much older than you before I could read, and I certainly didn't start out on books written for adults."

Genosa heard a warm resonance in her husband's voice, and it brought a smile to her own lips. There had never been much of that before now.

"Here, let me read you something." Sage's small voice was excited as he lifted the book and showed his dad a picture of a continent lying along the equator. "It says Bella Yareo is about four thousand miles long and is shaped like the letter Y. It says the shape has significance, but it doesn't elaborate."

"That's because the junction of the long stem of the Y on the West and the two arms of the Y of the East meet at a tri-intersection— an epicenter axis right at our Porturn City."

Sage nodded, "I like the words which describe interaction. The book says the word Porturn means a port where travelers always have to make a turn if they want to get to other parts of Bella Yareo."

"That's right." Thaddeus looked back toward the curtain, giving the appearance of knowing Genosa was taking everything in. "Mind if I sit and join you for a while? You could show me more."

The child made room for Thaddeus in the chair. "There's a whole section here devoted to Tidon. Did you know our planet was named after the tides caused by the moons? It's a sphere, over nine thousand miles in diameter. Some man by the name of Kautelius discovered that. Flat land thinkers are defunct. Defunct. I had to look that word up. It means they're no longer functioning or they no longer exist."

Thaddeus' chuckle and his acceptance made Genosa smile. At last.

"Voyageurs, in ships traveling the oceans, have discovered the smaller continents of Batakesh to the West and Orlandia to our East," Sage said.

"And Orlandia is where the pirates are from."

"Pirates?"

"Raiders who come in fleets, descending without warning on coastal towns and capturing any vessels they find in the sea lanes."

"Oh." Sage was quiet for a moment but soon he turned back to the book in his lap. "Still the book says no one has even sailed as far out to sea as the far side of Tidon, so no one knows what's there. They call it the dark side, but not because it doesn't receive Sintosy's light. It isn't really dark."

Thaddeus smiled, "That's right, Sage." He flipped a few pages. "Now here's something you might like to know: I actually wrote a section of the book you're reading."

"What is your section about?"

"The stars. I hoped that by writing it, I could help our university get an extra powerful telescope to learn more about our universe. We needed a stronger one with a curved reflective optical mirror. It's called a catoptic telescope."

The toddler shrugged, uncertain, and changed the subject. "Here it says that seven million people live in Porturn City and the total population of Bella Yareo is over two hundred million. Is that a good thing or a bad thing?"

"It's good for economic growth and development," Thaddeus replied.

"All right. I think I understand." Then, Sage held up a book with four moons on the cover. Genosa wondered where he'd found it, she hadn't seen him stop reading long enough to browse the shelves. "What's this book about?"

"Oh, that one." Thaddeus smiled. "It's a fairy tale, *Lunar Four*. It was written about twenty years ago. The author wrote as if he was able to see both ahead to the future and back in time."

"Is it any good?"

"I think…" Thaddeus looked down into Sage's openly curious face as though weighing how sophisticated his response could be. "I think the author hid behind a children's book."

"What do you mean?"

"I think he was unsure about whether his ideas would be accepted. He speculates about a time millions of years ago when Tidon had four moons. But he says the smallest one exploded due to the tremendous pressure of a pimple-burst volcano. Tidon and the three remaining moons were deeply scarred by the rain of debris that pelted their surfaces."

There was a long silence. Genosa shifted to hear and see better. She waited and waited, nestling her cheek up to the Kelboo shells on the curtain.

"Sage?"

"I feel I know that story already." Sage's words came slowly as though he was thinking very hard. "But how can that be?"

"Did you read it earlier today?"

"No, I just seem to know it."

There was another long silence, and Genosa's stomach churned the way it did whenever Sage did something unsettling.

"Puzzling, isn't it?" Sage asked his dad.

"To say the least." Thaddeus' voice betrayed no emotion. Something he was good at.

"You know, today I had a really good day." Her son's words were wistful. "Wish there were more days like today."

"Son," Thaddeus said, "you're not the only one."

Genosa silently went back to the kitchen. This was what she wanted. A child. A real child. Funny how that thought made her nose run.

· Ω ·

Genosa knelt beside her sleeping son, stroking his head as he struggled through the latest bad dream. The boy's hair was stuck with sweat to his forehead and his face was hot to her touch. He'd had an active evening, often a precursor to one of the nightmares that still, even at the age of three, disrupted his rest several nights a week. He kicked back the covers and let out a groan, eyelids flickering.

She lowered her head, hoping to make sense of his dream-talk, even though all of her efforts had yielded nothing. Still, as she strained to listen, Genosa was struck, not for the first time, by the thought that her son's babbling often sounded like two voices arguing.

When the murmurs and thrashing stopped, she slipped across the room to his dresser and turned on the big radio. In a few seconds, its vacuum tubes warmed and she adjusted the dial to find some music to sooth away the jangled nerves that Sage suffered on waking from a bad dream.

He was rubbing his eyes as she returned to his bed. "Was I dreaming?" he said.

"You don't remember?" She knelt beside him again, touching the back of her hand to his cheek.

He shook his head, sleepily. He never did.

"Try," she said. Then a thought came. "It sounded as if you were having an argument with somebody."

His face grew still, as if he was searching inwardly for some fleeting memory that had slipped from his grasp. "Yeah," he said, and she could see him struggle. Then his shoulders slumped and he said, "No, it's gone."

"Do you remember how your dream felt? Was it scary? Were you angry?"

He reached inside himself again. "Scary, I think," he said after a moment. "And, yes, I was angry."

"What about?"

He closed his eyes then opened them. "Being bossed around," he said. "Something wasn't fair."

"What something?"

But it was gone again. "Stop it. I can't remember," he said, turning to look at the stars she had painted on his ceiling.

She acquiesced. It would be futile to pursue it further. She held his shoulders lightly. "Sage." She waited until he looked at her. "You know that my concern is you, your protection. I want you to feel safe. These walls safeguard our family. You can count on that and your father and me."

He showed her a sad smile. "Can these walls protect me from my dreams? Can you and dad make me feel less tired and worn out than I feel right now?" He climbed to his feet in his bed and examined himself in the dresser mirror. He crumpled back down in disgust, his hair mussed and his pajamas twisted about his tiny limbs and torso. "I'm not normal."

"Oh, Sage." She reached out her two hands to take him into her arms, the only comfort she could offer. He was right, and they both knew it. He was not a normal little boy even when he wanted to be. But if there was a button she could push that would allow Sage to let go and totally trust her, she could never find it. Would he always be a befuddled prodigy, unable to figure himself out? Would he always see her attempts to reach him as, at best, well-meaning but unwelcome meddling?

Often, once he was fully awake after a bad dream, Sage could become angry to the point of black rage. It could happen now. Her arms faltered, and she lowered them to her side. At any moment he could turn on her.

"That's enough," he said in an unusually gruff voice. "I don't need your clumsy help. I don't need you or your husband. Leave me alone."

"When you feel better, we can get you dressed and have breakfast together. Here are your clothes; I'll leave them on the chair." She pulled the handle on the door behind her, leaving it slightly ajar, an invitation for him to come and join his family.

· Ω ·

At the age of four, Genosa and Thaddeus decided to enroll Sage in daycare. They quickly found that, not only did Sage surpass his own age group, he outcompeted the children even several years his senior. They burned through three separate daycares with their young prodigy Sage running circles around his caregivers. Eventually, the news reached Dr. Kent Lechmont, the official of the Porturn education authority responsible for administering school entrance tests to gifted children not yet of the statutory age. Genosa received a call.

Genosa was more than ambivalent about putting her son in school so young. However, she agreed to the testing.

On the appointed day, Dr. Lechmont seemed used to his subjects being nervous and looked at Genosa with surprise as Sage coolly regarded him back. The child was so small; the man had to pile books on the chair so Sage could see the materials on the table.

The process began with elementary numbers and vocabulary, and beginner's math and reading, and then scaled up, step-by-step, to give a delineation of how far this prospective student might go— how many numerals he could mentally handle in multiplication and division.

Half way through the testing Sage's legs started swinging from side to side. "I don't like sitting this way. I like to sit cross-legged on the floor. Can we do that?"

"Of course," said Dr. Lechmont. He rearranged things as the boy wished before beginning the test for reading comprehension. He concluded with a variety of multiple choice and spatial-relations puzzles.

When they were done, the doctor brought Sage back to his office and gave him a box of metal puzzles to untangle. He returned to where Genosa waited by his desk. "Sage scored only slightly ahead of older children at the start of testing," Dr. Lechmont said, reviewing the test results. "Then there came a moment when he seemed to get bored."

"I saw that." Genosa nodded. "It was as if someone had flipped a switch."

Sage watched them silently, as though he reserved judgment on their conclusions.

"After I aksed you to leave the room, his performance greatly accelerated," the doctor continued, ignoring the boy. "The answers came fast and he breezed right through tests that usually challenge highly intelligent children five to ten years older. He is, far and away, the most intellectually gifted child I have ever encountered."

Genosa sighed.

"There was one extremely surprising answer." Dr. Lechmont sat back in his chair. "When I asked about his favorite thing on Tidon."

"He said he liked the weather, but added that there were better places to spend time," Genosa laughed.

"He responded that his other planets were none of my business." The doctor chuckled, but his eyes were not warmed by the laughter.

"It would explain a lot if he turned out to be from another planet," Genosa said dryly.

The doctor nodded slowly. "Yes. Impossible, of course."

"Of course." Genosa felt uncomfortable under the man's piercing gaze. "So, is that it? Are we all done?"

"There is one other thing. The octostringet. Has he ever played it before?"

"No." Genosa shook her head. "Never."

"When I showed it to him, he ran his fingers across the strings. He stroked and plucked the metal wires. In less than a minute, he was making simple music. In two, he was using both hands and all eight strings, moving the central bridge to change octaves. He played a melody and made harmonies," the doctor pointed out, "like he was on his way to composing a symphony. Then he reached over and flipped the toggle switch to broadcast his music throughout the school on the public address system. Mrs. Rojan, your son does not lack for audacity."

She lowered her eyes in embarrassment and frustration. "No." Genosa was not surprised to learn that Sage's math wizardry was accompanied by an outstanding talent for music.

Dr. Lechmont went on to explain that the brain's cortex showed similar neuro-spatial temporal firing patterns for both disciplines. "Housed in common folds within the brain, I suppose," he said. "Centuries ago they used to burn people at the stake if they even remotely resembled freakishness. Even today, researchers are only now beginning to unravel the brain's secrets. Nonetheless, I'm sure some of them would be interested to take a look at Sage's."

"No," Genosa said in a tone conveying the discussion was closed. "Sage is having a hard enough time being a child, without becoming a lab specimen."

"I understand," said the doctor.

Genosa wasn't sure whether to be proud of her son or afraid for him. "What... what do you recommend?"

"It seems to me, Mrs. Rojan, it's not a question of whether or not Sage is ready for school, but rather a question of whether the school is ready for Sage. Apart from anything else, he is so young. But I'm going to suggest that we put him in the small, custom-built class we call High Intellect."

Genosa felt momentary relief, as if someone had lifted an anvil from her shoulders. An expert was telling her that Sage could be fitted into the school system, albeit by way of a special program for gifted children. Perhaps an enriched environment, with more outlets for his abilities, would take some of the strain from Sage as well as from her and her husband.

And, maybe... just maybe... it would bring an end to his nightmares and set him on the road to something like a normal life.

Chapter 3

IT WAS A BEAUTIFUL MORNING. Sintosy was rising in the eastern sky and it warmed them as they walked to Sage's school.

"What are those trees?" Sage pointed toward the few trees that broke the pattern of columnar aspens and flame-tapering cypresses. The crooked-leaning, reddish-brown tree trunks divided into twisting upright branches which overhung the roadway.

"They are Arbutus trees. The old leaves continually drop off as new ones replace them," Genosa said, tousling his hair. "They come from Batakesh."

"Batakesh," Sage recited. "A smaller continent than Bella Yareo. Across the equator, two thousand miles off Yareo's west coast. No pirates, though. Those are in Orlandia."

"That's right." Genosa couldn't help but be proud of her son's memory.

"It was the first conquest for the Bellan fleet," the boy continued.

"Right, again." Genosa kicked a drift of leaves, wishing her son would be more spontaneous. It was as though he had never been a child. "Those brave explorers from generations ago brought back a lot of non-indigenous plants which were new and useful to Bella Yareo."

"Why do you call them brave?"

"Well, they weren't sure if their sailing would take them off the edge of the world to fall off into nothingness."

Sage frowned and shook his head. "That's just plain silly."

As they passed a mini park fewer than a hundred paces from the house, Sage suddenly darted from the sidewalk to stop before a pile of leaves the wind had gathered up. He turned to face her, and then let himself collapse backwards into the multicolored heap. The leaves splashed over his head, a few settling to provide him with a colorful cap. "This is as far as I go this morning," he said, lying there, staring up at her as she crossed the grass to him.

A quiet joy rose inside Genosa. Perhaps her son might learn to let pleasure and sensation into his life. She'd planned to give him a lengthy walk to school then take a day for herself, but it was better — by far — to join the rebellion than to fight it. She smelled cut grass and rustic wetness. Somewhere down the block, someone was burning leaves and a light breeze brought thin wisps of smoke in their direction. Laughing, she too allowed her body to become limp and tumbled down into the leaves beside Sage. They tossed double handfuls on top of each other, tickling and giggling.

"Oh, look," he said, "one of Tidon's moons is sitting right atop that tall aspen. That's Sotus isn't it?"

"Yes. It's a full moon, Tidon's largest moon," she said, "and it's a long way from here and that tree."

"I know that, mom. It's the only moon on hand today; the other two must be hiding on the far side." He pointed, trying to make believe he could touch its scarred face. "Those craters remind me of a broken bubble after it bursts, like when you're making me porridge in the morning. Do you think that someday I'll be able to go to the moons and walk on the surfaces?"

She laughed. "Oh, Sage. No one can travel in space!"

"We can fly," he argued.

"Bellans are just getting used to the idea of air travel." She sat up in the leaves. "Space flight will be a long time coming."

"Not if we make it happen." He sat up, too. Back to being serious.

She sighed. Their moment of connection had passed. "Well, you could be right. Yesterday your dad told me he read that some tycoon was pushing the King and the Senate to start up a space program. We can wish that tycoon good luck. Who knows what the future holds?"

Sage's gaze suddenly sharpened. "What's a tycoon?"

"A business man."

Sage wrinkled his nose. "What does a business man know about space?"

Genosa shrugged, "I don't think it matters when you have enough money to do anything you want."

Sage grew quiet at that. After a moment he stood and brushed the leaves from his pants. Rebellion apparently forgotten for the day, Sage resumed his walk to school, and Genosa followed him.

Last week, she had enrolled Sage in a private class of so-called 'super mind' kids. The group was small, just three other boys and two girls; a good mix. Sage didn't seem to care, or even notice, whether he was playing with boys or girls; regardless, he was better at interacting with other gifted children, although they were really only a little like him. The contact seemed to make him feel less alone in the world. He often took a ringleader role and tutored them along. He even tapped them on the head when they did well. He'd say, "Here let me apply a star to your head for being so bright."

Later, he told his dad, "These are smart kids; especially the one girl. I call her Brainella when I want to antagonize her. She learns fast, like me. But it's hard to be friends. We try to outdo each other."

"Sounds all right, but be careful what you call people," Thaddeus warned. "How about the boys? Who's your best friend there?"

Sage shrugged. "The boys aren't interesting. Some days I try to teach them, but their attention span is too short. They want me to play, building things."

Genosa was glad that Sage seemed happier, now that he was part of a learning group. When she picked him up after class, they would actually engage in normal conversations, with him talking about the other kids in his class.

"Ango, the other girl, is jealous," he said one day, "because Brainella and I compete so much against each other. Ango stole her pencils and geometry set and wouldn't give them back to her. I had to negotiate a deal to spend equal time with both of them."

"Wait till you're sixteen," Genosa laughed. "Then watch the girls go berserk."

They reached the door to the school. It was closed and the yard, empty. Class had gone in. Sage stopped and stared intently — angrily — at the door.

"Sage?" she asked tentatively.

"Stop hounding me!"

Genosa tensed. She pulled back, unsure.

"I'm tired." he growled. "Stupid dreams, nightmares— call them what you will. Dackt!" He turned to glare at her. "Driving me nuts. Can't you understand?"

"Sage Iden Cosimo Rojan. I'll have none of that swearing," she scolded him.

Abruptly, his anger went away, and she was looking into the haggard eyes of a tired toddler. "Every day it's the same. Can we just do something different?" he said.

Genosa took a moment to think. This was a heartfelt request out of need. She shrugged and spread her hands. "Schedules can change. Doesn't mean the end of the world." She would not fight him. "Today we'll try being creative. Any ideas?"

He put his finger to the side of his cheek. "You know, I've never been to dad's lab. Can we go there?"

"Alright, so long as you behave. Here, lazy pants jump on my back, piggyback, and I'll carry you home. We'll call your teacher and tell her you're taking a day off for bad behavior."

He grinned.

"See? I can do sarcasm too. Just like you."

· Ω ·

There was a tap at the door. Thaddeus lifted his head from the microscope but before he could slide from his stool, Genosa and Sage entered the lab. She had seldom visited him at work. He grinned and performed a playful bow. "Welcome, strangers, to my dungeon. Gen, I thought Sage had class today?"

"Rough night. He's tuckered out. So, we decided to do something different like coming to visit you. If you have a few minutes, maybe there's something here to whet his appetite." Her face telegraphed a hope that Thaddeus might save the day.

"Sure, I'll see what turns his crank."

"Good." She disappeared into the corridor. "I need a washroom."

"Right." Thaddeus knelt to look Sage in the eye. "What do you want to see first?"

"Your office."

"All right, then." Thaddeus led the way. A compulsive tidier, he took a second to straighten some files on his desk while Sage inspected the collection of books shelved on the back wall. Running his finger along the spines of the books, Sage read their titles: "Modern Biology, Discovering Atoms, Astronomy, Sun Sintosy, Tidon's Moons. You have some fantastic books, Dad. Can I take those two back home with me?" He pointed to the last two on the shelf.

"Interested in the sun and moons?"

"Yes."

"Fine." Thaddeus retrieved the books from the shelf and placed them into his son's backpack. "Astronomy is one of my fields. On the other hand, I like to look inward into the tiny world of atoms as well as outward to the stars. You might say that within science I'm rather ambidextrous."

"I want to look in the microscope."

"All right." Sage climbed on the chair and managed to peer through the lens, excited with the view. A box of glass slides sat next to the microscope. He quickly discovered how to change them and examined several. "I want to look at atoms. Where are they?"

"Well, we haven't been able to see atoms yet." Thaddeus leaned on a lab stool. "Our optical microscopes aren't powerful enough to have the capacity to see something that small. However, we know they are the building blocks of molecules."

"Then, how can you say they really exist?"

"By conjecture. We formulate their existence by thinking hard about what matter is composed of in its tiniest pieces. We prognosticate that atoms are very tiny spheres. We're stating that an atom is the size of what we call an angstrom; many thousands of times smaller than the thickness of a human hair."

"So, what's this piece of junk I'm looking through, if I can't see atoms with it?" Sage pushed himself back from the microscope.

Thaddeus switched off the microscope's light. "One day someone will invent a microscope powerful enough that we might really see atoms clearly for the first time ever."

"When?"

"I don't know, Sage. It may be years away. We're in atom infancy right now. That's why I'm always pushing for more funding so we can build more powerful microscopes to see inward into an atom. And also more powerful telescopes so we can see further out to the stars."

Sage turned the microscope light back on and changed the slides on the microscope's platform, flipping through them faster and faster. "This one's all blurry," he said, pulling a slide out of the armature and carelessly dashing it onto the counter top, where it broke into several pieces. He snatched up another from the box and held it up to the light for a moment before throwing it down.

"Hey!" Thaddeus took his arm, arresting the boy's tantrum.

Sage's small face turned toward his father, a hard glint in his green eyes and his sunken cheeks as flat-planed as a tombstone. Watching his father, he swatted with his other hand. The box of slides flew across the room.

Thaddeus lunged to grab Sage's free hand, but missed. The microscope followed the slides, striking the floor with a crash and a tinkle of shattered lenses.

Thaddeus choked back a curse. He lifted the boy, squirming with surprising strength, and turned him face-down across his knee and spanked him.

The boy made no sound.

Genosa, returning, rushed toward them. "Thaddeus!" She slipped on the shards of the microscope and fell on her hands and knees in the glass.

Heat rose in Thaddeus. He spanked the boy again. Still nothing. Again.

"No!" Genosa cried. "That can't help!"

For a moment there was a silent staring contest. Then, Thaddeus let out a pent-up breath and glared into Genosa's pleading face. "Fine," he said, breathing hard. "Just— fine."

Genosa stood and reached with blood-smeared hands to lift her unresisting son from his arms. The boy made no move to hinder her.

"He's fine," Thaddeus said.

Genosa turned away from Thaddeus and set the boy on his feet. Over her shoulder, Thaddeus saw Sage's face, full of cold, blazing rage. If he could have, the boy would have killed him then and there; of that Thaddeus had no doubt.

"Did you see what you did to your mother?" he asked.

"She did that to herself."

"She wouldn't have slipped if—"

"Stop!" Genosa looked down at the wreckage of the university's microscope. She clamped her arms tightly about Sage's torso and said softly but firmly into his ear, "Your father had no right to hit you—"

"Genosa!"

She glared at him out of a corner of her eye. "—and he's sorry he did. But you had no right to break valuable equipment. We'll have to pay to replace the microscope and slides."

"Don't care," Sage said.

"It was your idea to come here," she reminded Sage. "Your dad welcomed you into his laboratory. Look at the mess you've made. He's your father, so he has to forgive you. But do that kind of thing to other people and they'll never let you in again."

The light of rage left the boy's eyes, as if a person was departing a room, slamming a door behind. Genosa's words had helped more than Thaddeus' spanking.

The small body relaxed. "My bum hurts."

"So do my hands and knees," she said. "And your father's reputation."

Thaddeus looked at the pieces of microscope on the floor. "Maybe it can be fixed," he said grudgingly. Blood trickled between Genosa's fingers, staining his son's shirt. "I'm sorry." His voice was harsh.

"I think we're all sorry," said Genosa. She held the boy out at arm's length. "Aren't we, Sage?"

He was subdued now. "Yes. I don't know why I get so angry."

"Maybe you get it from me." Thaddeus bent and picked up pieces of glass and metal, his movements feeling cold and mechanical. "I never thought I'd be a spanker."

"Can I still read your books? I promise I won't hurt them."

Thaddeus sighed. "Of course. Now let's get your mom cleaned up before she bleeds to death." At the child's look of alarm, he said, "I didn't mean it. She'll be fine in a minute. You can pick up the slides. Be careful not to cut yourself." He found a clean towel and some alcohol in a drawer.

Genosa perched on a lab stool and pulled shards of glass from her knees, while Thaddeus dabbed as gently as he could at the cuts, unable to look her in the face.

The child knelt and carefully salvaged any slides that had survived, placing them securely in the grooves of the wooden box, which had come through the encounter only slightly scarred. After a minute of silent work, he said, "Why does this happen to me?"

Thaddeus' fingers stilled on Genosa's hand.

"You're different," his mother said.

Thoughts flickered across Sage's face. "The other children in the high-intellect class are different," he said slowly. "But they don't have awful dreams they can't remember. They don't—"

The boy's fingers paused on the slide box. "They don't go up like fireworks."

Thaddeus shared a look with Genosa. "You have one good thing to cling to," he said, "It's the fact that you're asking questions." He picked a shard of glass from Genosa's thumb. "Just now, when I got angry at you, it felt like I was all boiling inside." He dabbed the wound with the towel. "Like my skin was hot and I needed to breathe hard. What does it feel like when it happens to you?"

Sage placed a piece of broken glass on several others that lay in his palm. "It doesn't really feel like anything," he said. "It's like I'm watching from a corner while my body throws things and my mouth swears. Sometimes I use cuss words that I don't even know. I'm learning them as I'm saying them."

Thaddeus sat back on his heels and looked up into Genosa's face.

Genosa's mouth silently formed the syllables *psychosis?*

He shook his head. He'd be darned if he knew.

Chapter 4

SCHOOL COUNSELOR Rictin Pivantis shook hands with the couple at his office door. "Mr. and Mrs. Rojan. Please come in." He indicated the seats before his desk then settled into his own seat, the chair creaking as it strained under the extra weight his wife had been urging him to lose all summer. "I understand you are interested in having a psychological examination of your son, Sage. That's one of the things Lodiash High School employs me for. As a psychiatrist, I deal with troubled students every day."

Genosa took one of the chairs and Thaddeus took the other.

"Well, we're not certain he needs a psychological examination," Thaddeus hedged, looking over the framed degrees on the wall behind Pivantis' head. There was a frown on the man's face that suggested he thought psychology and psychiatry hardly deserved being called sciences at all. Pivantis knew the type.

"That's what we're here to find out," Genosa said hastily. "If it would help." She had mentioned, when she first made the appointment, that it had taken a while to convince her husband that a psychological examination was a good idea. Pivantis looked over the spectacles that hung on the bridge of his nose and wiped his balding head with a tissue. "Tell me about your son. Then we'll decide."

The couple did their best to put all the strangeness of the past twelve years into a few words. Pivantis made notes, twice stopping them to ask Sage's age at the time of the milestones they were describing.

"And the dreams are continuing?" he asked.

"Yes," said Genosa, "though they're not as frequent."

"And he's never been able to remember even one of them?"

"Never. Is that so unusual?"

Pivantis shrugged. "It's not a matter of being unusual, but indicative of something."

"What kind of something?" Thaddeus said.

"I'll have a better chance of answering that question when I've met Sage." He consulted his calendar. "But it might be a few weeks before I can get back to you with my diagnostic evaluation." He peered at the anxious couple over the top of his spectacles. "If whatever's troubling him is deep-seated, it might be a while before he trusts me enough to let me see into his behavior."

· Ω ·

There was a rap on the counselor's office door. The smallest high school student he had ever seen came into the room, holding a hall pass. But the eyes that regarded him were full of intelligence and the piping voice was not lacking in confidence. "You wanted to see me?"

Pivantis leaned forward on his desk. "You're Sage Rojan?"

"Yes." The boy took in the details of the office once, and then turned to him, dismissing them.

"Then, yes, I wanted to see you."

"Why?"

"Good question. Take a seat young man."

Sage positioned himself on one of the too-large chairs. Pivantis took note of the boy's fair hair and sparkling green eyes. *Quite athletic looking.* "How old are you?"

"Twelve."

"And you're in high school?"

"I'm smart. I might be short, but none of that bothers me."

"That's what I hear." Pivantis shuffled papers across his desk. "What else are you?"

That got him a sharp look. "I don't know what you mean."

"Neither do I, yet. In fact, that's what we're here to find out."

He watched the play of expressions over the child's face: puzzlement, a tinge of suspicion, giving way to cautious curiosity. "You're supposed to understand me?"

"I'm really supposed to help you understand yourself."

Sage's laugh was more cynical than a twelve-year-old should have been able to manage. "Good luck with that."

"I don't rely on luck," said the psychologist. "And neither, I suspect, do you. How about we get started?"

"I've had a lot of tests."

"I understand you have." Pivantis knew Sage's intelligence scores were off the charts and did not, as was often the case with prodigies, tend to clump in one area while remaining close to normal in others— his verbal, mathematical, reasoning, and spatial manipulation results were all beyond exceptional. So, too, were his physical strength and coordination. On any scale that Pivantis could think of, Sage ranked *at* the top— a top that no student had ever reached before.

"So." He noted himself being coolly studied by the boy he was supposed to assess. "You're exceptional."

"I'm in grade eleven on a custom-built acceleration program." The small shoulders lifted and dropped. "Even with that, they're holding me back."

The counselor was impressed. "Okay," he said, "If you're so smart, how come you're not happy?"

"I don't know."

"Tell me what you do know about yourself."

The boy sighed. "I can do things other kids can't and I know all kinds of things they don't. But I don't know what happens to me when I'm asleep. And I don't know why I sometimes get angry — really angry — and then act like an idiot."

"Maybe you're angry because you're unhappy."

Sage glanced at the certificate over the counselor's head then brought his eyes back to the counselor's face in a way that said, *you need a doctorate to work that one out?*

"Bear with me," the man said. "Just because something is simple to say, doesn't mean it's not complex when you get into it. If you don't believe that, wait until you first hear yourself saying, 'I love you.'"

That one got him a different look, one that suggested — whatever plan the counselor had in mind — Sage was willing to give it a try. "What do we do?"

"To begin with, you just do what you normally do. And I'll watch."

"And then?"

"Then we'll do some digging around in your head, to see what we find."

Sage stiffened. "My head is private."

"Don't worry," said Pivantis. "You'll do the digging. I'll just help you interpret what you turn up."

He watched the twelve year old consider what he'd proposed. "All right."

· Ω ·

During the counselor's interviews with the staff, many of Sage's teachers described the boy as the strangest student they had ever known. Now the counselor was seeing it firsthand, during biology class, Sage had one of his so-called daytime 'episodes'. The boy's shoulders slumped, his head bent forward as if he was sleeping.

Sage began to rock back and forth in his desk, his whole upper torso slowly beating time. Pivantis, even from the chair he filled at the back of the biology lab, could see Sage's lips moving, forming sounds. The attention of the rest of the class drifted surreptitiously toward Sage until the teacher tapped her chalk sharply on the slate. Apparently, such behavior from Sage was not all that unusual.

Pivantis slipped from the back of the room until he was level with the rocking, mumbling child. He squatted to watch and listen.

Dissociation— altered state of consciousness, was the term that popped into the psychiatrist's mind. Like a daydream but all-encompassing. He watched for another two minutes, straining to hear what the child was saying. But the sounds were mostly indistinct, and the few syllables he could hear clearly made no sense.

Finally, he rose and went to the door, beckoning the teacher to follow him. Out in the hallway, he said, "I take it you've seen this before?"

The teacher was an older woman, from a generation when a misbehaving pupil would be reprimanded with a sharp slap from a wooden ruler. But she shrugged at the question. "Nothing takes Sage out of it. We've learned to ignore it. In a while, he'll stop."

"And then?"

"And then he'll be normal— well, as normal as the Brumbler gets."

"The Brumbler?"

"I've heard the children call him that. It's short for Brilliant Mumbler."

"Does he know the children call him that?"

Again she shrugged. "Can you imagine high-school students not letting an oddball in on his own nickname?"

· Ω ·

The counselor's last interview was with Vice-principal Gladys Nesiber. One of her duties was to substitute when a teacher was temporarily unable to take a class, and often that class contained Sage Rojan.

Pivantis liked Gladys. She was a sharp-minded, observant woman, who generally knew whatever needed to be known about what was going on in her school. That tended to make his job easier. So when he knocked on her door and put his head in at her office, he was not surprised to hear her say, "Rojan, right?"

"You got it." He eased himself in and shut the door.

"Heard you were making inquiries." The vice-principal rose to take off her sweater. She closed the shades of her office window, as if to prevent anything she might say from escaping into the outside world. "He's the central topic of our administrative team chats," she said, sitting down again. "Gifted, brilliant, exceptional, multi-multi talented. On the flip side, inexplicably troubled and infuriatingly bad-tempered. A golden child, but tarnished. A true prodigy, but also the kid you're most likely to dream of strangling."

"So I gather." Pivantis took a seat.

Gladys had been the driving force behind establishing the gifted student's program at Lodiash. "I know gifted," she said, shaking her head. "But Sage Rojan is the most diverse polymath I've ever come across. He's exceptional at everything. I bet if we enrolled him in auto shop, he'd build a race car. And it would probably win."

"But he's also a case study," the counselor said.

"Yes," said the vice-principal, "but a study in what?"

"Ah. There you have it." He bit his lip. "I think — I'm almost certain — my diagnosis will be Dissociative Identity Disorder. He has the panic and anxiety attacks, and mood swings."

"Multiple personality." She nodded thoughtfully. "A primary personality and one or more alters. Could be. I've noted the sudden anger without a justified cause. You've seen loss of subjective time?"

"His parents report it." Pivantis folded his hands across his belly. "Psychotic-like symptoms. Hears voices. Obsessive, compulsive.

If I'm right, we'll have to watch for suicidal behaviors and self-injury. He may question his own sanity."

"During one class," Gladys said, "he went into one of his brumbling states— could be a pseudoseisure or spontaneous trance state."

"That's associated," Pivantis confirmed.

She nodded. "While he was unconscious, his hands drew intricate diagrams and schematics. He talked through the drawings, giving nonsense names to unheard of parts, which he muttered were needed for a thing he described as an electronic brain."

"Electronic brain? Did he mean a calculator?" Pivantis asked

"This was nothing like any calculator I've ever heard about," Gladys said. "When he woke I asked him what an electronic brain was. He didn't know."

Pivantis shook his head. "Memory loss that goes beyond normal forgetfulness. Classic."

Gladys pressed her lips together. "He became sad and ashamed when the students teased him. I've come to know that Sage can change his mind-set and scale up to the top of the next mountain. But once he gets there, he's not pleased or satisfied with himself. Something inside won't let him stop to enjoy the moment. It's like he's always being prodded from within. Something drives him, but it's not the joy of accomplishment." She sighed. "A lot of prodigies burn out early — prodigy means 'spendthrift' after all — and most end up miserable failures. With Rojan, whether he's a failure or a colossal success in everything he tries, he's still miserable."

"What good is greatness if no happiness comes from it?" Pivantis supplied.

· Ω ·

Thaddeus and Genosa Rojan entered the counselor's office and took the same seats as before. Pivantis opened the file on his desk.

"First of all," he said, "Sage is a good kid. He doesn't hurt anybody, doesn't even try. Doesn't play hooky, doesn't smoke or drink."

He's only twelve," interrupted Thaddeus.

"Makes no difference. Trust me on that." Pivantis went back to the file. "But he's an unhappy child."

Genosa nodded, "That's partly why we're here."

33

"I'll be frank with you— I've never seen a child like him. Nobody here has."

Thaddeus opened his lips to say something but his wife's hand gently touched his arm, so he subsided.

Pivantis acknowledged the unspoken reaction. "But you already knew that, too. You've likely known it since he was born." He straightened the glasses on his nose. "There is a school of psychology that holds that the mind is made up of different components, and only one of them is the conscious mind."

"You're going to tell us Sage has an unconscious mind? And that it's in conflict with his— what do you call it?" said Thaddeus, in a tone that made clear that he thought the idea was ridiculous.

"More than that," said Pivantis, "something inside Sage drives him, eats at him, and sometimes gets in his way. Call it his unconscious or subconscious. In psychiatry, we would refer to Sage's condition as Dissociative Identity Disorder. Some people call it Multiple Personality Disorder."

"You're calling my son crazy? Mentally ill?" Thaddeus spoke as if he thought Pivantis was the crazy one.

Genosa covered her husband's hand with her own, her face pale.

Pivantis leaned forward, grieved by the couple's pain. "I know this is not easy for you. But the dreams are a clue. You've heard him arguing with himself, nagging himself. You've seen him fly into rages, and when he does, he seems to become — for the length of the tantrum — another person."

"That's right." Genosa said, leaning forward, moisture glistening on her cheeks. "When I look into his face, I don't see my son. I see a stranger."

Thaddeus shifted uncomfortably, lips pressed closed.

"Forget the mechanism that creates the effect," Pivantis said softly. "This is not a lab experiment. It's a real-world problem of a real boy who's been made terribly unhappy. The only question is: what can we do to make Sage's life better?"

"And you've got an approach?" Thaddeus managed gruffly.

"I do."

Pivantis could almost feel Genosa's gaze on him, as if it had actual weight and pressure. "What is it?" she said.

"One last thing, before I tell you," he said. "When I was evaluating Sage, I tried hypnosis."

Thaddeus sputtered.

The psychiatrist held up his hands. "I was once as skeptical as you are, but I can assure you that therapeutic hypnosis has nothing to do with stage performers who make people cluck and bark. Beyond the popular misconceptions, hypnosis is just a way of clearing the mind and allowing it to focus without distraction from the thousands of sensory signals that bombard the brain moment by moment. In the hands of a responsible practitioner, it's a reliable tool."

He hadn't entirely convinced Thaddeus but at least he had his attention.

"Well, one thing I learned is that Sage can't be hypnotized. Or won't be hypnotized." He leaned across the desk and recounted what had happened.

"I lowered the lights, offered Sage a comfortable chair, and began my standard relaxation technique. When your son's posture loosened and his eyes closed, I began the first stage of inducing a trance."

Thaddeus looked at Genosa, but said nothing.

"I asked Sage to visualize a white screen with a black dot at its center. I asked him to concentrate on that dot and think of nothing else but that dot and to listen to my voice and only my voice. Usually, the more intelligent a subject is the easier they are to hypnotize," he said. "It's a matter of the mind's capacity to focus, and Sage's mind can focus like a microscope."

Thaddeus grunted at that, but didn't speak.

"Sage was doing very well. I asked him some basic questions about his feelings, to see if there was any resistance— did he like his parents? To which he answered yes. Did he have any friends? No, he said, which was not a surprise. Geniuses tend to be solitary. But then I asked him if he had any enemies."

Genosa's eyes bored into him. "What did he say?"

Pivantis read from his notes. "'Oh, yes. It pretends to be my friend, but it isn't.'"

"'Who is it?' I said. And that was where things got interesting. Sage opened his mouth to answer, but in an instant his mouth snapped shut and his eyes flew open. I found myself facing a very enraged child I didn't recognize. It was as if something inside of Sage, some part of his mind," he told the boy's parents, "intervened and shut him down. It was as if a sleeping guard dog had suddenly awakened to find that I was in its territory. It came to life and was growling at me in an instant."

"I tried to end the session then and there, but Sage carried on, cussing me with a repertoire of foreign and contrived words. He berated me until, finally, the vitriol subsided. Then he calmly got up to walk out of my office. Before he left, I asked him, 'Do you remember belittling me?' but he was completely puzzled by my question. You can believe what you want to believe about how the mind is organized, but at some level your son is convinced he has an enemy. And I think he's right. Whatever you want to call it, there is a force inside him, a force that overpowers him when it comes out. I am certain that, whatever it is, it is the source of his nightmares and episodes when he flies into a storming rage."

"Something inside him?" asked his mother.

"Possessed by a demon? Is that where you're going?" Thaddeus asked Pivantis.

"In an earlier time, that would have been the quick verdict," Pivantis chuckled, "But, today, analytical diagnostic rules over superstition and the more useful term is Multiple Personality Disorder."

"What can we do?" Genosa asked.

Pivantis rose to his feet. "There is a technique I can teach your son that might help him deal with whatever's going on inside him."

"What is it?" said Genosa. "Please."

"It's called lucid dreaming. It's new to psychology.

"Can this — this lucid dreaming — hurt him?"

Pivantis spread his hands. "I'll be honest and say I don't think so."

"You're not sure," Thaddeus said.

"Here's what I am sure of: Sage's unhappiness is tied up with his nightmares— which he never remembers. This technique may finally allow him to know what's going on in his own dreams."

Thaddeus and Genosa looked at each other, skeptical and worried.

Finally, Thaddeus said, "If you've got an enemy, you at least need to know who or what it is."

Chapter 5

AS FAR BACK AS SAGE could remember he had always been aware of his 'shadow.' At one time it had behaved much like Orlandia's pirates: showing up to overpower him for its own purpose. But, as Sage grew older he was aware of it simply as a *presence*, scarcely felt, but never far away. His 'shadow,' unlike the dark version that Sintosy threw on the sidewalk when he walked to the park with his mother, was shapeless, without definition, and forever present in the privacy of his mind.

When he was three, Sage asked his mother, "How come I can see my outside shadow but never my inside one?"

His mother had been puzzled by his question and, he could tell, a little frightened too. He saw a familiar sadness in her eyes, the same sadness he saw every time he asked her a question she couldn't answer. "What inside one?" she said.

"Never mind. Just something I was thinking about."

Sage had tried playing tricks on his shadow, thinking about a complex chain of logic then, all at once, switching his awareness to the whatever-it-was that he could feel was mentally observing him; turning the table on his personal paparazzi. But no matter how quickly he attempted the transition, the shadow withdrew before he could bring it into focus.

Even though he'd never seen it or heard its voice, Sage knew the shadow came to him in his dreams. He would awaken to find his mother and sometimes his father looking down at him, their faces contorted with worry; the covers wrapped around him, or tossed in all directions. He would realize that he had been twisting and thrashing. His dreams fading in a faint echo;

words he'd spoken vaporizing like wisps of mist. He never managed to hold on to them long enough to grasp their meaning.

And there was always one other thing he was aware of in those moments: the shadow withdrawing from him, like something lithe and sinuous disappearing into a hole in a wall.

· Ω ·

Dr. Pivantis' suggestion of hypnosis allowed Sage to feel something new. He felt the equivalent of a twitch inside him. The shadow had been startled, or at least discomfited in some way. Of course, every time after that when the time came for the counselor to lull Sage into a trance, the shadow would intervene. He did not know how it was done, but whenever Sage tried to follow the doctor's suggestions — imagining a black dot on a white screen, watching the pendulum swing before his eyes — something prevented him from settling. He could not make the connection, and finally the doctor told him he was one of the minority of intelligent people who could not be hypnotized.

Sage was disappointed, but in the weeks that followed, the counselor suggested something that might help reduce the ill effects of his sleep deprivation. "It's called lucid dreaming," Dr. Pivantis explained.

"I think I've heard of it." Sage strained to remember; which was odd. He normally remembered everything that he had ever read, heard, or seen. In fact he often imagined he was a machine that could crunch facts and analyze data; although even those terms felt foreign in their own way. He knew that he had been doing so, at full throttle, since he came out of the womb. In fact Sage was surprised to learn, early on, that in comparison to him, other people usually operated at half-speed.

Why don't I remember what I've read about lucid dreaming? he asked himself, even as another part of his mind was taking in what the counselor was telling him. It seemed the techniques for lucid dreaming were similar to self-hypnosis; controlled breathing, clearing the mind of stray thoughts, concentrating on being completely involved with the moment.

"I can do that," he said.

They did some practicing in the counselor's office, and Sage soon found that he could achieve a state of clear-minded calm and maintain it indefinitely.

"Excellent," said Dr. Pivantis. "Now all you need to do is perform the technique just before you fall asleep. Tell yourself that you can achieve this state of mind whenever you call upon it."

"Sounds easy."

The counselor held up a cautionary hand. "It can take a while before the dreaming mind makes a connection with what the conscious mind is telling it. But once the connection is made, it's yours."

Sage tried it that night. He lay in his bed breathing rhythmically and focusing on a single continuous sound voiced in his mind. Once asleep the bad dreams came. He tumbled into a maelstrom of images and sounds, sensations and thoughts, swirling around him, buffeting him from all sides.

As always, he was not alone. His shadow-self was with him, and he realized, as he always did in his dreams, that this other was a part of him— and yet entirely separate. Still, he could not bring the shadow into clear focus. It was darkness, a presence — above all, a voiceless voice — urging him to do more, to try harder, and most importantly, to permanently integrate everything into his mind, to learn, learn, learn!

Sage resisted, fought to assert his own independence, but in his dreamscape, the shadow was stronger. It pushed and bullied and drove him like a beast of burden, whipping and spurring him with the force of its will, a will so powerful it defeated dreaming Sage, for all his resistance, and bent him to its bidding.

This night, in the midst of the struggle, Sage recalled what Dr. Pivantis had taught him and reached for the lucid technique.

The shadow batted it aside.

Sage reached again, felt the technique being pulled from his grasp. *Still too strong* he thought and gave up the effort. Instead, he let himself be sucked into the whirlwind of sounds and images the shadow threw at him. This was another part of his dream world— where he seemed to live fragments of other lives, in other worlds, under different suns and constellations, in strange landscapes, towering alien cities and grubby little villages, jungles and deserts, high in the skies and down in the ocean depths where sound did the job of the missing light.

Here, he was an old man, there, young woman, then, an abandoned child in rags, now, a princeling in silks, sometimes, an astronaut jettisoning through space. He was a darting, flying thing; a massive, slow-moving denizen of the deeps; a fleeing herbivore at one moment; a thing of bunched muscles and razor claws the next. The life-shards came and went in dizzying succession, and from each episode he drew some knowledge, some awareness, and saw it packed into a great mosaic floor that always stretched before him in his dreams.

The mosaic surface went on and on, into an immense distance on all sides, a swirling, complex pattern of shapes and symbols and colors that he realized was, somehow, a kind of schematic. The mosaic was his mind, and it was being built, night by night, dream by dream, to the commands of his inner shadow. Sometimes, too, the work went on during the day, during the times when he seemed to those around him to be disconnected from the world, closed in on himself, his eyes vacant and lips mumbling. In the dream he knew all of this, and knew that he would forget it entirely the moment he awoke.

He could feel the shadow moving around him, though he couldn't see it. Even here it was more a suggestion than a solid presence. But he could sense that it was interacting with the mosaic, forming connections, nudging elements into a desired alignment with each other. And he knew that *it* was impatient to complete something; that *it* was already looking beyond this work to a larger and grander plan. And he understood that it was driven by a barely contained rage at his slowness to accomplish the great work.

Sage watched, as if from above, while the shadow flitted from place to place over the pattern, working, always working. Then he saw it stop and Sage knew, as he knew every night, that time had run out and soon he would wake to drag himself, tired and unrested, through another day of learning and doing and becoming.

The shadow emitted no feeling of sympathy or empathy as it slunk back to wherever it lurked during his waking hours. With the shadow receding Sage remembered Pivantis' technique of lucid dreaming.

As the mosaic floor began to fade and break into patches around him, he reached for the clarity of mind he had developed before he fell asleep.

Now, Sage stood on the patterned floor. It was no longer dissolving. In the distance the shadow continued to withdraw, the dark amorphous smudge dim and heedless of Sage's new found stability. *Not so fast*, Sage thought to himself, and willed himself to follow. His dream body reacted to his desires and he flew across the endless mosaic, faster and faster, his dark and shapeless companion receding before him.

But not receding fast enough. Sage gained. And now he saw that there was indeed a limit to the great floor. It ended at a black wall, and in that wall was a narrow, bluish opening. The shadow reached it, paying no notice to Sage's pursuit, and slipped through.

Sage exerted his will again and put on a burst of speed. As he approached the opening, it occurred to him that it might be a threshold leading to a radically different state. The opening narrowed as he drew closer, and resolved itself into a watery curtain. *This should be easy.* He pushed, but the water transformed into a barrier of solid ice.

But there was a space, and a sliver of time to look through the narrowing frosty gap. Beyond, a golden light illuminated a seemingly endless hallway floored in black glass, its sides lined with closed doors. The shadow stopped at one and entered. Then the gap closed and the vision disappeared.

Sage woke, his mind still lit with golden light. He remembered the closing doorway, the corridor of doors. He remembered the shadow making its exit. He found he could not hold on to the whirlwind of dreams, and had only a dim recollection of the mosaic over which he had been flying before he looked through the crack in the icy barrier. But at least now, for the first time, *he remembered something.*

He was tired, as he usually was in the morning, but he went down to breakfast happy.

· Ω ·

Sage sat quietly in the passenger seat as his mom drove the Raffer Canal roadway toward school. His mind was mulling over the memories of the mosaic and doors from his dream. He felt healthier this morning. It had worked out for him, the act of sharing those remembrances with his parents over breakfast. Most times, after a bad night had left him tired and groggy, he felt unsure as to whether, as he once put it to himself, *reality was really real.* Sometimes he found it necessary to reassure himself that it wasn't all some ridiculous arrangement of the shadow's.

He allowed his senses to open and receive. He took in the beauty of Chaffler's Bridge as they approached, rolling down the window to let the fragrance of the hanging flowers fill his nostrils. Too, his ears picked up the squeals from the squeaky wooden boards. His senses strained hard, seeing, hearing, smelling; providing him proof that this morning was real.

The auto jerked Sage's head forward as his mother stepped on the brake and stopped in front of the school. She wished him a good day as he slammed the car door shut and ran up the front walkway. His legs were tired, but today he felt an unaccustomed exuberance.

He took the concrete steps two at a time in upward leaps, remembering how he'd sped across some now-vague landscape in his dream. He closed his eyes, the better to recapture the fading memory.

Instead of flying through empty space, he collided and sprawled, his arms and legs entangled in the limbs and clothes of another person —

A girl. "Watch where you're going, you clumsy oaf!"

He scrambled to his feet as the girl stood, gathering her scattered books.

"I'm sorry," he said. "My fault." He reached down to help with the books, but she ostentatiously ignored him. As she dusted off her blouse and skirt and swept back the hair from her face he realized she was of his own size with long blondish hair and sapphire blue eyes.

She snatched the books from him, gave him an unforgiving look. "Look where you're going, not where you've been."

Then, as if he'd ceased to exist, she turned and walked away, still straightening her clothes, her back stiff and her nose at maximum elevation. Instantly, he knew he liked every part of her — even her long white knee-high socks and her flashy low-cut red shoes — except for the part where she preached to him.

Sage had never cared to have a girlfriend, nor a friend of any kind, but for the first time he genuinely regretted the effect his behavior had had on another human being. He would like to have made a better first impression.

Oh, well. He sought to push the matter from his thoughts. He wouldn't be seeing her again, and after the breakthrough of the night before, he had more important things to ponder.

Arriving at his class, Sage took his usual desk. The seat next to him was empty, and had been since a high-strung boy named Jattro had transferred out. The lack of a neighbor suited Sage; he liked the elbow room.

The other gifted students filtered in. Sage paid them little heed, and no one took the time to say hello to 'the Brumbler'. Then a motion caught his eye— blonde passing the classroom door. A moment later, she was poking her head in the door, looking around. Her eyes slid over him as if he wasn't worth a closer inspection. "Is this the accelerated group?" she said.

The teacher looked up from his desk and confirmed that it was. "Are you Tamara Young?"

"Yes," she said.

"Well, come in. There's a free desk over there." He pointed to the empty desk beside Sage.

Sage watched her glide in, the red shoes coming towards him. He felt odd. Somehow she was *more real* than anyone else in the room; as if she was somehow drawn in brighter colors than his surroundings.

For her part, she paid him no attention at all. She made for the empty desk, opened the lid and placed her books inside. He watched her fold under her skirt as she sat down. It was a familiar motion he'd seen a thousand times, but somehow when she did it, it had more... he didn't know what it had more of, only that it did.

Settled, she glanced over at him. Their eyes met, and she gave him a long, penetrating look. She snorted and looked away, shaking her head, her long hair continuing the motion after she stopped.

He felt himself blushing, and couldn't remember ever doing that before. Nor could he recall ever being nervous about what he was about to say. He cleared his throat. "Are you sure you're in the right class?"

She gave him a cool look. "Was I supposed to get your permission?"

Sage's embarrassment deepened. The teacher called for the class's attention. "Today we welcome a new member to the accelerated group. Tamara Young. She becomes the youngest person in the class, being a month younger than Sage."

One of the oldest boys sniggered.

"Well let's get started. Today I've prepared a pop quiz," the teacher said, but then broke off and peered at Sage. "Are you all right, Sage? You look a little off-color."

"I'm fine," Sage said, sinking down into his desk.

The teacher handed out the mimeographed quiz. Sage was always the first to finish and always scored one hundred per cent. Today, the test was somehow invested with more importance.

He raced through the questions, his pencil flying, then, proud as a wide-winged rain bird showing off its plumage, strutted to the teacher's desk. When he returned and sat down again, he was pleased to see that Tamara was still at the top of the page.

Blinking, he realized, much to his horror, that Tamara young wasn't on the first question but was, instead, working at the top of the second page.

The girl rose to take her test to the teacher, then returned to her seat and sat down primly without acknowledging Sage's existence.

The heat flashed back to Sage's face. He would not make a perfect score, and worse, he was beginning to suspect that she would—

· Ω ·

The next weeks established a pattern. For the first time in his life, Sage Rojan knew what it was to have competition... competition that mattered to him.

Somehow, Tamara Young seemed to be nearly as intellectually gifted as he was. They fell into a habit of trying to outdo each other, and Sage did not always win. Sometimes they tied, and sometimes she was just a little bit more focused, a little bit more detailed in providing the right answer, and at these times he could feel the shadow boiling inside him, wanting to lash out. Sage did his best to control the burning rage inside him, sometimes struggling to reach for the calm of lucid dreaming. And, at times, he caught her watching him.

But the real difference was that the girl, for all her singular abilities, was able to make friends with other students, even though they were much older. Sage remained solitary.

Their competition was not impersonal. She resented the casual know-it-all tone in which he more-or-less unconsciously spoke, and didn't forbear to ask him if he would soon need a new hat— "two sizes larger, to accommodate that swelled head."

Sage was perplexed by the way Tamara was able to get the better of him. Often he performed below par when around her. During their confrontations, they tongue-lashed each other, as though Tamara needed to put him in his place every chance she got.

"Sage, you've got this huge ego, as big as all outdoors. Maybe someday you'll come down to Tidon."

"And maybe someday you'll quit being goody-two-boots." But Sage's comebacks were lame. Tamara had a knack for getting under his skin.

Often, the best he could come up with was to call her a teacher's pet. Their bickering amused the rest of the class but exasperated their teacher. It became common practice for Sage and Tamara to find themselves both escorted to the principal's office for causing excessive class interruptions.

One afternoon, as Tamara received another award and grinned and sashayed her way back to her desk, Sage's shadow rose in rage. He struggled to push it down.

As she passed by his desk, Sage's leg, without thought or reason, shot out sideways catching Tamara's foot, causing her to sprawl onto her hands and knees. In an instant she jumped up, grabbed him by the scuff of his shirt and pulled him backwards. Sage and his desk tumbled over.

The teacher raced into the fray and exiled them both to the office, together. They sat for a very long time on hard chairs outside the principal's closed door, as the shadow raged within Sage— fixated on Tamara. Strategically, Sage closed his eyes, forcing himself into a trance and calling upon lucid dreaming, his outside awareness severed for an indefinite amount of time.

When he finally opened his eyes, all he could see was Tamara gazing at him, mouth open, and concern in her eyes. He turned away.

"You were mumbling crazy things."

Sage tensed. Her pity felt worse than her anger.

"I'm not going to call you the Brumbler," she said it decisively as if she was making up her mind about something....

Chapter 6

ONCE AGAIN, Sage glided at high speed over the vast mosaic. This was part of the sea of knowledge he'd been drawing from for his entire life. No, not drawing; the shadow had been pumping the knowledge into him.

Again, the mosaic ended at a black wall that went up forever, a wall pierced by a single blue barrier. The threshold was open and the shadow, seemingly unaware of Sage's pursuit, passed through it. Sage willed his dream-self to greater speed. This time, he would not just peek through the barrier. He would enter the realm beyond.

As the aqua barrier narrowed, Sage put his hand forward and felt the watery curtain, a cold liquid crystallizing into solid ice. He snapped his hand back and waited. The diminishing barrier became a rush of burning steam. Still, he waited and watched as the barrier contracted. This time atoms of hydrogen and oxygen moved apart, separating into shimmers of pure gas. Rewarded, he squeezed through the vacuum of their disassociation.

Behind him he heard the aqua curtain close with an icy *crack*.

Ahead he saw the endless corridor and recalled the vague darkness of his shadow disappearing through one of the myriad of doors.

Behind him the great wall and gap through which he had arrived disappeared, as things do in dreams, and he found himself in a vast circular foyer, with a floor of glossy black tiles. The atrium was the hub of a great wheel, each one of its hundreds of corridors, like the one the shadow had taken, lined with countless white doors.

Above the ground-level corridors were even more hallways, tier upon tier of them, fading into the distance. He willed himself to float up one level, then another, rotating his body as he rose. He saw doors, thousands upon thousands of them. *What*, he thought, *might lie behind them*?

He rose to the topmost level and willed himself to one of the corridors. The first white door was marked with numbers and symbols, *67-047 and* ▲▼178♦✿.

The next was marked *67-048*. The next, *-049. Sequentially*.

He dropped to the level immediately below the top level. A door read, *66-049* again with the same combination ▲▼178♦✿ configured above.

Now, though he was sure he had done nothing to cause it, level sixty-seven began to move clockwise, while the level below it rotated counter-clockwise, as if someone had just started up a series of carousels, stacked one on top of the other, all sliding soundlessly.

An automatic defense mechanism to confuse intruders? Or, open for business? His interest was now acutely piqued. He decided to see if he could open one of the doors.

Door *66-453* passed before him. He extended a dream hand and pushed on the panel. It gave no resistance and opened to complete blackness. He reached within and felt around for a light switch, as if he was entering a darkened room. His fingers brushed a button, and he pressed it.

He expected a light to go on. Instead, the space framed by the doorway erupted in a kaleidoscope of colors that flowed outwards and sucked him inside. The stream of images plunged him into action.

And the action was terrifying.

Screaming men, women, and children hurtled past him through dense foliage.

"Zorphians!" a panicked voice screeched. "Run!"

Sage bolted, adrenaline electrifying his muscles and he realized he was experiencing the events around him through the senses of another conscious being.

Dodging a stump, the body he inhabited threw a quick, panicked glance over its shoulder.

A carnivore bore down on him, three times his height, huge—

He stumbled over a log, thrashed through willows and plunged forward.

A blast of fetid breath and two arcs of jagged teeth, upper and lower, clashed together above him in anticipation of savaging his flesh.

He dodged left, around a trunk, down a short embankment. A woman ahead of him shrieked as another monster sank its teeth into her thigh.

The thing behind him butted Sage in the back, trying to knock him down. If it succeeded —

He stumbled through a rocky stream and dove to his right —

It would crush him to the ground, eat him alive.

It's a dream —

The beast's hot breath hit his back in wet gusts.

A dream within a dream —

Abruptly, the scene disappeared. No light, no sound, no texture or temperature — Sage was adrift in nothingness, weightless and motionless.

He twisted about, trying to see, to hear, to feel — *anything*.

A white oblong formed itself in the distance. That was better.

Sage willed himself toward it. He felt no motion; the fact that the rectangle grew steadily larger was the only clue that he approached it. He passed through a portal of white light, and found himself, as he had been before, in the great foyer near the top of a column of corridors.

Before him was a door numbered 66-559. A different door.

His chest tightened.

Inside would be a dream. But what kind of dream? Could a dream kill him? Or could he overcome whatever was inside through force of will?

He smiled. Never had he felt such challenge, such uncertainty, such sense of being — he was truly *alive*.

The door opened to his touch and again he pressed the button that turned darkness into color and action. He felt himself drawn into another being —

Although he was inside the new creature, he also hovered and observed himself in action; it was surreal. A silent narrator placed information in his mind, so wherever he focused, he knew what he was seeing and what it meant.

He resided in a non-human male, intelligent but unsophisticated, and he stood naked and shivering within a group of his peers, inside a dirty encampment near the reeds of a scummy lagoon. The reeking stench of the murky squalor burned his nostrils.

66-559 was the only individual identification Sage could access, though the word 'Calmor' came to mind as a species name. Sage drifted about this creature, noting details of the life it lived. 66-559 possessed four arms, two legs, and two heads, each with one cyclopean eye. Like the others near him, he was emaciated. Starvation had left him torpid. The silent narrator summarized from years prior, when 66-559 had been snatched from its home world by an alien species which called itself the Kispil. The reasons for the abduction were unclear, but 66-559, along with dozens of others of his species, had been relocated to a distant planet and confined to a research facility, where samples of flesh and fluids had been taken by the Kispil.

Eventually the researchers stopped coming and 66-559 and his comrades were able to break out of their confinement only to discover that the vast hive-like structure in which their captors dwelt was choked with the skeletal remains of dead Kispil, slaughtered by some unknown force.

66-559 and his comrades, unable to operate the spaceships they found, tried to make lives for themselves in this world turned mausoleum. But the soil of the planet lacked the key nutrients their metabolism found essential. They were dying and 66-559 would be the last to go, starved to death and consumed by the insects of the Kispil planet.

Sage left the compartment. The dream had been disturbing in a way he could not define. He was not certain he wanted to know so intimately any other creatures.

But still his veins hummed with sensation, with life. Sage tentatively pushed open another door, then another, and another.

Behind each one was the memory of a life that he could either plunge into or observe from a position of neutrality.

Each door lead to different alien landscapes, strange looking people— some humanoid, many not. He observed places that no Tidonese had ever seen, creatures so diverse they amazed him. He experienced pain and pleasure, triumphs and defeats, the magnificent and the tawdry, moments of intensity, and years of tedium.

How could these experiences be here? They were not his memories. Were they fantasies? But why were there so many? Could they belong to the shadow— the shadow that was a part of Sage. Could Dr. Pivantis' diagnosis of *Multiple Personality Disorder* be incorrect? But, what else could they be? Perhaps past life memories, like he'd read about in a theology book once?

Sage returned to the foyer and willed the black wall with the aqua barrier to appear. The threshold came as he bid, and he passed back through to the great mosaic.

The pattern stretched in all directions, but its scope was not limitless, merely large. He used the skills Dr. Pivantis had taught him to will that the limits be made known to him, and at once his distance vision sharpened.

Far off, he saw another wall, black like the one behind him, but speckled with dots of white. *There*, he commanded. But this time there was no sense of flying across the great pattern. At one moment he was outside the aqua, and in the next he was at the foot of the second towering black wall. This one was full of windows, each glowing with light.

He chose a window at random, and pressed his face against the pane. But his view was obscured. All he could see was diffuse, featureless light. He stepped back and searched for an entrance, but saw none. He experienced a moment's frustration, but then his training reasserted itself. *Make an entrance*, he willed.

A pair of tall, wooden arched gates, large enough for a cathedral, appeared. He bade them open and they swung outward, light spilling onto and around him. Sage felt a sense of wonder— a sense that here was something more than the collection of existences he had sampled across the way.

And, with the wonder, came worry. So far, he'd been able to deal with whatever he encountered. But there was something about the windows, the flooding white light, which stirred a sense of foreboding.

He looked back over his shoulder. All he had to do was wake up and he would be home, with his parents, competing with Tamara, jumping through hoops for teachers and psychologists. Back with his unhappiness.

He faced the arched gates. *I've come this far. Nothing has the right to scare me away. Not even myself.* He placed one dream foot in front of the other and stepped inside.

His first impression was of some kind of vast catacomb. Again, there were tiers upon tiers, rank upon rank of metal vaults— like the ones he had seen in pictures of ancient sealed tombs. They went up and up, disappearing into mist. And even when he tried to use his skills to will the obscuring clouds away, they lingered unresponsive.

Dread fluttered in his chest.

He pushed the fear back and crossed the wide floor, approaching one of the vaults. It was wider than he was tall and its lintel was high above his head. A handle wrought from dark metal was set near one edge. *A burial ground with thousands of tombs? If I open one will I find a wrapped body or worms eating away at a corpse?*

He reached for the handle, he felt the coldness of death in his dream hand, and pulled the thing downward. Vibration wracked his grip and protesting metal screeched. He summoned his willpower, prepared to force the mechanism open.

The shadow.

It was close by. Dread bloomed into panic he could barely hold down.

Something high overhead plummeted toward him. Leathery wings and a long jaw filled with sharp, conical teeth.

In an instant he knew he faced the shadow's will.

He turned and ran, racing for the open gates.

A piercing shriek turned his blood to ice. The sound knifed through his spine.

Faster!

It was as if his feet were sticking to the floor, as if the air from his waist down had become as thick and as clinging as springtime mud.

Another shriek reverberated above, closer— much too close. And he was too far from escape.

A shadow fell over him, then a gust of foul breath—

Pivantis! He had taught him—

Wake! Wake! Wake!

Teeth snapped in his ear—

Then he was lying on the rug beside his bed. His bedroom dark, his sheets soaked with sweat and his pillow on top of him. He threw them off and shivered in the silence.

The light snapped on. Genosa and Thaddeus stood in the bedroom doorway. Sintosy's first light was just graying the window. "Are you all right?" asked his mother.

It took Sage a moment to settle his breathing. "Better than all right."

He remembered... the mosaic, the thousands of doors, the snippets of the lives behind them. The last place he'd been and the shadow — his other self — resolute to keep him out.

Chapter 7

SAGE CLOSED THE DOOR to his bedroom and drew the shade to prevent the glow of the streetlamp outside from flooding in. He turned off the overhead light so that the room was illuminated only by the small intrusion that leaked underneath his door from the hallway beyond.

He pulled back the covers of the bed but did not get in. Instead, he sat on the exposed bottom sheet, his upper body upright, spine supporting him, his legs crossed. He felt comfortable. The position had become natural to him over the past several days. He had gone back to Dr. Pivantis and asked for help. He had told the counselor what he remembered of the mosaic and the tiers of corridors lined with doors.

The psychiatrist had listened silently as Sage described what lay behind the white doors, how he had experienced life after life, on world after world; and about his shadow.

"You don't believe me." Sage read the look of doubt on Pivantis' face. The doctor rubbed his fingers unconsciously on his upholstered chair. "I think you should have a more thorough assessment."

"Then you think I'm insane."

The psychiatrist's expression remained professionally neutral. "You have to consider the possibility that you — at times — experience psychotic breaks with reality."

The words felt like a blow. Because these were the words he had been dreading; the words he had expected to hear. "So I should be locked up."

"No, Sage." Pivantis had leaned forward, brows knit with concern. "Researchers are learning more about the subconscious all the time. There are medications that are showing promise—"

"No medications."

"Sage, don't make up your mind until—"

"No medications. I don't want to be a sleepwalker."

"Your decision, of course. Or, perhaps I should say, your parents'. You are, after all, still a minor."

Sage brushed the qualification away. His parents wouldn't make him do anything he didn't want to do. Still he huddled miserably into the corner of the couch.

"And each white door was sequentially numbered?" Pivantis said thoughtfully. Professionally. "Sounds as if it's organized like a bureaucracy."

"Don't condescend to me." Sage couldn't keep the petulant sound out of his voice. "You've made up your mind. You're thinking, if my subconscious creates a bureaucracy, what does that say about Sage's hallucinations?"

"It's too soon for anyone to make up their mind," Pivantis said severely. "You, or me. I'm just trying to understand you better."

"Don't lie to me, Pivantis."

He leaned his elbows on his knees. "Sage, work with me here. Yes, you have a working diagnosis of Dissociative Identity Disorder. Not much is known about it. You say you want help, but you don't want medication. There are other things we can try, but I need to know more."

Sage let out a deep breath. He wanted to believe Pivantis. The doctor and his parents were the only ones who seemed to be on his side. "I wonder if what I'm experiencing is some sort of connection to a realm outside the day-to-day universe we call reality. One in which we return, time after time, after we die and are reborn and die, again, and again."

"In that case," the doctor said, "is that next life a random one or is it chosen for us, and we're just told to get on with it."

Sage found himself wondering the same thing. "I find it hard to imagine that I picked this life."

Pivantis nodded thoughtfully.

"Either way," Sage continued, "I was out of my league when I tried to open the vault in whatever that other structure was. My shadow conjured a monster. I don't know what it might have done to me if I hadn't torn myself from the dream..." The lucid-dreaming technique had its limits.

"You want to know if there is something more to strengthen your hand," Pivantis finished for him.

"Right. I can't go toe-to-toe with my shadow— my other personality." Sage was certain of this. "Not when it can create things like that."

"Sage," Pivantis said. "A mouse doesn't have to be stronger than a cat. It just needs to out-maneuver the jaws and claws."

· Ω ·

Seated cross-legged on his bed, Sage practiced the relaxation exercises he had already mastered. When his breathing was ordered and his thoughts were clear, he moved on to the new techniques Pivantis had shown him. With his arms extended so that the back of his up-turned hands rested on his knees, he closed his fists and at the same time transferred their sense of controlled power to his mind. He felt his mental faculties powering up, his ability to focus his thoughts becoming both stronger, and more controlled.

So far, so good. He closed his eyes but could still picture in his mind the board he had hung on his bedroom wall that afternoon. Pivantis called it a 'vision board' and had told him to print on it, then to repeat over and over, words that expressed his dream-goals. Now, feeling his own mental abilities as a tool to be used, Sage repeated to himself the first mantra: *Find out what's in the shadow's vaults.*

In his enhanced, meditative state, the words took on a power that went beyond sound and symbol. He felt them as an expression of his strongest will, a determination that came from the deepest part of him. It was like stories he'd read in which magicians memorized spells so they became part of the wizard's being, to be focused and directed, to make the world do as the spell-caster willed.

He called up the second mantra: *Use the new technique to remember the dream state.* Information was power, especially for a mouse. More than that, Sage had a right to know what was going on in his own mind. He'd felt, in the past, that he had been invaded, that he was harboring an uninvited, unwelcome guest. He meant to know just who the second personality was, and what it was up to.

About the third invocation, Sage was not so sure: *Find a way to converse with the shadow.* Logically, the most direct way to find out what it was up to was to ask it. But Sage wasn't sure he'd receive an answer. And if he did get one, he wasn't at all sure it would be something he wished to hear — if mice could converse with cats, they probably wouldn't like the message.

He chanted the words in the clear chamber of his focused mind, until the third affirmation joined the other two as shining steel cords binding and supporting his will.

He opened his eyes. It was too dim in his bedroom to see the vision board, but the white oblong was nonetheless filled with meaning for him. It was real, just as his determination was real. As Pivantis had said, these matters were ruled by what he called an 'act of attraction.' The disciplined mind could make manifest that which it most clearly envisioned.

"Sounds like magic," Sage had said, with a tinge of skepticism that sounded, in his own ears, like something his father might say.

"Maybe," Pivantis had responded with a small smile, "but in the world of dreams, to be armed with potent magical powers is probably not a bad thing."

Sage felt ready — like one of the mariners who had sailed off to find the new land of Batakesh — to start his own voyage of discovery.

He willed his heartbeat to slow. His eyelids closed and behind them his eyes rolled slightly upward. His right hand moved to the back of his head, where his index and middle fingers slowly tapped the nape of his neck. Then, he took a long, slow, deep breath and held it for three seconds. He softly breathed the word *lucid.*

He repeated it, knowing only the persistent tapping on his neck. The beat of his own fingers would be like a shaman's drum sounding in his dreams, giving him the power to cast out and drive off any dream-beasts the shadow might throw his way.

Still drumming, he unfolded his legs, and lay down upon his side, resting his head on his pillow. *When I draw up the covers,* he told himself, *I will fall into a sound sleep.*

· Ω ·

Sage became aware of himself standing on the vast mosaic. He looked about, but saw no sign of the shadow. He focused his vision on the far distance, willing himself to see, and there was the towering black wall with its aqua door. He turned and looked in the opposite direction, and there was the wall of windows.

There, he said to himself, and in an instant he was before the cathedral gates. He focused his will and said, *Open*, and the great arched portals swung out toward him, bathing him in light. He stepped through.

The vaults rose above him, each metal door firmly closed. He stood still and let his awareness of the place grow, while his mind formed the question: *what are you?*

The answer came back, not in word, but in knowing: a library. And more than that. He knew this space was not part of him in any way. It belonged to his shadow and was in some way sacred to that other self within him.

And then came something else— an awareness that there was something illicit about the library's existence. It was as if he held stolen goods. The knowledge resonated through him: *This should not be here.*

No wonder his adversary had summoned up a beast from a nightmare to drive him out. This place wasn't just private property; it was a secret the shadow dared not let be known. *Known to whom?* Sage thought, but that knowledge did not come. Still, he had *something*.

Suddenly the illumination in the great space dimmed. Sage looked up and saw a winged beast circling on its sails of ribbed leather. Then it folded its wings and dropped toward him like a thunderbolt.

Sage was prepared. He tapped his fingers on the nape of his neck with renewed vigor and the beat of a drum filled the great space. Sage gazed into the black and yellow eyes of the dream-beast and this time he did not flinch. Drumming continuously, he extended his free hand and pointed one finger at the plummeting creature while he drew all his strength into his imagined lungs. Then he opened his mouth and screamed, in a voice that rang like clashing gongs, *You have no power over me! Be gone!*

The winged beast was almost upon him, its talons reaching, when the force of his will struck it like a hurricane buffeting a butterfly.

Without sound, the beast blasted to shreds. Sage watched it dissolve to ash, and then to nothingness before even the tiniest flake could touch him.

He looked up into the mists again. No new threat made itself known.

He scanned the structures around him; free now to look around. The vaults up the side walls were lighter in color than the rest, a silvery gray that shone with reflected light. *That's where I'll start*, he thought, and focused on a particular vault on the lowest level.

He willed himself to stand before it. A handle, like a golden bar mounted horizontally, invited his grasp. He touched it, cool against his fingers. But as he made to pull it downward, a chill presence appeared beside him.

Had he been in his own skin subject to the free play of nerve endings he would have jumped. Instead, his fingers tapped rhythmically on the back of his neck, and he turned.

It was his shadow. Nothing but a vague darkness, radiating cold.

"Show yourself," Sage commanded. "It's time we had a talk."

Knowledge appeared in his mind; the shadow would not show itself; it had no form which Sage would be able to discern. The emptiness beside him churned.

"Very well," Sage said. "Now, who are you, and what do you want of me?"

As soon as he asked the questions, he knew that he would not be answered. He sensed anger, hostility, above all pride. The darkness surged, as though it would surround him.

"You don't like being questioned?" Sage held his ground. "Tough. I want answers."

An image materialized in his dream-mind: a riding beast bucking and fretting at its reins, the rider firm in the saddle, its whip poised to deliver punishment.

"You can try." Sage gripped his strength. "But it's not going to work. There is a quick way out."

A frisson of alarm escaped from within the darkness, quickly suppressed, and the shadow boiled.

But Sage had struck a nerve. "You didn't count on me having a will of my own?"

The shadow writhed, its vapor arching over to encompass him, yet unwilling to touch him.

"Well, get used to it. I'm tired of having my life disrupted, twisted out of shape. I can end it." Sage formed a mental image and it appeared as if on a screen in front of him. It was of himself, down at Shingle Beach, filling his pockets with rocks. Then his image turned and faced the water, marched determinedly into the sea, the waves washing over his knees, waist, chest, his throat...

A surge of denial came to him and the shadow blackened and roiled.

"You think I wouldn't?" Sage challenged. "Why not? Name me one single thing *I've* got to live for. So far, it's all been about you— whatever you are."

The image: Himself. Smartest boy in the world. Great future. Limitless possibilities.

"But none of it is mine." Sage turned slowly, addressing the thing rising up on all sides of him. "And none of it means anything to me. If I walk into the sea, what would I be giving up?"

The shadow drew back into an amorphous cloud before him. Had he shaken its confidence?

"Here's what I want," Sage pressed. "First, no more of the whip and spurs. I'll learn, but I won't be driven."

The creature shifted, difficult to see in the dimly lit dream world. Sage could not tell whether it acquiesced or gathered itself for another assault.

"Second." He went on as though the thing did not oppose him. "No more shutting me down in the middle of the day, for whatever purpose takes your fancy. I'm tired of being seen as a mumbling idiot, rocking back and forth."

He waited, and after a moment, he felt the shadow's agreement. Not willing agreement; begrudged, but it was still a victory for Sage.

"Last, but far from least, I want to know what this is all about."

The response was instantaneous and rock-solid. *No.* The shadow became thick in its utter blackness and rose up, towering above him.

Sage held onto his power, his control, and his calm. "This place feels wrong, illicit. I don't know who you are hiding this from, but I've no doubt they'll want to know it's here. This," he circled a finger to take in the place where they were standing "is not supposed to exist."

No. The answer was slippery, convoluted, deceptive, and the roiling shadow flattened, grayed, curled before him like a prowling cat. Sage had struck an important chord.

"All right," Sage said, "if not stolen, then misused for sure. And who knows what kind of trouble you'll be in when the rightful owner comes around? Because I've got a feeling he's a lot bigger than both of us."

It had been a shot in the dark, but the shadow flattened, paled to wisps.

The whip and spurs will be withdrawn. The creature shifted as though with a breeze, almost fawning. *The daytime fits will cease.*

Sage would not be told everything.

But, it offered more. *Visit these vaults and any of the other lives stored behind the white doors of the aqua.*

"But I still won't know what it's all about?"

And then, into his mind, came a partial answer. *A great achievement. A wondrous accomplishment that will astonish.*

"Astonish what? Who?"

The answer was vague but Sage understood the shadow looked forward to a golden moment of triumph; a victory.

The shadow was intending to *make* something; an act of creation to astound... again, the knowledge was not shared. But Sage caught a glimpse of the shadow's desire for a day when all creation would recognize its worth.

"You want to create something," Sage said. "Did it never occur to you to just ask for my help?"

No. The shadow almost solidified into an oblong cloud before him, neither threatening, nor manipulative. *You would not.*

"Okay," he said, "You could be right. But for now we share this body, why not work together?"

The diffuse darkness before him simmered a hesitant, cold assent. Cautious acceptance overlying wounded pride? The rider might agree to ease up on his mount's reins, but that didn't make them best friends.

"Then leave me," Sage said. "I've got some exploring to do."

The shadow faded, just slowly enough to let him know he was not in command, and Sage was alone again in the place of vaults. *The library,* he reminded himself. Well, if there was one thing Sage Rojan knew how to use, it was a library.

He extended his dream-hand again and pulled on the handle of the vault with the silver-gray door. Smoothly and silently, it swung open toward him.

Within the vault was darkness, and he peered into it, wondering whether he should stick his head inside. Instead, what looked like a transparent tapestry rose before his dream-eyes, marked with figures and symbols.

At the center of the tapestry a dazzling circular core bulged, surrounded by a myriad of bright dots forming into spiral arms that tapered off into tails of individual motes. To Sage, the design resembled one of the saucer-shaped pinwheels that children played with in parks and schoolyards. As he studied the image, he realized that it was slowly spinning. When he first glanced down at the legend beneath the rotating figure, the symbols printed there were alien shapes that meant nothing to him. But as he focused on them, they shimmered and rearrange themselves into characters he could understand. *Spiral Galaxy Tolasious: 200 Million Stars.*

He put out a hand to feel the tapestry, but his fingertips passed through it. Startled, he moved his hand to the right; immediately the image shifted. Tolasious vanished and a different wheel of stars took its place. *Spiral Galaxy Fregom: 150 Million Stars.*

Sage put out his hand again, but this time carefully moved his fingers down through the nonexistent fabric. New information appeared: *UR67; Quadrant 22; Cluster 14, Spiral Galaxy Fregom 542.* A classification and a location.

And there was that number again. Sixty-seven, the same number on all the doors of the top floor in the room of doors. *Coincidence?*

His hands played over the tapestry, dragging the images first left then right, and each movement took him to another spiral galaxy, revealing additional details when he moved his fingers down. There were thousands of entries — more — in what seemed to be some kind of catalogue. He closed the vault door and opened the one next to it. Up rose another transparent tapestry, this one with a different arrangement of stars and a legend beneath that told him he was looking at a numbered and coordinated galaxy of the elliptical type.

He had time to think to himself: *What would Dad give to see this?* Then he went on to the next vault; *Barred* galaxies. Beside it, *Irregular*, and beyond that, *Nebulas.*

He moved from vault to vault, surveying galaxy clusters and individual stars. Then he came to the vaults that focused on individual planets— not just more than he could count, but more than he could even guess at.

Could he find Tidon, with its three complexly circling moons?

Sage pondered his discoveries. His father had talked about the possible enormity of the universe, and how he was sure that future astronomers would find far more galaxies than their

Tidon-bound telescopes could see through the distortion of the atmosphere. There was even talk of building large radio receivers and pointing them at the sky, because if stars gave off light and heat, they probably radiated in other segments of the electromagnetic spectrum, as incoming radio — and even X-ray — waves.

Dad was right. More right than he could even imagine. There were still thousands more vaults to look at. It would take Sage millennia to go through every one. *Work enough for a god.* What was important now was to gain an overall perspective. Gradually, probing and sampling among the vaults, Sage started to put a picture together. Knowledge flooded into his mind — he imagined the mosaic outside the library changing and growing as he explored, each tidbit adding in. He'd always liked to learn, the shadow's whips and spurs notwithstanding, and was delighted to move from vault to vault, discovering, evaluating, thinking through the facts he was amassing.

The universe was impossibly, achingly big. His whole world, moons and all, was no more than a speck in the vastness. He'd never felt so small. He put two and two together and it added up to billions and trillions. The lives he had glimpsed behind the thousands of white doors must have occurred on many different worlds. Life must be spread throughout the stars and galaxies. He remembered as a toddler being impressed to know that there were hundreds of millions of people on Bella Yareo. Now he knew Bella Yareo was nothing on the cosmic scale. He was no more significant, he thought, than one of the billions of bacteria that lived in and on his own body.

Enough for one night. He wondered how much of this he would retain when he returned to the waking world. He certainly knew more about the universe now than any other human being on Tidon. He could imagine himself casually dropping some amazing fact into a classroom discussion.

Then he caught himself. He had gone in a moment from sheer awe at the scale of the universe, to wanting to score points against another bacterium.

Time to quit. Get some rest. He stepped back to get the whole edifice in perspective, so he would know where to start next time. He took a dream-stroll across the wide foyer, taking in the entire three-dimensional span of the vaults, working to understand the layout and thought-structure behind the arrangement.

At the farthest end of the great space, a rectangular arch-way interrupted the rank upon rank, tier upon tier, of vaults. At the top of the arch was a glowing sign that grew clearer as he moved closer.

EMPYREAN.

Interesting word. Sage had no idea what it might mean, but crossed under the arch.

The walls of the vast room were shelved with books from floor to ceiling and more corridors extending outward from the center like the spars of a wagon wheel; too many books for anyone to ever read in a lifetime. *Now I know why it's called a library.* He ran his gaze along the close-packed spines on the nearest shelf. No titles, only numbers. He opened one at random. Its pages were dense with small print, too small for him to read without magnification.

He had put the book back before he remembered that he could conjure up a lens in a moment. But his eye had fallen on something else; a wooden structure, resembling a short, broad pillar in the middle of the room, like a pulpit where a preacher might stand to deliver a sermon, or an orator a speech. Atop an angled shelf rested a solitary tome, its closed cover black and its pages edged in gold. An ornate lock latched a broad strap of metal-encased leather, but into the lock's keyhole was already inserted an old-fashioned key.

For me? Or for the shadow? Or some sort of trap that was prepared for me while I was exploring the vaults?

He tapped the back of his neck to summon the power of the drum. When the room reverberated with the rhythm, he reached for the key and turned it. The lock opened smoothly, the metal clasp at the end of the strap falling free. Still drumming, Sage set his fingers to the edge of the cover and, with a sense that he was doing something momentous, opened it.

He blinked, then ducked as the multi-colored word EMPYREAN jumped off the page and jettisoned over his head. The word replicated into hundreds of duplicates, swirling around him.

The next page opened of its own accord, text swimming briefly before his eyes, an ornate and fanciful form he had seen before in old documents, in large cursive calligraphy. A directory. Headings rolled down the page, coming into view, disappearing then running through again.

He reached for the page to intercept and trap a heading before it disappeared again. But he pulled his hand back—

Really, should I?

Still, Sage had wanted knowledge. He'd threatened his shadow with suicide if he didn't get what he wanted. So could he back away, now? Now, that he realized the gigantic mouthful he had let himself in for?

He looked back over his shoulder. No shadow waited. No monster.

Chew, he told himself, *chew and swallow.*

He touched the page, and the directory's Secrets stilled. He felt awed by what he saw. In particular, the word 'Artisan' made him flinch. It was a term some Bellans used for what they thought of as a creator or omnipresent being. There was too much information here, too much he didn't understand and already the weight of the night was dragging on him. If only he could make a copy of the page and take it with him back to the world of the wakeful. But no, lucid dreaming was dreaming nonetheless. He'd need to rely on what he could remember when he woke from the dream.

EMPYREAN DIRECTORY

EMPYREAN	E01:01
ARTISAN	A01:01
FIRMAMENT	F01:01
RECYCLIUN	R01:01
GENESIS	G01:01
UNIVERSE AGE	U12:22
LIGHT	L10:18
BLACK HOLE CATALYSTS	B21:14
PLANET STAGES	P09:28
STAR DEVELOPMENT	SO5:13
GALAXY FORMATION	G02:05
SPACE	S12:17
TIME	T11:24
VISITATIONS	V07:11
REINCARNATION	R13:12

"Wow." He shook his head slowly in amazement.

His finger traced the page, and came to rest on PLANET STAGES— and the notation P09:28. The heading dissolved as though the page was made of water disturbed by a dropped pebble. A new directory appeared. Sage touched a heading: STAR DEVELOPMENT— S05:13.

STAR DEVELOPMENT left the page, flying up to the alphabetically lettered shelves above. Volume S05:13 came pulsating downward, surrounding him with text and diagrams floating in the air. He raised his hand to brush through the information. Texts scrolled, explicit instructional diagrams expanded, and models enacted movement.

As he examined the contents, he recalled that his father had similar books on a shelf in the garage, which explained how to repair and service the car's engine and other systems. But— no. This book had more in common with the half-dozen grease and flour-smeared volumes his mother kept in a cupboard near the stove. Not a how-to book; a recipe book—

—and what it told was how to make a star, from scratch.

He pulled out another section, this one on REINCARNATION. Suddenly, he had trouble holding the page in focus.

No!

His body, lying in his narrow bed in his small room on a tiny planet, was waking up.

He squeezed his eyes closed—

The books, the shelves, became insubstantial.

Dackt! If he left everything open like it was then surely something would find out he'd been here. The Shadow— or maybe something, or someone, bigger; someone who owned what Sage had begun to think of as an unsanctioned library.

With an immense effort of will, he closed the great directory of secrets, the swirl of information disappearing back into its pages. Sage pushed the metal clasp into its receptacle and locked it with its key.

He would come back.

He must learn what the Empyrean had to offer.

Then, in a flicker, he passed from the library through the foyer of the vaults, through the cathedral gates, onto the mosaic.

Somewhere along the way he became aware of the presence of indistinct darkness, without shape or substance.

The shadow seemed to be studying him. Then in a moment it was gone and he was alone on the mosaic, fading into nothingness.

· Ω ·

Sage awoke in his bedroom, Sintosy's morning glimmer seeping past his window shade. He forced himself to remember what had happened. Vaults, tapestries, books. The great directory.

Yes.

Details were missing, but the shape of it was there. The shape, and a great hunger to return.

He rolled out of bed and tripped over his shoes; he didn't remember leaving them there. Something urged him to wonder at that, but images of vaults and books swept the feeling aside. He went down to breakfast; exhausted but triumphant.

Bright spring sunlight bathed the kitchen table, set with trivial, almost laughably blasé objects. A bowl and a spoon. A jug of milk. His mother, humming a trivial melody, spooning cooked oats into his bowl, his father scanning insignificant events in the newspaper. How could such mundane things intrude on his mind? He slumped into his chair, almost angry at the scent of honey and tea.

His mother caught his look, her spoon hesitating over his bowl. She slopped the rest into his dish and withdrew to rinse dishes.

Sage watched the miracle of steam rising from his cereal, the only interesting thing in the room. He poked a figure eight into his porridge. How infinitesimally young he was, compared to what he had seen. To his parents he must seem like a lunatic.

Still, the wonder of the last hours infused him, and he couldn't contain his excitement. "Dad, our universe is so gigantic. We need to invent a better word. Gigantic doesn't do the universe justice."

His father looked up from his newspaper. "How about humongerrific?"

"I'm serious," Sage put his spoon back into the bowl irritably. "What do people know about how it got started and where it's going?"

His father lowered the newspaper and peered at Sage over his glasses. "There's a philosopher at another university who theorized that the universe began in an immense explosion that simultaneously created space, time, energy, and matter."

Sage pushed his irritation back. He listened.

"It's not yet a universally accepted explanation," his father said. "One of its detractors called it the 'Bang Theory.' The name was intended as an insult. Interestingly, it's now become customary shorthand for the concept of a perpetually expanding universe."

"And, is it true?"

Thaddeus Rojan removed his glasses thought-fully. "Too many holes in it, to my thinking. Still, it has caught on with this generation of astronomers. Seems they believe in it as devoutly as their great-grandparents believed that the world was flat."

Chapter 8

IT WAS GARDENING DAY. Like everyone else on Bella Yareo, Sage's family grew their own vegetables in the yard. The weeds grew themselves and regularly had to be dug out, especially among the rows of low-to-the-ground bushes that provided the sweet mu-gevity berries which even Sage had to admit were best on ice cream. His mother worked steadily, slashing through the unwanted intruders, while his father's forearm muscles bulged, his hoe rising, falling, and chopping.

Sage leaned on his implement. He'd been trying to see if exercising his will would make real-world weeds wilt as they would in his dreamscape. They wouldn't, to his chagrin. He hated gardening, and he was unable to fathom why at the age of thirteen he was still required to do such ridiculous chores. He swatted at a bee that came nearby. Then, he watched a caterpillar climb over one cabbage leaf and onto another.

"Sage." His mother's voice, reminding him that the vegetables were being grown for the family's benefit, not for any opportunistic insects looking for a free meal.

He flicked the crawling thing over the fence, where it landed on a neighbor's crops.

Thereafter, under his mother's eye, Sage's weeding became more energetic. But only slightly— most of his attention was drawn to his inner world. Perhaps he could reside in the Empyrean...

Sage's dad ceased weeding and straightened to look through the gap between their house and their neighbor's. A man in uniform was approaching their front door. "Genosa, I think there might be someone at the door," Thaddeus said.

Genosa put down her hoe and went through the house to answer. Sage followed her. Any excuse to give up weeding was a good one. He caught up to his mom as she opened the screen. The uniform had suggested a postman or maybe a courier service driver, but the serious, middle-aged man on the doorstep was neither. He was tall, and wore a red tuxedo-style jacket with matching joppers, black high-top boots, black leather gloves, and a black cap that looked like something a sea captain might wear. The ensemble reminded Sage of the time he and his dad had attended a polo match at Mullen's Field.

"Good afternoon," the gentleman said, in an accent that sounded very proper to Sage. "My name is Jamison. I am chauffeur to Mr. Duggin Elhandro Bristol. His limousine is parked down the way." He pointed. Sage's father joined the tableau on the doorstep and the three Rojans craned their necks to catch a view of the long, reddish limousine parked down the block. "Mr. Bristol wishes to speak with Master Sage Rojan."

"That's me," replied Sage, glancing at his mother with a puzzled shrug and continued, "He can come in if he wants."

The chauffeur looked down at both of them. "Mr. Bristol does not meet people in their homes. He sees them either in his office or his automobile. Today, it will be the auto."

"That's weird," Sage said.

"Mr. Bristol? The entrepreneur?" his dad said. "The man pushing to start up a space program?"

"Yes. Mr. Bristol would be happy to meet all of you." Jamison extended his arm in an elegant gesture. "If you please."

Sage, followed by his parents, trooped curiously down the sidewalk to the long, sleek vehicle. Sage was impressed by the limousine. He'd never been in one, and had only ever seen the occasional one in the city center. As they passed the hood, long enough to shelter a twelve-cylinder engine, he ran his finger along its sparkling polished surface. Immediately, the chauffeur produced a spotless white handkerchief and briskly rubbed away the lingering smear.

With a cold look at Sage, Jamison opened the rear door of the limo and stood at attention. But Sage's mother put out an arm to hold her husband and son back. "That name. Bristol."

"What?" his dad asked.

His mom stepped away from the car, out of earshot of the driver, Sage and his dad did likewise. "I've heard talk at the bank," she whispered. "His company is lax in meeting financial obligations. He's a bit of a libertine. Shady."

"What are you saying?" Dad said.

"That maybe the smartest thing to do right now, is to walk away."

The blank-faced chauffeur stood, holding the door as if he had done it since the beginning of the world and could continue right through to its end. The interior of the car was cloaked. Anything could be waiting in there. But something — Sage's shadow, or just his own curiosity — drew him toward the meeting.

"It's all right, mom," Sage said. "Whatever the man proposes, we can always say no."

"I'm with Sage," his dad said. "This guy has been chasing the government to start up a space program for years. If we don't take five minutes to hear him out, the curiosity might kill me. I'd never forgive myself."

Genosa hesitated. "Don't say I didn't warn you."

Sage approached the car and stepped tentatively into the dim interior. He'd heard of plush carpet, but was still surprised to find how soft it felt underfoot. The interior of the limousine was finished in polished hardwood and red quilted silk.

A thick-bodied man, with a broad face that had seen a lot of weather, lounged comfortably on a luxurious seat. Mr. Bristol had the thickest pair of eyebrows Sage had ever seen, and a pair of dark, intelligent eyes that closely inspected the boy after the merest glance at his parents.

"May I offer drink?" The entrepreneur's strong accent placed his origins from the farthest west coast of Bella Yareo, where an entirely different language was spoken. "Trecenta wine," the big man said lifting a cut-crystal decanter from a small side cupboard. The offer was only good manners in Porturn City and good manners required that the offer be accepted, so Mr. Bristol poured the amber liquid into a selection of clear crystal glasses.

This was Sage's first taste of Trecenta. He enjoyed it and, despite his mother's down-drawn brows, he smoothly emptied his glass.

"You have good boy there." Their host cozied back into his seat.

"Thank you." Sage's dad stretched back in the soft fabric as well. "We're proud of him."

"Let me tell about myself," said Bristol. "I am businessman. Make things. Also make things happen."

"Your name is well known," his dad said. Sage thought his father was a little nervous, but was covering it well.

"My father was famous *builder*— merchant sailing vessels." Mr. Bristol twirled the stem of his wine glass between two fingers. "He moved here, Porturn City, where market opportunities best. Built new shipyard— not only made ships but founded profitable shipping line. I diversified into land transport. Do even better than ships."

"I've heard you deal with more than just shipping," Sage's father said.

"Yes. That was, early in career. Since, Bristol Industries more diversified. Emerging technologies where nobody seize high ground. Drive out competitors. Establish monopoly. It work for me."

Sage's father let out a small breath of air, "Ah."

The portly man shrugged, "I know where world goes." He finished his wine. "I always be first there."

"Isn't breaking new ground always a little risky?" Sage's mom asked. She perched at the edge of her seat, as though she would dart from the vehicle at the first sign of trouble.

Mr. Bristol smiled at her, but Sage noted that she stiffened as though slapped. "My financial empire largest, cannot sink with stiff wind Mrs. Rojan. Also Bristol handshake send message. If Duggin Bristol approve it, change and progress happen."

"I'm sure it does," his mother said coldly.

"Which is why you here," the big man said.

Genosa's face was a study in suspicion, "What do you mean?"

Instead of answering directly, the man turned to Sage. "You want access of Bristol resources?"

"What?" Sage said.

"You sent diagrams, plans, proposals."

Sage stared at the man; he didn't remember doing any such thing.

His mother turned to him, shock making her skin pale in the dim light. "Sage. Why didn't you tell us about this?"

"Your ideas," Bristol continued, "connecting thinking machines, big network, satellites in space, bouncing signals round world. Telephones like radios. Future ideas. Kind of ideas Bristol Industries wants. Tell me." His hard bright eyes stayed locked on Sage. "Where your ideas come from?" The eyes slid across to Sage's dad sitting dumbstruck in the seat across from him.

Sage's dad spluttered then finally got out, "Don't look at me. If Sage contacted you directly then those ideas are all his."

"Sage! I can't believe you didn't talk to us about this." His mother glared at him but Sage couldn't ignore the faint hurt in her eyes.

He stared at his parents feeling the world falling out beneath him. He hadn't sent Bristol anything! He wouldn't even know where to start to do so; though in all honesty it wouldn't take him long to figure it out. Then he felt a tug of impatience from somewhere within and suddenly he was aware. Somehow the shadow had contacted Bristol. But how was that possible? Something bubbled from the inner portions of his mind. A knowledge, a vague memory, of drawing plans in the middle of the night, of a trip to the post box at the end of the street. Strings being pulled and Sage was the marionette. The night he had spent in the Empyrean... It would have been the perfect time for the shadow to take Sage's body where it wanted. The realization shook him to his core but he pushed past the sensation.

Bristol leaned back and surveyed the three of them. "For five years I chase Senate to begin space program. But they say, 'Don't know even what is on other side of Tidon.'" He growled and poured himself and Sage's father more wine. "Sage's satellites will map whole world. Cheaper than sending ships or planes."

Sage's dad blinked in surprise. "That's true."

Bristol shrugged. "Finally, they saw sense for agency."

"Really?" His dad perked up, his enthusiasm impossible to hide. Even Sage felt a stirring of excitement.

"Since receiving Sage's package, I buy up companies that are ground floor to new industries. Now, I own telephone company, airplane manufacturer, military radio factory, and machine factory. Sage get offer to come work for me now."

Genosa cut in. "But Sage is only thirteen!"

"Age not important," the entrepreneur said. "Only ideas matter." He turned back to Sage, "You draw diagrams, make working models?"

All three of the adults faced Sage.

Sage felt the pressure of his shadow and nodded.

"Then all settled. Sage work for me."

"Now wait just a minute here," his father said, "he hasn't even finished school!"

"He genius. School not matter. No school smart enough. Besides, Bristol Industries already register ideas. You refuse and they get built anyways."

"What?" Sage's dad half-rose in the confines of the limousine. "You've *stolen* Sage's ideas?"

"I own rights, Rojan. Not you."

"That's theft!" Thaddeus cried.

"Theft? Maybe. Who say your son first to come up with ideas? He has gigantic imagination. Some say he psychotic." The pudgy man shrugged. "Doesn't matter. Fact is, you try to build those ideas without me, I sue you into hole in ground."

His dad set his wine glass down. "That's it, I've heard enough."

His mom reached for the door handle. But something stirred inside Sage.

"Fine," Sage heard himself say. "Go ahead. Try to turn those diagrams into prototypes. But you don't have the data."

Bristol's brows narrowed, his gaze riveted on him as though he would burn Sage into compliance with his eyes.

Sage and his shadow remained composed, seated in the plush chair as though born to luxury, his eyes never leaving the older man's.

The entrepreneur slapped his knee and laughed. "Okay," he said, "I never say before, but you got me over barrel."

"Which is why you're here today," Sage said, "instead of watching your technicians build communication satellites and portable phones."

"Then we don't have to listen to this." His dad took his mom's arm.

"No wait." Sage heard himself say, but he wasn't sure if it was him or his shadow talking or maybe both this time. "Bristol's right. I want this opportunity. Only I think we'll want a lawyer because the offer Mr. Bristol is going to make will be complex. And likely written in his favor."

"Some kid you got," Bristol said.

His parents glanced at each other and slid back into their seats.

"Okay, here's offer. Sage come work for me; Senior Project Manager. Provide detailed designs — oversee production teams — communicate directly with me. I pay competitive wage."

His mom zeroed in. "How much money?"

"Senior Project Manager not cheap— might be hundreds of thousands per year."

His parent's eyes widened.

But the shadow stirred in the back of Sage's mind. "No," Sage said.

"Alright, more. Millions."

His dad's breath caught.

Sage shook his head, "It's not about the money."

Mr. Bristol's lids lowered. "Then what?"

Sage looked at his mother. "Mom?"

The banker in her caught on fast. "Shares," she said. "Profit participation. Public identification with the products."

The man's eyes narrowed. "Know way round business world?"

Genosa put her hands together in her lap. "A little."

He smiled. "Then we work something out."

"Also," Sage held up his hand. "My parents will work with me."

Mr. Bristol shrugged. "That also fine. Family stay together."

"You'll pay them well and provide my father with a research budget. My mother will have a senior accounting position."

Bristol frowned but finally shrugged, "Agreed."

His dad looked a little dazed, but Sage could see his mom's mind turning over. Now she nodded and said, "Send us a proposal in writing. We'll have our lawyer look it over and get back to you."

"Then we have deal," said the industrialist.

She cleared her throat. "Don't try to low-ball us," she said. "You're a multimillionaire. My boy could make you Bella Yareo's first billionaire; the first multi-billionaire."

Bristol smiled a knowing smile. In his dream-lives, Sage had seen that same smile on the faces of kings and emperors.

His dad was still a little behind the rest of them. "What kind of research budget?"

Bristol folded his hands across his belly. "Think biggest research budget at university. Double it."

Sage's father's brows lifted.

Then Bristol said, "Now double it again."

"Gosh."

"And more, if not enough." Bristol said with a huge grin on his face, "Now Rojans, please excuse me. I go draw up contract."

Jamison opened the door and the family stepped out onto the sidewalk. The red limousine pulled smoothly and soundlessly away.

Thaddeus shook his head. "How about that?"

Chapter 9

BRISTOL TOWER WAS the newest and tallest building in downtown Porturn. Its twenty-three stories made the surrounding buildings look like a huddle of toads. In a city where ancestry was revered, many had opposed its construction. Anti-change activists had nick-named it the 'Porturn Penis.' To them it was an eyesore in a cityscape that, not too long ago, had forbidden any structure of more than four stories. But even staid Porturn City Council had been coerced by the hard-pushing Duggin Bristol to rubber-stamp his plans. Those councilors he couldn't buy had been blackmailed into compliance.

This was the first time Sage had been up in the tower, and the penthouse view allowed him to survey the surrounding panorama. Through the floor-to-ceiling windows he could scan the bay area and the beaches that led to the open sea. Upland, King Ferdason Palace dominated Castle Hill. Beyond lay the nation's Senate and Parliament Buildings; imposing their dignity on the landscape. Farther south, in the distance, he could see Bristol's new airplane landing strip— reminding everyone that this was a new age.

Sage inched closer to the window. With his nose right up against the glass, he looked down past his shoes to the sidewalk, far, far below, where a group of protestors jostled together like aphids on a leaf.

The Alliance for Traditional Values.

That's what they called themselves. He'd heard about them on the radio. 'Knuckle-draggers and mouth-breathers, people who wouldn't know the value of progress if it came up and vaccinated them in the rump thereby saving their lives from germs that would've brought them a miserable death a couple of generations before', his dad had said. Duggin Bristol was their idea of a sorcerer incarnate.

Those people down there didn't know it, but to Sage this day would be the day everything changed, forever.

He wished that he could throw his shadow over the side, out the floor to ceiling window, and smash it on the pavement below.

Instead a gull flew by; soaring then diving, before it wheeled and flew off toward the bay.

Sage turned around and assessed his new office. It was spacious and decorated in the deep blues and cool greens that made him feel most at home. His desk, designed to be comfortable for his size, was spacious, and his chair swiveled to bring file cabinets and work surfaces easily to hand. There was a large conference table in the center of the room that would allow him to lay out his designs during team meetings. In one corner of the room, a set of large wooden bookcases faced a comfortable looking couch with a reading lamp already on. The desk was already strewn with memos and lists; but this morning would be consumed with the task of orienting himself to his new role.

He pulled air deep into his lungs, then let it slowly expel from his nose. He was trying, with not much success, to muster his courage. *I'm not sure how this is going to work out.* Part of him wanted to be on one of those boats sailing out of the bay, past the Entural Islands, out into the open sea.

The prospect of coming here, having the freedom to let his mind run with his ideas, to feel challenged, had been exciting. But how much of that excitement had been his? He wondered how much of his interest in inventions and science — especially space science — came from his own nature, and how much of it was slipped in under his mind's door when he wasn't looking. He was already painfully aware that his shadow was the source of much of his intellectual energy.

He felt uncertain. For a year now, he and his shadow had lived uneasily by the agreement they had made but Sage wasn't sure how he felt about the knowledge that, somehow, the shadow had used his body without his consent. In his dreamscape, Sage had tried to call the shadow to account, but it would not respond. *The shadow reads me right. This isn't reason enough to make me fill my pockets with stones and walk into the bay.*

75

And now he was apparently about to put himself under the whip and spurs of another hard-driving taskmaster. Sage hadn't switched taskmasters; he had acquired a second one. The shadow and Bristol seemed to have much the same agenda, which was a relief on one hand, and a source of further worry on the other. Duggin Bristol made no secret of his intention to get what he wanted out of Sage Rojan. *Still*, he told himself, *this is a chance to prove myself. How it works out is largely up to me*. The rewards were excellent, he knew, but decisions about what projects would get priority would never be his to make.

On the other hand, his father was delighted with the research facilities he'd helped design with a budget that left his colleagues at the university pale with envy. And even Sage's mother was coming around to the idea of managing a hefty and growing portfolio of shares, stock options, and income for the three of them, on top of her position in accounting.

He squared his shoulders and took the elevator one floor down to his father's work space.

His dad looked up from a box of books he was unpacking. Like Sage, he would be spending a good deal of time in *Idea Development*, even though the bulk of his work would be spread out among the research facilities and manufacturing plants. Thaddeus wore his usual professor's garb of tweed jacket and knitted vest, but he looked years younger and full of the optimism Sage himself would have liked.

"Well, son." His father spread his arms to indicate the generous space. "What do you think?"

His enthusiasm was contagious. "Dad, you and I could invent things even if we had to set up shop inside of a garage. We're going to change the world."

"And for the better."

Sage smiled, feeling some of the weight on his shoulders lift. "That's the plan."

His dad clapped him on the shoulder. "Let's go find your mother?"

· Ω ·

Genosa was dressed like a bank executive, in a conservative skirt and jacket combination. The Bristol contracts were piled high on her wide desk, its satin-wood top polished to a deep gloss.

"Are they good?" Sage said, nodding at the stacks of paper.

"Everything we asked for, in plain language," she said. "They look good to me financially, and the lawyer couldn't find any built-in time-bombs or trapdoor clauses."

"Then we sign?" Thaddeus reached into his jacket pocket for a pen and clicked it into readiness. "I'll witness for you, you witness for me."

"We sign," she said, and two minutes later, the deal was done. Sage's father pulled from his vest pocket the old watch he always carried on a short fob, flipped it open, and read the time.

"You've got somewhere you need to be?" Genosa asked.

"Nowhere else but here," Thaddeus said. "I'm just noting the time when our lives changed forever."

· Ω ·

They spent the rest of the day setting up the lab and their offices, and getting to know some of the people they'd be working with. Duggin Bristol put in a brief appearance between meetings, crushed their hands with his firm shake, then opened his briefcase and took out a copy of the late edition of the morning newspaper. Centered on the top half of the business news section was a photo of Sage. Beneath, the caption read: *Sage Rojan, pint-sized whiz kid, leads Bristol's charge into the future.*

Sage scanned the article. Beneath the headline was a rather breathless account of his new role at Bristol Industries, with predictions of how communication satellites, interconnected 'thinking machines,' and work-anywhere personal phones would revolutionize society.

"Isn't it a little early for publicity?" Sage said.

"Stock market react," the millionaire said, with a knowing tap of one finger against his nose. "Share price up ten per cent at close." He looked at Genosa. "That mean you make plenty money just for keep breathing."

"Is it wise to raise expectations so soon?" Thaddeus said. "We haven't even started yet."

"Publicity good," said Bristol. "Good publicity even better. Don't worry. I hire PR genius, work exclusively with Sage. Pretty soon, you be most famous kid on planet."

"It's my image we're talking about," Sage said. "I'd like to have a say in how these announcements are made."

His new employer smiled a smile Sage had seen in past lives. The one that said the cat got the mouse. "I would like to be foot taller," Bristol said, then spread his hands and shrugged. "Universe say, sorry, Duggin, no can do. Duggin say to you, sorry, Sage, read your contract. PR my decision."

And with that Bristol was gone.

Sage looked at his parents. Thaddeus made his mouth into an *eh-what-the-heck* shape and said, "Son, a little fame won't hurt you."

But Genosa's eyebrows were now divided by a deep vertical line. "We'll see," she said.

· Ω ·

It was three days later as Sage cut across the rear parking lot heading for his parent's car when he found out why Bristol couldn't be trusted to handle PR. From behind him, he heard a man's voice yell, "Hey, he's not just some kid! He's the whiz kid! Get him!"

Footsteps, lots of them, coming fast. Sage ran for the car. *Who would—*

The Alliance for Traditional Values.

Oh.

Sage sprinted. The angry mob streamed after him.

Ahead Sage could see his parents talking to a short blonde woman.

"Everybody in," Thaddeus yelled as he started up the vehicle and backed it out of the parking stall.

Sage put on a burst of speed and came up on the car from the rear, diving headlong through the back door.

He smacked his skull against something hard, then flew back against the seat as his dad floored the gas pedal. The car took off, the momentum slamming the door closed behind him.

As they peeled out into the street Sage sat up. "Ow," he said, rubbing his head. Someone must have been leaning forward to try to catch him as he crash-landed on the seat. And he'd come in at a perfect angle to ensure that their heads knocked together with a shock that went all the way down his spine. He glanced at the person in the back seat beside him. Blue eyes glared back at him.

Sage froze. The *woman*, who was nearly his own age, was rubbing a red and rising bump of her own. "Do you store rocks in that noggin of yours?"

"Tamara Young? What are you doing here?" asked Sage, as the car took another corner and began to accelerate on a straightaway.

His mother answered from the front seat. "Remember Bristol saying he'd hired a genius to do PR?"

"No," Sage breathed.

"No, you don't remember?" Tamara shot him an accusatory gaze. "Or no, you hate the idea of working with me?"

"How," he swallowed, staring at her in astonishment, "how did this happen?"

The girl was pleased to inform him that after Bristol had learned about Sage's brilliance he had sent scouts to the Accelerated Learning Program at Lodiash High School. Tamara had heard about Sage's brilliant step into Bristol Industries and decided she could do one better so she came prepared with a presentation about the future of information handling and communications and a process she called 'engineering public consent.'

"Oh, my gosh." Sage had been so caught up in his own whirl-wind, he'd barely spared a thought for Tamara. He realized that part of him had been unaccountably sorry he'd end up missing out on their rivalry— that he'd miss… he wasn't sure what. But, now that she was back, he wasn't all that sure he wanted to deal with her again on a daily basis. And— now she was in his dad's car?

"So here we are," she said, "I was just introducing myself to your parents since we'll be working closely for the next little while. I need to learn as much about you as I can in order to set up your PR."

Sage noticed a copy of the 'whiz kid' story on her lap, and groaned. "PR? You're responsible for that?"

"Are you kidding me? I can do a lot better than Duggin Bristol. He's responsible for this mess."

"Excuse me for butting in." His father slowed the vehicle to a reasonable speed. "But Tamara is just what this effort needs. It's clear those people in the parking lot know we're going to change their world, and they resent it. It's going to take more than inventions to build the kind of society we want your children to live in. It's going to take a change of mind-set among people like them— or at least we need to make sure they are never more than a noisy minority. Tamara's already set up to be a key part of that effort."

"Thank you," said Tamara. "But when you said 'your children' a moment ago—"

"Good grief!" Heat flooded Sage's neck and he scrambled as far as he could against the door. *Ok yes, he liked Tamara, but— children!*

His mother turned and looked at Tamara with an evaluating eye. "They'd be awfully bright kids," she teased.

"Forget it!" Tamara snapped, at the same time as Sage blurted out, "Never in a million years!"

"Make it a billion," she said.

"Well," chuckled Thaddeus, "at least you agree on something. Now back to the problem at hand. Tamara how about you join us for dinner."

"What?" *Were they all crazy?* He never could think straight when she was near him. "Why?"

"Thank you," Tamara sneered.

"Yes that's a wonderful idea," Genosa said. "That gives us plenty of time to get to know each other. Maybe we can share some of Sage's baby pictures."

Sage nearly died. "No. Absolutely not!"

Tamara sighed. "Listen, Brickhead. I don't like this any more than you do. But we need to develop a clear message, *and* we need to present a common front to Bristol, before he springs any more publicity bombshells on us. The faster we get this under our own hands the faster Bristol will leave off with his," Tamara said.

Sage rubbed his head again, he didn't want to admit it but she had a point. He would rather not be the focus of another angry mob. "Fine," he mumbled, then winced at how petulant he sounded.

"Cheer up Son," his dad grinned through the rear-view mirror, "at least you got a pretty lady out of the deal."

Both Sage and Tamara glared at him.

Chapter 10

SAGE, IN A SIMPLE PLAID SHIRT and gray slacks, followed his parents into the outer reception area of Duggin Bristol's twenty-third-floor corner office next to the conference room. It was their first Bristol Industries senior management meeting. Sage knew he looked like a kid and wondered how the meeting with Bristol's high-powered executives would go.

It had been a productive few weeks. His first inventions were on the drawing board and he knew he had free rein to plot the course of their development. It excited him that those coming inventions could change the Bellan nation.

As Sage entered the conference room, he applied his fingertips to his temples and tried to rub away the low-grade ache of fatigue and tension that filled his head.

"You all right, son?" asked his dad.

"I will be, when the meeting's over and we're back at work."

Bristol's assistant, a bird-like older woman, poked her head into the room and waggled her eyebrows. "He's ready."

The rest of the executive team stood from their seats as Duggin Bristol entered the room. Everyone, including Sage and his family, sat back down as Bristol sank into his chair.

Over the past several days, Sage had individually met each of the senior managers. No friendships had been formed. Bristol Industries was a tight ship, not a happy one.

There was a small flurry of nods as the grisly-faced crew of money-handlers and has-been engineers acknowledged their boss. Bristol nodded to the assembly and pulled some papers from his briefcase, arranging them before him on the polished tabletop.

Sage's samplings of a thousand or more past lives had given him a good perspective on Bristol. He knew that a lot of what came out the man's mouth was braggadocio and that Bristol expected his employees to absorb it without argument. But behind the bluster was a single-minded determination to remake the world in a shape that better pleased Duggin Bristol. And if anyone got in the way of that aim, the industrialist's first instinct would be to trample that person underneath; and thereafter own every possible inch of that person's world.

Now the effervescent, ever-exuberant Bristol looked up from his papers and snapped a quick *Beya*; the signal that it was time for business.

He pointed at the man to his right, his Executive Vice President of Operations, who launched into a brisk summary of outputs, shipments, sales forecasts, revenues, and operating expenditures.

When the report came to an end, Bristol grunted. Sage deduced it must have constituted a positive review since the reporting VP let out the breath he had been holding. Now the stubby finger pointed to the next man, the Vice President of Acquisitions, who outlined the latest achievements. In each case, Bristol Industries had acquired one hundred per cent ownership. When Duggin Bristol ran an enterprise, he ran it without quibbles from anyone on the sidelines to interrupt building a financial empire.

The reports continued. The company's finances were rock solid. Operating profit was up eight per cent on the quarter, forty per cent over the past year. A new issue of non-voting preferred shares had been oversubscribed two hours after its launch; the corporate treasury was swimming in cash and positioned to make any new acquisitions Bristol might target. The physical plant was in tip-top condition, except for some technological upgrades, but all of that was proceeding on-budget and on time.

Bristol looked out from under thick eyebrows. "On time only?"

The Chief Engineer cleared his throat. "We're two days ahead of schedule on refitting the automobile assembly plant, and it looks as if the truck factory will re-open at least a day early."

Bristol grunted again. "Make it two days. Need trucks for distribution of new products. Bristol Industries does not lease."

"Yes, sir." The Chief Engineer made a note on a pad. Sage thought it highly unlikely the man would need the written reminder— as soon as Bristol had spoken; beads of sweat had broken out on his forehead.

Now the industrialist's square head swung around and stared straight down the table at Sage. "Now we talk new inventions," he said. "Some of you," he looked around at the senior staff, "don't think it good idea to bring in kid; give him and family big budget."

If any of the executives harbored such feelings, none of them thought it was a good time to own up.

"But Sage Rojan is future of company. Is future of world." He listed the products, still in their infancy and yet unknown to the public, which they would be bringing to market: jet airplanes, helicopters, televisions, computers, communication satellites, fiber-optic networks, and wireless phones; first in the big cities, then expanding along the highways and coastal shipping lanes.

"A year, two, three most, whole of Bella Yareo depend on what we provide, won't know how they ever lived without gadgets. And will pay us every time they buy plane ticket or nice new car."

He looked about the room again, his chin raised as if daring anyone to contradict his vision. Then he looked back at Sage. "So," he said, "how is coming?"

Sage stood and surveyed the table of dubious faces. "Well, each of these large inventions is made up of a series of smaller innovations: many require complex circuits, chips, capacitors, and integrated circuits. We have to get each component right before we can build larger systems."

Bristol frowned in dissatisfaction.

Heat flashed in Sage's chest and he stared down the line of executives into the industrialist's face. "There is a progression. These components are only drawings and they need to be modeled and tested. You can't have the cart before the horse."

Bristol's complexion darkened.

Sage's father stood next to him. "Also, there are several rare metals we need for these inventions. You own a number of industries, Mr. Bristol, but very few rare earth mines."

In silence, the senior staff turned toward the man at the head of the table.

Bristol intertwined his short fingers on the desk in front of him and looked at Sage without speaking.

Thaddeus shakily took his seat.

Sage returned the big man's gaze with cool detachment.

The heavy man leaned his hands on the table and rose to his feet. "I buy mining company; foremost producer of rare metals.

We take one hundred per cent production. Give all you need."
He snapped his fingers and the VP of Acquisitions scribbled
the note on his paper. Bristol moved his chin around as if his
collar was too tight. "What else problem you got?"

"We're still constrained by a shortage of lithium," Sage
said. "We've got to have it for the batteries. No batteries, no
portables." On Tidon — indeed on most planets, as he knew
from his readings in the Library — lithium was not found
in its pure state, but had to be extracted from compounds it
formed with other elements. 'Hard to find and to process.'

Bristol held up a hand to stop the boy. "You mentioned
this yes. I already have covered. Papers all drawn. Tomorrow
I buy lithium mine in Bragian Salt Flats. Brine sludge brews
like beer. Just suck up from below crust and make nice."

"When we have the lithium, we can start building models
and testing them," Sage said. "Of course you're aware that
during processing, lithium is separated, captured, and stored
as a fine powder in vacuum-packs because it is very reactive
to air. Pressurized lithium is then mixed with ether and forced
into the battery shells. If the refining process doesn't do it
precisely that way, it will be useless. And, the refining process
produces lots of pollutants. We have to take care of those, as
well."

The millionaire shrugged. "I aware." He snapped at his
assistant, "Write that down. Tell refinery." He smiled up at
Sage. "Pollution not a problem. Old saying where I come from:
difficult we do right away, impossible take a day or so."

Sage thought he should introduce the man to his shadow;
they had a lot in common. "You're the boss," he said.

"Right, and you genius." The meaty fist thumped the table.
"We mine rare metals. You think up inventions. Then I patent
everything. Break neck of anyone who gets in way."

Sage inclined his head to the room at large and took his seat.

Bristol straightened and addressed the room. "Fiberglass
plant already retooling to make fiber-optic cable. Soon we lay
network all across continent. Complete monopoly. Hook up
portable phones, other communication devices; and create
nation-wide-web and access." Sage hid his smile. Bristol understood little of the meaning of the words he parroted.

"Now with work out of way, we move to space program."
Bristol waived his meaty hand at a man Sage didn't recognize

from the company sitting at the table with them. "Bella Yareo Space Agency— BYSA, has sent new Director Brantford today to confirm. Senate agrees, we pay part budget and patents belong to Bristol. Now we develop rocket. Someday man on moon." Brantford nodded and Bristol's smile beamed like a thousand suns.

Whenever Sage heard Bristol talk about his long-desired space program, he got a thrill of anticipation from his deepest fires. Dad shared it, too. And sometimes Sage thought that going into space was at the real heart of Duggin Bristol's drive to own and control. Maybe it wasn't just greed that drove him, or the need to be on top of any heap he came across. Maybe, underneath all the bluster and the thick ugly skin, the man harbored a noble dream?

In the past lives stored within him, Sage had been part of cultures that went to space; he had stood under the different-colored skies of other worlds and watched strange suns set on alien landscapes. But those experiences were only the half-life of a memory. He longed to rise up from Tidon, in this flesh that clothed him now, to see with his own eyes the vastness of infinity. He wasn't able to remember the first few weeks of his life on Tidon, but his mom had told him how she'd taken him out one sleepless night and laid him down in a gondola on the canal; how he'd looked up at the stars, hungry to touch them.

Sage hoped this desire was his, and his alone; that there was a noble purpose to his otherwise driven life. He had so much talent and ability, enough to astonish all who encountered him — except, perhaps, for one annoying girl — but how much of that came from the shadow within him? Was he no more than a beast, ridden where the rider directed, spurred on by whips and carrots? Half of him wanted to know the truth, and half of him was afraid to hear it.

His thoughts were interrupted as his dad stood once again. "Mr. Bristol, I'm delighted to be working with Sage on the inventions, but when you mention the space program, I hope you realize that in my heart that's where I'd love to work. Is that possible?"

"Yes," said the industrialist "We make inventions, money, but end-point is space program." He looked at Sage. "You make me inventions," and said, in the gruffest tone Sage had yet heard from him, "Then you make me space ship. We go up, see whole world. Like— Artisan."

Thaddeus practically glowed and a shiver of sheer delight traveled from the base of Sage's spine to the nape of his neck.

Maybe this would work out after all. Sure, he might tire of Bristol's carnival act. But for today at least, he was willing to ride along.

"All right." Bristol clapped his hands and sat, lolling in his chair. "Last report: marketing."

A lean well-dressed man by the name of Ryze Feldstrum had been fidgeting like a caged animal. He immediately launched into as slick a presentation as Sage could have imagined.

Ryze erected a folding easel and filled it with a succession of bar charts, artwork and draft slogans for the new products, and quoted statistics. "What it comes down to," Ryze finished, "is that the consumers can't wait to get their hands on the goods. They don't really know what they're going to be like or how they're going to use them, but they know this is the future and they want in!"

"The ones who chased Sage across the parking lot didn't want it," Genosa pointed out quietly.

Feldstrum smiled a marketer's smile. "But those people represent a shrinking minority view." He put another chart on the easel and tapped its multicolored bars. "When we have the communication network up and running— eighteen months maximum," he glanced at Bristol to confirm, "we will be able to provide communication for, and broadcast to, more than ninety per cent of the population; we will effectively control public opinion. Without a doubt, it's time for our sparks to cause a real fire; to ignite that flame which can fan across the entire country."

Bristol leaned forward. "And political opinion?"

"The politicians will have to come to us," Feldstrum said. "All of them." His eyes took in the room and he cleared his throat uncomfortably. "Even the King."

The industrialist smiled an ugly smile. "That would be agreeable."

"We're already designing our strategy." Feldstrum left the easel and gestured to the door. "If I may, I'd like to bring in the architect of our communications strategy." At Bristol's nod, Ryze opened the side door. "May I introduce, Miss Tamara Young," Ryze said.

Wow. Sage had to look twice to assure himself this was the same thirteen year old Tamara Young he bumped heads with in his father's car. She looked more like a young woman than a girl his age. Her long blonde hair was tied up in a bun showing off her elegant neck which was adorned with a jeweled necklace. She wore a sharp cream-colored business suit, a pair of red pumps, and ruby lipstick that made her lips full and flush.

"Whiz kid number two," Bristol beamed. "Pretty soon I have all genius in Bella Yareo working for me."

To Sage it seemed that the senior executives accepted Bristol's new hire with much more warmth than they'd responded to him.

Tamara's eyes roved the room then locked on Sage, and when she saw him notice, she smiled the same beguiling smile he'd seen that first day in school, when she'd aced the test he'd blown.

With that, Bristol abruptly adjourned the meeting and the group broke up; Bristol bustling to his next appointment, assistant in tow. Tamara stayed as the executives slowly filed out, chatting with each one individually.

On his feet now, Sage sidled toward Tamara. For the first time in his life, he had a real urge to be near her, though he felt the shadow inside, resisting. He caught her as she left an informal grouping, tongue-tied, unsure what he should say. "I guess I'll be up here in research and you'll be down below with Ryze."

"No," she said, looking straight at him in a way that made him feel that he was being weighed and found slightly wanting. "Bristol's always had an interest in PR. I'll be working on this floor so I can be handy when he wants to bounce ideas off of someone." She winked at Sage's horrified look. "Don't worry, I'll keep him in line." She touched two fingers to her chest and said, "Vice President, Corporate Communications."

Thaddeus looked at her with approval. "Well, good for you." Then he glanced at Sage. "Besides, son, won't it be good for you to have someone your own age close by to talk to?"

"Lucky me," Sage said, remembering at the last minute to roll his eyes. He did want her close but there was no way he could say it.

Chapter 11

THEY ROLLED OUT the communication system by the end of that first year, transmitting by way of antennae but working around the clock to install the fiber-optic network that would eventually connect every city and village on the continent.

From his desk at Bristol, Sage led the charge of speedy inventions. Within months, television became the new rage with broadcast programming adapted from popular radio shows — especially the daytime dramas and evening musical-varieties. But mixed in with the entertainment were news shows, and a great deal of the programming involved enthusiastic coverage of the changes that the Rojan's Revolutionaries — as *Now Magazine* had dubbed Sage and his team — were bringing to Bellans in the near future.

Now and then a dissenting voice was heard — especially from those who traveled widely enough to notice the slag heaps and deforestation around Bristol's open-pit mines — but the constant thrust of the messages broadcast to the people of Bella Yareo were that the changes brought by the technological revolution were happening at a speed faster than light — and that that change was good. Bristol Industries' polling department — which Tamara Young had created — reported, week after week, that the overwhelming majority of the population agreed.

Sage spoke to Bristol about diverting a percentage of the budget toward developing renewable energy sources and supporting the workers laid off by the mechanization of his plants, but Bristol would hear nothing of it. Money was to be spent on company priorities; not frittered away on useless environmental or social programs.

A year later, when more than half of the continent's homes boasted at least one fiber-optic connection, the station based wireless phones were ready for market.

So, two years after Sage joined Bristol Industries, the communications revolution was in place and the first reliable silicon chips were making desk-top computing devices possible. Sage was elated. He was spending eighteen-hour days in the lab, goading, guiding, directing, refining, and routinely engendering quantum leaps in the understanding of the twenty-plus engineers and technologists working under him.

That was what made it the best of times. What made it the worst was the constant niggle that his shadow was back in the saddle, driving him forward at a pace that drained his energies and made him look like a victim of some debilitating disease. He was haggard, his shoulders stooped, and there were dark baggy circles under his eyes. Tamara told him they were big enough to be saddle bags.

It was bad enough that the shadow drove him from within, but Bristol never let up, either. The industrialist hammered Sage on the need to develop jet aircraft. The deep mines were producing the rare minerals needed to build engines that wouldn't melt or deform under the heat and pressure jet propulsion required. The swept-wing designs were working well in the wind tunnels and it looked as if the first real prototype would be able to approach the speed of sound and overcome threats of metal fatigue.

For Sage's fifteenth birthday his mom and dad bought him a brand new motorbike to go with the driver's license he'd received for acing the test two months prior. On a rare lull in his work schedule, he decided to take his bike out of the city limits on a wooded country road he remembered driving once with his parents early in his life. He enjoyed the drive until he began passing hill, upon hill, upon hill, of unsightly gray rock, miles of earth stripped of vegetation where Bristol Industries had dug up coal for the steel factories. He told Bristol about it on his return, but Bristol brushed him aside, saying he had no money — or time — to invest in re-planting trees. When Sage told his parents, they thought the local trees would eventually cover the unsightly mines and slag, once the coal was exhausted. But they hadn't seen the devastation of the landscape. Only Tamara seemed saddened by the news of the destruction.

"What do you want to do about it?" she asked when they were alone in her office.

He shrugged, "What can I do?" Over the past year he'd grown comfortable in her presence, sometimes even able to speak his mind. Sometimes he caught himself thinking she was the only person who could understand him. "Bristol is all generosity when he's getting what he wants. But tell him something he doesn't want to hear and he's ruthless."

She agreed. "When I brought up the fact that some of the consumers are turning away from Bristol Industries because of the pollution they're seeing, he told me it was a PR problem. That I need to find some way to shut those — extremists, he called them — up."

Sage shook his head. "I hate to admit it — especially to you—" he grinned, "but Bristol is one problem that has me stumped."

She grinned back and the acknowledgement — a rarity — warmed him. "Me, too." But then she turned away, all business again, and the pleasure of her smile disappeared. "For now, we just have to toe the line. Let me think about it. Maybe there's a way we can get him to see value in conservation."

But even the astounding pace of Sage's creative innovations was too slow for Bristol; there was no convincing him to divert attention to things of the past. In fact Bristol began interfering in the design work, arbitrarily ordering changes or rethinks; pushing Sage to the breaking point.

· Ω ·

Sage rapped lightly on an engineer's office door and pushed it open; flipping through the file he carried in his hand. "Kreidn."

The engineer lifted his head from a spread of blueprints on his desk.

Sage stopped dead in his tracks.

Next to Kreidn was Bristol, pen in hand, marking up Sage's new blueprints — a prototype of a long-haul passenger jet — with circles, arrows, and lines.

"What are you doing?" Sage snatched the blueprints from the desk. The engineer who'd been working on the plan with Bristol eased himself out of his chair and slipped out of the office.

"Is too big." Bristol stated. "Is need to be smaller, more—" He pronounced the word carefully "—maneuverable."

The office door clicked closed.

"No, it doesn't." Sage slapped his file on the desk. "It's a big plane to carry a lot of people. It will make wide turns, fly straight for a thousand miles, make another wide turn and land on a long, long runway."

"No." Bristol's face took on an expression Sage couldn't read. "Fly fast, make sharp turns, climb and dive, zoom-zoom."

"Half the passengers will lose their breakfasts." Sage rolled up the drawings.

"Maybe not so many passengers," Bristol said.

"It's designed to carry three hundred, plus cargo." He snapped an elastic band around the roll. "Lots of money in cargo. You like money, don't you?"

The industrialist shrugged.

"What's going on?" Sage tapped the desk with the rolled-up blueprints. Duggin Bristol usually jumped at the idea of making money.

The man looked at the ceiling, as if the answer to Sage's question might be found there. "Passenger and cargo plane is good," he said. "But not what we need now."

Sage said again, "What's going on?"

"You want space program?"

"What's that got to do with what we're talking about?"

"Everything."

"Explain." Sage crossed his arms.

Bristol shrugged again. "You, me, your old man, we want space program. Duggin Bristol, first man in space."

"Better wait until we've tested the spacecraft. Things can go wrong."

"I trust you." said the industrialist.

"Then trust me with the truth."

"Okay." Bristol raised the blinds behind the desk and waved generally at the sky. "Who does space belong to?"

It was Sage's turn to shrug. "Nobody."

"Ha!" Now the big man's hands clapped together. "Tell that to King and President." He looked from side to side as if there might be unseen eavesdroppers. "Tell it to heads of army and navy."

"Spell it out!"

"Is simple. I say to government, 'We go to space.' Government say, 'Not so fast. Got little job for Rojan Revolutionaries.'"

"What kind of job?"

"Pirates."

"Pirates?" Sage understood now. "You want me to make war-planes."

The man spread his hands again. "Not me. King, President, admirals, generals. Make warplanes. Drop fire-bombs into pirate ships made of wood."

Sage, unlike anyone else on Tidon, had seen the effect of fire-bombs on human beings, the burning gel that stuck to the skin and burned through to the bone, while the screaming man — or woman, or child — tried to scrape the stuff off with hands that were also soon ablaze.

"No," Sage said.

"Yes," Bristol said. "I already told them."

"It's wrong."

"You ever see town after pirates come? They hit my home when I six years. You don't run fast enough, they kill you, or steal you away. You never see home again."

Sage opened his mouth to refuse categorically. But no sound came out. Instead, the lab and Bristol faded from his senses.

No! It had been a long time since his shadow had exercised its power over him, but it demonstrated now that it was still more than capable of taking over his body.

Suddenly, Sage was in a cold, dark, dimensionless place. The shadow was there; a darkness within the darkness. Knowledge. If Sage did not produce warplanes for the government of Bella Yareo, all of Bristol Industries' permits and licenses would be withdrawn. There would be no space program. If he refused now, the King would only command it of him personally, and if he refused then, he might find himself facing a charge of treason. It'd been a long time since the headsman's axe had been taken down from the dungeon wall, but Sage didn't doubt it would still be sharp.

The shadow released him.

"You do not," he heard Bristol say as the lab came back into focus, "make bombs. Navy already has firebomb weapon. Is needing delivery system."

Sage put a steadying hand on the desk, sickened.

"No choice," said Bristol.

"No." Sage's voice was hoarse in his own ears. "No choice."

· Ω ·

The pirates from Orlandia usually came after the rainy season, with winds in their favor. This year was no different. They appeared far off Bello Yareo's northeastern coast— entering from the Sea of Cortalone out in the Saltron Ocean; more than one hundred and eighty under sail, coming in fast, riding atop the waters with the morning sun. Their target was Sulley, a coastal city of some twenty-thousand people, the main port for a hinterland that grew grain and vegetables, fruit and wine, and just happened to also include one of Bella Yareo's largest gold mines.

Within minutes of the Royal Navy's observation of the ships on the horizon, Bristol Industries' reporters had their cameras ready to broadcast, and Tamara Young was knocking on Sage's door. A moment later, Genosa and Thaddeus silently joined them as the distant events marched across the small screen in Sage's office.

Sulley Harbor was fortified with bastions and batteries of cannons seemingly from an age long past; an age which in fact was only yesterday amidst their mad dash for the future. The smallest of the raiding ships mounted at least forty guns, and some of the multi-deckers had three times that many.

A camera — likely mounted on a hill overlooking the harbor — panned over to a lean, chiseled-jaw reporter. "...the pirate admiral, scanning the town of Sulley in the dawn light from the command deck of his great flagship, will see nothing amiss," the reporter was saying. "The pirate's telescope will not be powerful enough to show the slim antennae which rise from the top of Sulley's tallest buildings," — the camera panned away from the reporter to said antennae — "nor will he spy the other towers bedecked with gray stereovision dish transmitters. And even if he were to see them, he would have no way to know them for what they are. News of Rojan's Revolution has not yet reached the ears of the elite of Orlandia."

The small group in Sage's office, along with most of Bella Yareo, watched as events unfolded. The pirate's lighter sloops and single-decked frigates sailed nearest to the shore and drew fire from the town's cannons; most of which missed their targets. The locations of the batteries became exposed to the heavier men-of-war ships, which returned fire, their cannons thundering ceaselessly.

Slowly, the camera rotated inland to a small figure on Sulley Watchtower, who was peering into the gray murk of the offing. The look-out picked up his wireless phone and dialed.

"I'll bet he's calling central intelligence at the Royal High Command Headquarters," said Thaddeus.

Next, a buzzing drone became audible behind the barrage of guns. The camera panned, went out of focus, and then zoomed into a patch of sky. "There they are," Thaddeus breathed beside Sage's ear, his arm outstretched toward the screen, finger pointing.

They came in low and fast over the water, at little more than twice mast-height.

There was a flash of metal aircraft as the planes roared over the harbor.

Then spindle-shaped, silvery cylinders tumbled lazily from their wings. At deck-height, the canister igniters blew apart and set off the jellied petroleum they carried. The first salvo struck the pirate flagship.

"These pilots have been on constant stand-by for weeks." The reporter's voice was calm as the screen showed the Orlandian ships disappearing into a swelling blossom of flame. "Once the orders came from the Chief of the Bellan Admiralty General Staff, they had their planes in the air within minutes. The Table Mountain Squadron joined up with eight aircraft from Bozra at a pre-arranged assembly point, twenty miles inland from Sulley, where they formed two strike wings, turned seaward, and aimed for the pirate fleet."

For the first-hit ships, every external surface, and every man on deck, was on fire. The cameras zoomed in to show liquid from the weapons dripping down open hatches and companionways, igniting every flammable surface.

"What many Bellans may not know," the suave voice continued, "is that this enemy admiral does not consider himself a pirate, but rather the upholder of an ancient tradition of seaborne warfare. However, the last minutes of his life will be a horror of shock and terror, culminating in hideous pain. I doubt if the Orlandians will send their ships against Bella Yareo again."

The flagship went up, a blast so powerful it blew out the fire on one of the nearby frigates, but the blaze soon reignited from the petroleum burning on the water. A moment later, another of the smaller ships exploded, followed by a three-decker man-of-war. Debris and dead sailors, all on fire, flew in every direction, some landed in the water, some crashed into the rigging and woodwork of ships that had been outside the fireball and only scorched by its heat. Tarred ropes and deck seams ignited as sailors scurried about, closing the hatches to the powder magazines.

The camera zoomed back to the handsome reporter. "A little background for Bellans who have never experienced the horrors of piracy. In past attacks, Bellan defenders would normally fire until their own cannon were silenced and most of their own crews dead or dismembered." The reporter shook his head in anger, but his voice remained calm. "After winning the cannon barrage, the pirate ships would bombard the town while its population fled, then land thousands of armed sailors to mop up any resistance before they begin the looting. And the slave-taking."

Behind him, the second flight of the first strike wing roared overhead, low and invisible against the glare of the rising sun, and new fire blossoms bloomed where moments before there had been ships.

"I've seen enough." Sage stood to turn off the monitor.

"No." His mother laid a hand on his arm, eyes damp with tears.

"How can you watch this— this—" Sage's stomach twisted in knots.

Explosions and crackles from the small box were the only sound in the office. The rest of the pirate fleet's main body, which had been sailing in line astern in four columns, broke formation and turned toward the open sea. But sailing ships could go no faster than the wind blew, and this morning the offshore breeze was scant. Two flights of the second strike wing roared in on the tails of the first attack and turned the sea into a lake of fire.

Sage reached for the knob.

"No!" his mother lifted a stricken face. "You will watch this. All of it."

"It's sickening!" He was disgusted with her. "I can't believe you can look."

Her nostrils widened in fury. "You did this."

Her words wrenched his stomach.

"You."

"We all did," Thaddeus said softly. "We are all part of it."

"Yes," Genosa said. "You. Me. All of us. And we will all watch the consequences of our actions. We will not turn it off and pretend that this horror can happen to someone else and wash our hands of it."

Stunned, Sage sat. He turned his eyes back to the screen.

Bomb loads used up, the aircraft circled high into the sky, reformed into pairs and then came in low to hammer the unburned vessels with automatic cannon fire, exploding shells and tracer rounds penetrated to the powder stores of three more ships and blew them to pieces; all of the weapons designed and built by Bristol Armaments. Just as the jets used up their ammunition, a third strike wing of twelve planes from the Gredag Air Base, two hundred and twenty miles away, arrived to prolong the carnage.

Tamara reached out and took Sage's hand.

When, with its magazines and bomb racks empty, the third wing turned for home, the Orlandian pirate fleet had lost every one of its multi-decked men-of-war and most of its frigates. Three of its reconnaissance sloops had been sunk by cannon fire, and the only vessels undamaged were the unarmed store ships which would have carried off into slavery any citizens of Bella Yareo unlucky enough to have fallen into the raiders' hands.

These ships were abandoned, their crews having rowed to the one relatively undamaged frigate whose captain now found himself commanding what was left of the pirate fleet once thought of as invincible.

"What a victory; most of the pirate fleet have found their final resting place at the bottom of the sea," the reporter shouted, his face filling the screen with a triumphant smile. "I have no doubt that any remaining ships of the shattered fleet will be made short work of by the King's ships."

The camera panned back to the bay and a cloud of shrieking, diving, squabbling gulls dove over the mess of charred wreckage.

"Most Bellans believe that those pirates seeking to surrender should be given no quarter, but be killed on the spot, unless they are captured for intelligence purposes."

"Now." Genosa stood, trembling. "Now, you may turn it off."

· Ω ·

The streets of Porturn City overflowed with fanatics crowding the victory parade as it snaked up Castle Hill to King Ferdason's Palace. A spectacular leading float hoisted the national flag and preceded the King's carriage, drawn by a white steed of Carthusian pedigree. Its thick mane lifted in the breeze, its nostrils flared, and its ears stood at attention as it gently pranced over the cobblestones, through the oldest city district. The driver, in top hat and tails, held the sprightly horse in check for the cheering well-wishers. Traditional shields and the King's coat of arms — dating back centuries, to when a divine Balan had been the last emperor to rule the country — reflected garish sunshine.

Sage, standing on a float behind an obscene throne that couched Duggin Bristol's rump, dutifully waved to the ecstatic crowd lining each side of the parade roadway ten-deep. Both his arms ached, and so did his heart. Beside him, sailors and airmen seemed to revel in the adoration. Sage did not.

In fact, he was sickened by the overblown display of admiration for the slaughter. For days, the repulsive carnage had played over the network— over and over; the massacre of the Orlandian Armada, now known only as 'The Great Battle.'

Sage wanted to crawl under a rock when he thought of his role in the destruction. He would've arranged to be left out of the festivities, if he could have, but his position in Bristol Industries — and Tamara's campaign — forbade it. And his mother's condemnation of his actions meant that he must face this charade and accept responsibility for his part in it.

The one ray of light in this fiasco had come from Tamara. When Sage had spoken to her about the horror that filled his heart, she wasn't sure what she could do to help, but said something enigmatic about her talent being persuasion. A few days later, Sage heard that King Ferdason had sent a delegation to Orlandia to sign a treaty of peace. That treaty included regular surveillance of the Orlandian coast by Bellan ships and planes, but at least it was a step forward, and the apprehension of any threat from future piracy was gone.

So. Here he stood. Waving, in the brilliant sunshine and heat, dressed in a ridiculous military suit of royal blue, like an actor in a low rate broadcast portraying a 'man' of the air force. On a gaudy float decorated in patriotic bunting, behind an ornate chair graced by the buttocks of Bristol himself. The name 'Bristol' incongruously spelled out in large letters on every square inch of cloth; just in case anyone didn't recognize the billionaire who'd manufactured the aircraft that won the battle. It was all Sage could do to keep from vomiting.

But, nonetheless, he and Bristol were both heroes now. Sage swallowed hard as fans in the street below reserved their most ecstatic roars and whistles for him. Whenever he lifted a hand in a diffident acknowledgement, a wave of adoration erupted from the people in the streets. Many of them chanted 'Cosimo,' rather than Sage, using his third name which the media had fallen in love with. At Bristol Industries there was also the new line of Cosimo products, capitalizing on his even greater fame.

After an eternity, the coach and entourage of floats came to a halt at Ferdason Palace; the horse puffing and snorting from the climb. For eight centuries, the palace had stood atop Castle Hill overlooking River Porturn. The modern stately stone castle, restored in gothic style with its flying buttresses, had forgotten its fortress features of long ago. In the past hundred years, under the sovereignty of the House of Ferdason, its prime purpose had changed from protection to pomp.

King Ferdason stepped from his coach and held his arms aloft in acknowledgement of his subjects' applause as he walked onto the draw bridge overhanging the moat below. He turned and took his congratulatory bows. For the monarch, in charge of foreign affairs, there had been little to brag about, until this victory.

Then it was Duggin's turn. He waddled up the steps, a willowy wife on one arm, both bathing in the renewed cheer of adoration. Bristol media controlled these people, their thinking spoon-fed to them by the conglomerate.

Sage was next and he jumped from the float to make his own walk across the drawbridge. The police line almost broke as sobbing, shrieking girls and women tried to break through to reach him. During the broadcast battle — produced by the Bristol Network — the people of Bella Yareo had seen the pirate ships burn. But subsequent shows prominently featured the young genius whose miraculous planes and bomb delivery systems had removed the ancient scourge of piracy forever. Tamara's public relations campaign had centered on the prodigal child who cared nothing for fame and riches, but only wanted to change his world for the better. In three short years of invention and now war, the sixteen year old had become a national hero; his name and face more recognizable than the King's.

Inside the palace, colorful wall tapestries, frescoes, immaculate murals, and shimmering stained glass of statelier eras, adorned the walls and lofty ceilings of the huge atrium. Sage imagined himself to be one of the high columnar pillars which stood in front of him; they reminded him of the strength he would need to muster, to meet the challenges ahead, working for a tyrant.

Bristol bowed to accept a long, praise-filled speech and a knighthood for his war-mongering.

Then, Sage knelt before the King and lowered his head. The King spoke first of Sage's accomplishments — an embarrassing number — then waxed on about a new honor. King Ferdason had commanded that Sage be decorated unlike any Bellan had ever been decorated in the past. With that, the King personally placed a scarlet ribbon and medallion around Sage's neck, then knighted him with a sword touching his right shoulder. The King then reached down and showed the large medallion embossed with the House of Ferdason, proclaiming Sage Iden Cosimo Rojan the sole member of the Order of the Purifying Fire.

This event, too, was nationally broadcast. News reports noted that many Bellans stood to attention in their living rooms when Sage turned to face the cameras.

Sage lifted his face to the cameraman and forced himself to smile. *Never*, he vowed. *Never would he wage war again.*

· Ω ·

That same night, back inside his dreamscape, the way to the tiers of white doors stood open, as did the cathedral gates to the Library. Sage stood on the vast expanse of mosaic that he knew to be, in some way, a representation of his own mind, and watched for the shadow. After a timeless time, he caught a flicker of motion from the corner of his inner eye and willed himself in that direction. He came across the vague darkness of the shadow, suspended mid-air over a complex subroutine in the great pattern. As Sage, hovering, looked down at the design, he saw that subtle elements were rearranging themselves, forming new alignments, reaching out branches that made new connections between curves, and excrescences.

"Putting on some final touches?" he asked the shadow.

Usually, when he came across the shadow and tried an interrogation, he was ignored. But then, how many riders entertained queries from their mounts? This time, however, something seeped back to him: a sense of completion, of satisfaction even.

"Want to talk about it?" Sage asked.

No response.

"Well, I've got something I want to talk about. All those men burned to death."

He felt something like a shrug, followed by a succession of images he recognized: deaths he had witnessed behind the myriad of white doors, some not only seen from without but also experienced from within.

"You made me be part of it." Sage said. "It was no choice of mine." He felt another shrug and the sense of the shadow turning away. "I won't do anything like that again. I'd rather die."

He sensed a pause in the other's connection to him, as if the shadow was weighing up whether or not to tell him something. Then he was aware that his earlier comment about the work being almost complete had been accurate.

"So we're almost there?" It was as if he received a nod in reply. "And then what? You leave me be and I get to live a normal life?"

To that there was no answer and he felt the darkness withdraw from him. But at least it hadn't been a 'no.'

· Ω ·

"Sage, can you hear me?" Someone was shaking him. He came back to the world, sitting at his computer-assisted design workstation, a complex diagram on the screen and his hand on the vector tablet. Involuntarily, he switched the screen image to a schematic of Sintosy and its seven circling planets.

Tamara stood over him, a sharp line between her brows. "Where were you?" she said, and something about her expression made him feel that he should confide in her, tell her everything. "I spoke to you three times and you might as well have been on another planet."

He didn't have an answer for her. Last he could remember, he'd been finalizing the engineering schematics for the finely tuned motors that would move the great dish of the giant radio telescope Bristol Space was building as part of a joint venture with the Bella Yareo Space Agency— BYSA. It was his father's favorite project, and Sage worked on it whenever he had a free moment, as he had this afternoon while waiting for Tamara to come over to discuss the public relations campaign for the annual products launch.

In the year since the destruction of the pirate fleet, Sage's public approval numbers had soared and stayed in the stratosphere. Once Tamara showed Bristol the polling results, even the conglomerate's egomaniacal founder saw the wisdom of letting the boy who had won the hearts and minds of ordinary Bellans be the public face of Bristol Industries. Whatever Sage Rojan wanted, the people demanded that he get; whatever he blessed, the public adored.

Tamara Young was one of the few who didn't fall down at the national idol's feet. Now she poked him on the shoulder she'd just been shaking. "Tidon to Sage, are you receiving?"

"I was thinking," he said. "It's what I do." He let his eyes slide up to her for the first time and he blinked at her attire. Wow. She made clothes look fabulous. He looked away quickly, lest she catch him blushing.

They were both seventeen now, the age when Tidonese boys and girls tended to group themselves into couples in preparation for high school graduation. Neither he nor Tamara had need for a graduation ceremony yet Sage had found himself gravitating towards her as time went on. He had a troubling internal dynamic that saw him constantly swinging between wishing heartily that she would leave him alone, to fearing desperately that she just might. Whatever Tamara's feelings toward him might be, they were opaque to his sensibilities and he often chastised himself for desiring her companionship. 'Who would want a prickly cactus in their side?'

"You're not the only one around here who uses their brain," she was saying to him. "It isn't all just you and your team of robots." She gestured to the prototype of the automaton still sitting in the corner of his office.

Lately, he'd designed and built an assembly line that consisted of a series of automata that took their instructions directly from his own workstation via a secure fiber-optic link. The system was particularly useful when his work required him to create components on a nano-scale.

"At least the robots don't pester me with dumb PR questions," he said.

"There are no dumb PR questions." She pulled up a chair and sat beside him. "Just dumb answers." She looked at the monitor's screen. "What were you working on just now?"

Sage glanced at the screen. He couldn't answer, because he couldn't remember. Lately, the shadow's mental kidnappings happened more and more often; his master was homing in on the conclusion of all that had been building through Sage's short existence. Sage both resented the usurpation of his free will and at the same time welcomed the implication that soon this

master-slave relationship would be over. One thing was clear—
he wasn't going to discuss it with Tamara Young. She thought
him weird enough as it was.

He turned his back to the computer and faced her. "What's
on your agenda?"

"New product launches." She laid a number of placards out
on his desk. They showed a series of image-and-text mock-ups
of advertisements for the latest outpourings from the Rojan
Revolutionaries, most prominent among them 'intelligent' wireless phones that could access data from the rapidly developing
continent-wide web. The phones also had built-in cameras that
could capture hours of digitized imagery, and Ryze Feldstrum,
Bristol's head of marketing, was expecting teenagers to create a
whole new genre of folk-art, once they could start manipulating
and sharing the images and sounds via Bristol's communications systems.

"Ryze approved these?" he said, glancing at the mock-ups.

"Absolutely," she said.

"Then why are you showing them to me?"

"Because long ago you laid down the law that there could be
no use of your image unless you'd personally signed off on it."

"Oh," he said. "Well, from now on, if Ryze says it's okay, then
it's okay. You don't need to bother me with it."

"Oh?" she said archly. "Then you're not interested in this one
either?" She'd held back one of the boards and now produced it
with a casual flourish. It showed Sage in a space-suit — someone
had pasted his face over the model's — against a backdrop of
Tidon as seen from space, surrounded by its moons and a vast
star-scape. The slogan read: *First in our hearts, first in space.*

"That's been approved?" He snatched up the placard.

"By the King, by the government, by Bristol, although he
wanted the honor for himself. But you're the most popular figure
in Bellan history. The people want you up there."

He stared at the image, saying nothing. Inside, a turmoil
of emotions erupted. He wanted so much to be 'up there,' as
Tamara put it; but at the same time he wondered if the strong
emotion that accompanied the thought of blasting off from the
BYSA complex was genuinely his own, or if it had been planted
in him by his shadow. Perhaps, he allowed himself to think for
a moment, once he was aloft the shadow would depart from
him. At one time Sage had wondered if the shadow could have

been an alien, somehow trapped on Tidon, and was using him as a means of escape. But, no, he thought bitterly. His shadow was no alien being. No matter how much he tried to justify it to himself, whether he thought of himself as reincarnated or prodded by a personal demon, the fact was, Sage Iden Cosimo Rojan was a sham.

"Hey," Tamara said, "you're really excited about this."

He shook off the self-pity and grinned. "Wouldn't you be?"

"I'd be excited to be a national hero and the most recognized face on Bella Yareo," she said, "not to mention the person who is almost single-handedly changing the world. Unfortunately, you usually mope around like somebody's ruined your day. Every day."

"I—" He cut himself off. He wanted to confide in Tamara, to tell her everything he kept secret in his divided mind, confess his Dissociative Identity Disorder diagnosis. A part of him thought — hoped — that she, more than anyone, would understand. But what if she didn't? He wasn't sure he could take the rejection. The only people he'd ever confided in were his parents — who'd seen first-hand his dreams and nightmares — and Dr. Pivantis who'd made the diagnosis. But not Tamara, never Tamara. He couldn't bear to let her think of him as some pitiful creature no better than a finger-puppet to a psychotic personality.

"What?" she said.

"Nothing." He handed her back the placard. "I like the picture."

"Yippy, thanks," she said. "Your approval means so much to me."

He ignored the sarcasm. "I've got to get back to work."

"Another super-duper, ultra-secret wonderment?"

"Yeah, something like that." He wanted her to leave. But no. That desire came from his shadow, anxious to get back to whatever it had been working on. What Sage wanted was for Tamara to stay.

Instead, he shook his head and said, "Yabe," although he did not turn to his chair until she had gathered up her materials and walked out.

Sage touched the display. 'Quantronix.' It said. A complex diagram of circuitry appeared on screen. The next thing Sage knew was that the clock in the corner of the display screen had elapsed more than four hours.

His back and neck were stiff. His mouth was dry and his eyes felt like boiled eggs in deepened sockets. He must have been working like a machine at full throttle. When he tried to find the design, he saw that the work had been erased, but there was a log entry indicating that before erasure, the file had been transmitted to the robot assembly line to begin manufacture. When he queried that array, he was told that access to the process required a password.

Sage had no idea what that password might be.

Chapter 12

THE PRIVATE JET lifted from the end of the runway and climbed to twenty thousand feet before banking to begin the two-hour flight to the BYSA space center, deep in the continent's interior. Sage was the only passenger with the pilot. Normally, his father and a team of radio telescope technicians would have accompanied them, but the telescope was largely done now. What remained was to install and calibrate the electronic equipment that would sort and analyze the wavelengths captured from the universe so they could be translated into images. Sage hoped that his dad would find, along with the raw output of stars, the modulated signals that revealed the presence of other intelligent life.

"Why are you going on your own?" his father had asked, as they waited in the airport cafeteria for his departure.

"It's something—" Even after all these years, it embarrassed Sage to talk about his shadow. "I can't help it, Dad. It's my... illness."

His father's face reflected the same mix of emotions that often troubled Sage. "Sage, I worry about you. You live two lives. You don't get enough sleep. I've said it before, Sage. We need to go back to Dr. Pivantis. Or some other doctor—"

"No drugs." Sage pushed himself from the table. "Dad, I need every ounce of control, every brain cell I own, to keep the shadow down. I can't dull my mind with drugs."

"Perhaps you could go somewhere. Rest—"

"No! Dad, don't lock me up! I'll go crazy — crazier — I swear!"

His father had acquiesced and Sage shouldered his duffel bag and smiled his gratitude.

During the flight, Sage worked on a couple of projects, using his prototype intelligent phone as an encrypted connection to his system back at the lab. A little while before they were to begin their descent, the pilot came back into the cabin — the plane flying on autopilot — and asked if 'Cosimo' wanted to take the controls. For all his accomplishments, Sage was still only seventeen years old. He'd flown a couple of times in the co-pilot's seat, but this was the first time he would handle the sleek corporate jet on his own. Sage jumped at the chance even though he knew there was no real challenge in it. After all, the skies over Bella Yareo's deserts were not yet as crowded as those over Porturn and, besides, Bristol's personal aircraft could go where it liked with the knowledge that any other aircraft except the King's would be told by air traffic control to get out of the way.

Sage enjoyed the feel of the airplane, the power when he pulled back the yoke and increased the throttle. He soon realized, however, that the pilot had an ulterior motive in inviting him into the cockpit: the man brought their conversation around to the space program, and from there to the selection process for the elite group — all pilots — who would be the first Bellans in space after Sage himself. Sage couldn't fault the pilot for wanting what he himself wanted. He told him the names of the BYSA officers who would be vetting the applicants and looking for a particular kind of flyer; someone who combined sheer courage with a coolness of mind. "They don't want hot-shot cowboys," Sage said. "They're looking for the calm, clear-headed type, people who will react the right way the first time, because there might not be a second time."

And then they were only fifteen minutes out from the space center. The pilot took the controls and Sage went back to his seat. The landing was so smooth Sage barely noticed they'd arrived. He pulled himself away from the circuit design he'd been tinkering with and decided that he would mention the pilot's name to the space program people. Besides, Bristol might be annoyed if he lost his private jet-jockey. And Sage didn't mind annoying Duggin Bristol.

BYSA's space center had been built in Tasil Flats, on the edge of the huge brush-desert that stretched, another two hours flying time, to the Kalico Mountain Range. The Kalicos created a rainshadow that left the area permanently arid, so there wasn't much between Tasil and the Kalico interior except sage brush, cacti, lizards, and a large ranching operation built around deep-drilled wells.

Sage stepped down from the plane into bright sunshine, surprised that his motorcycle wasn't waiting for him. Across the tarmac stood the large BYSA control-tower headquarters, soon to be converted to Mission Control; and a mile farther out into the desert, the space launch pad. Closest to him, atop the only hill in the flats area, was a white geodesic dome that housed the radio telescope. It had been built for Sage by BYSA as part of the collaboration between the Space Agency and Bristol Industries. He'd nicknamed the observatory 'Cos-Ob,' for his now famous middle name, Cosimo.

A driverless utility vehicle arrived to collect him. He climbed in and read a computerized message explaining that the road to the observatory was under construction and not recommended for two-wheeled travel. Vexed, he commanded the vehicle to take him to the observatory.

The joint venture between Bristol Space and BYSA was working well. Bristol, along with capital input into the program, provided the expertise of Sage, Thaddeus, and their team of engineers. In return, BYSA provided the Bristol team with work facilities at the BYSA complex. Together, the teams came under one umbrella for collaboration on the space project.

The four-wheel-drive vehicle climbed the long hill and delivered Sage to the barbed-wire perimeter security fence that surrounded the observatory. Sage inserted a data card into the gate's control panel and put his eye up to the retina scanner. The lock clicked and the fence gate slid open.

It had been a while since Sage had been inside his dome, overseeing, along with his dad, its construction and assembly. Insulation of the interior walls and ceiling had been completed, coated and sealed to keep the inside temperature constant. The large telescope at the center of the dome had been exorbitant in cost, with its fifteen foot wide primary mirror, comprised of twenty hexagonal segments, and smaller optical and infrared mirrors for gathering spectra from galaxies and stars deep in the celestial expanse.

Sage was pleased to see how much floor space was left, now that the dish itself was up, the shakedown was complete, and all the construction equipment and debris were gone. His sense of pleasure, he realized after a moment, was echoed from within by his shadow. Whatever was going on here at the space center, it was important to the shadow.

Sage let himself become inert, interested to see what the shadow would do. Immediately, he felt his legs and feet moving without his specific guidance as the shadow exercised its will. Like walking in a dream, his limbs moved as if they belonged to someone else— which, at the moment, they did.

His shadow walked him across the concrete floor, to the wall opposite the entrance where the radio telescope control system was housed. He picked up a multi-button remote and at the same time threw the main power switch. When he heard the dish's electric motors hum to life, he aimed the remote. The huge wheel of metal above his head turned to the left; he thumbed another button to make it stop and track back to the right. A different sequence of buttons altered the system's mode, and he could elevate the dish so that it could point at any angle from the unseen horizon beyond the dome to the zenith overhead.

He punched 'rotate,' and the almost half-wide interior turntable rasped to life. The large telescope moved slowly to his left, until it rotated halfway 'round. Then he pressed the buttons that lowered into place an enormous insulating curtain meant to protect the delicate instrument from dust and magnetic fields.

Perfect. It's out of the way. Nothing but room here now. But his shadow hadn't walked him over to the workbench to play with the dish. *What was it up to?*

A moment later, he had his answer. The closed-circuit telephone mounted on the wall behind the bench chirped. Sage picked it up, identified himself, and was told that a semi-trailer had arrived at the main gate with a delivery personally consigned to him at the observatory.

He'd ordered nothing, but he could feel the excitement from the shadow within him. "Send it up to the observatory loading dock. I'll meet it there."

As Sage waited outside, he leaned against the side of the dome, his back against the fortress of concrete and iron.

A half mile down the hill a large transport truck was chugging slowly up the rough road, raising dust as its tires churned.

The Bristol Transport semi-trailer maneuvered its rear up to the loading bay. The driver climbed out of the double cab, followed by a man wearing coveralls, and threw a sketchy salute to Sage. "You really him?"

It was a question Sage heard often on the rare occasions he went out in public. "Yep," he said. He shook hands with both men and signed the driver's clipboard accepting delivery.

"Thirty cases in total," the man said. "Some of them are real big. So we brought our own forklift. Where do you want them?"

The answer appeared in his mind. "The ones marked RTEC — Rojan Telescope Extra Components — go over there; they won't be needed right away," he pointed off to the side near the control bench. "The rest go right here, close to the center of the room." Sage watched the men unload and then depart. He was alone.

Sage examined the shipping labels. Some came from the tools department of his father's inventions lab. The labels whose point of origin was identified only by 'Q' and a coded string of numbers told Sage their contents had been boxed and shipped by the robots on his own private assembly line.

"Now what?" he said aloud. His voice echoed in the great dome. The answer was provided from within: *open the smaller boxes first.*

The smaller cartons contained chains, pulleys, hooks, bolts, screws, pneumatic wrenches, and auxiliary tools. *In a shed behind the dome you will find the machines you need: a boomer, a cherry picker, and a scissor-lift.*

He was not surprised that, when he went out to the shed and started up the first machine, he already knew how to operate it.

"What am I making?" Sage asked. *You don't need to know.* He suspected the moment he had the machines inside the dome, he would black out and be aware of nothing until he woke, exhausted and dehydrated, lying on the concrete floor next to some unfathomable device.

But Sage had an amendment to that plan. As he steered the cherry picker up the ramp and into the observatory, he eased into lucid dreaming and when the moment came for the shadow to banish him, Sage slipped into his dream-state, and hovered above the great mosaic. Substantial parts of it glowed with a new energy.

Instantly, the shadow was beside him, surrounding him, roiling above him like the black smoke of an oil fire.

"I'm not going," Sage told it. "You may use me like a rented mule, but I won't do it sleepwalking."

The shadow darkened, flickers like inky lightning crackling within it.

Sage braced himself for an attack.

But then, the shadow grayed, calmed.

It took Sage a moment to grasp what was seeping his way, and then he grinned. "You're a show-off…"

The shadow withdrew slightly.

"You like having an audience."

The shadow writhed, snakelike. If the shadow had had a body, Sage was sure it would have sneered and shrugged. *If you want to see what your body is doing, fine.*

Then Sage was looking through his own eyes at the interior of the dome. He was still sitting in the driver's seat of the cherry picker. But for the next several hours, he sat in the passenger seat of his own body, as his shadow used him to open the larger crates marked 'Q' and assemble the strangest machine he had ever seen.

Utilizing the chains, pulleys, and fork-lift, he positioned an eight-hundred-pound, cast-iron receptacle: the device's base. He tied it down with steel bolts drilled into the observatory's turntable floor and then tightened them against the base's flanges with a pneumatic torque wrench. Next, he built up a structure of metal parts, a framework, which eventually reached almost to the top of the dome. He realized, somewhere along the way, that his impulse to play with the dish's controls had not been idle: he had needed to move the radio telescope out of the way to make room for what he was now building.

The great machine's sections fit, one by one, into place as it climbed upward from the floor with the addition of each new section. The shadow worked quickly and efficiently, with a precision colored by feverish intensity. Sage had to remind the shadow to let his body pause to take in nourishment and rest. "Besides," he queried, "if you work me to death before the job is finished, who will operate it for you?"

· Ω ·

At the end of the second day, Sage stood on the platform of the scissor lift, fingers resting lightly on the hydraulic controls, more than forty feet above the floor of the dome. There, from the strut work just below the ceiling that allowed a portion of the dome to open, he hung an arrangement of chains and pulleys to lift a cannon-like barrel, central to the mysterious machine he was building, into place.

The barrel was light-weight and slipped smoothly into position. Sage articulated a knuckle-lift from a turntable work platform mounted on an extended arm that was bent to reach around the barrel. Methodically, he — or more properly, his shadow — tightened each bolt to its maximum. Then he withdrew the chains and let the machine stand free.

Sage, himself, stood motionless, aboard the platform station high in the air, trying to make sense of the completed device. The barrel, since it was pointing straight up at a part of the domed ceiling that could be retracted, put him in mind of a telescope. But there were no lenses, nor a mirror to focus the light.

"It's called a Quantronix, isn't it?" he said out loud; though it was directed to his shadow. "That's why the boxes were marked with a Q."

He sensed a moment of surprise, quickly smothered.

"What does it do?"

No answer. Instead, his hands worked the cherry picker's controls to lower himself to floor level. He stepped off the platform and looked up at what his inner-master had built. From base to apex, the thing was some forty feet tall. The cannon barrel extended down from the aperture at the top of the dome to the middle of the device, and resembled a large funnel. Below that, the central belly of the machine was a sixteen-foot wide sphere containing two large magnetic turbines— set adjacent but counteractive to one another. The belly fit into a thick, curved armature firmly bolted to the base.

The thing reminded Sage of a huge army tank that someone had set on its hind end, with the gun barrel pointed straight up. "Are we going to shoot something up into orbit?"

His body was put to work again.

"Then why go to all the trouble of developing heavy-lift rockets?"

On legs so tired their long muscles trembled, he went to the workbench and found the remote. His fingers pressed buttons and the rooftop aperture slid open with a grating sound. He set down the remote and opened a panel just above the Quantronix's base where he'd installed its controls.

He watched with trepidation as his hands threw switches, set a couple of dials, and then pressed a button. He heard the sound of the turbines revving and stepped back, looking up. The long barrel grew longer, telescoping toward the top of the dome. A component built into the tube now extended itself like the reticulations of a worm, becoming the very tip of the machine, widening like the jaws of a cobra, as it passed through the aperture provided by the hexagonal panels at the top of the dome, and out into the daylight.

Daylight. How long had he been in here, building this thing? "What's it doing?"

And this time, he received an answer from his shadow: without hesitation, he was in front of the computer, schematics flashing in his eyes.

Rays of light, which had departed Sintosy eight minutes earlier, were striking the device at the end of the extended barrel. Image after image appeared showing how the light particles were captured, forfeiting their freedom for millions, perhaps billions of years.

The machine's complex internal parts each embarked on their assigned tasks. In the long wormlike extension, a receptacle captured rays of light and sent them down the barrel. There, they were subjected to an ultra-fast push that converted the light into a Quantronix wave and passed it through an array of prisms, causing the energy to bend and curve abnormally. The Quantronix wave emerged from the prisms precisely aimed into the machine's wide middle belly, where the bent light encountered twin turbines. These further spun it at incredible speed forming the specified atoms. Now locked up as matter, the internal parts of the atom spun, but could not escape their entrapment. The newly created atoms streamed deeper into the machine, much like a baby heading through the birth canal, to their final destination in the base. There, they were spat out, a finished product— comparable to a spaghetti maker spewing out lengthy stands of homemade pasta to form a ball. Nearly invisible traces of matter accumulated in a crucible.

"What type of matter?" Sage asked.

Whatever its controls were set for. Strands of elastic light were stretched; then cut precisely to required lengths and spun into the specific arrangements of neurons, protons, and electrons to produce the desired atoms. This time the Quantronix was set to produce pure gold, atomic number 79.

The machine withdrew its light receptacle from the air above the dome and shut itself off.

Sage peered into the crucible. A gleaming pea-sized sphere of yellow metal. He reached in and picked it up. Cool to the touch, and heavy in his hand. He rolled it between his palms then held it up for study.

"Well, now, that's something," he said aloud. "I've read books about the ages of antiquity when alchemists unsuccessfully hoped to transmute common metals into gold. Many of them were burned as witches or heretics. But this… this is unbelievable." The shadow had done in minutes something alchemists and scientists couldn't do in centuries. *Wow. Truly amazing.* In less than two decades the shadow had taken the planet Tidon from the bare boned beginnings of a technological revolution to the incredible feat of creating matter. *What next? Do we invent the panacea cure for every disease? Make an elixir of life to make us immortal?*

Inside, reflected exultation.

"This creating matter really means something to you, doesn't it?" Sage placed the nugget on the nearby workbench. "This is what it's been all about. To do something no Tidonese has ever been able to do?"

Almost, he got what he was hoping for: that in its excitement, the shadow might let slip the nature of its true goal. If Sage knew what the end of all this was supposed to be, he might have a lever strong enough to counterbalance the power of the shadow that used him like a pirate's slave.

But then, just as he sensed the knowledge was about to appear in his mind, the shutters rolled down. The shadow had let him have all that he was going to share, this day.

Still, Sage had been sincere in his admiration of the machine. If it could produce, in seconds, appreciable quantities of the rare minerals that were laboriously and expensively dug up and processed by Bristol Mines — generating mounting poisons in the land, the air, and the water — the expansion of the aerospace and information-technology sectors could truly accelerate.

Sage could already envision himself in a space suit. The faster the Quantronix could spin precious materials, the sooner he might become the first Tidonese in space, feeling its weightlessness and emptiness, stepping out of an airlock to perform the first spacewalk.

For all the exhaustion of his two days of almost sleepless labor, for all the joylessness of his life as the shadow's fetcher-and-carrier, the prospect of that future moment thrilled even Sage.

Chapter 13

COS-OB CAME EQUIPPED with a bare bones residential suite. It was for those occasions when someone might have to put in a double shift, if not longer, scanning the heavens. Temporarily set free by his shadow from the labor of alchemy, Sage dragged himself to the little one-room apartment. He was almost too tired to realize he'd put a soup bowl into his new radio wave cooker and flicked the switch to jolt the volts into warming the broth. He ate. Then collapsed on the cot and slept straight through the night. Luckily, his dreams took a hiatus. Sage suspected the shadow was taking it easy, allowing his body to retain the energy necessary to make more precious elements.

When Sage woke, his natural and augmented resilience stood him in good stead. He felt good. In the mirror above the little sink, he saw that the dark pouches beneath his eyes had faded from yesterday's murk.

He ate a breakfast of cereal and dried fruit then returned to the Quantronix. He felt loose and light as he approached the machine. "Just tell me what you want to do," he said to his inner-self. "I'm as interested in this as you are."

He received a sense that the shadow considered any such comparison laughable, but his body remained in his own command. He opened the control panel. "More gold?" he said. "Is that the idea? Invoke the golden rule: he who has the gold rules?"

It was not the idea. The shadow had no interest in worldly goods. Sage received a mental image of Bristol, swimming in a sea of banknotes, coins, and precious materials. The feelings that overlaid the picture conveyed ridicule and contempt. The shadow, on the other hand, pursued a dream. The dream was noble, of immense significance, and far more than Bristol, or even Sage, could ever comprehend.

Sage shrugged. "If you say so." He ran his fingers over the Quantronix's controls. "So," he said, "what now?"

The answer came. He changed the settings, meticulously calibrating dials. It was a euphoric rush to play at nanotechnology, manipulating structure and composition on a subatomic level by controlling the spintronics of light into matter; varying the formula for cutting the length, then enforcing the stretch and tightness of each ray of light to be spun for a specific element.

"So we're making batrillium?" he said, the settings done. It was a transuranic element, atomic number greater than 92, which did not exist on Tidon. He had supposedly encountered it in other lives on other worlds. It would be a great help in creating ultra-sophisticated devices.

Sage activated the machine and watched its light-catcher pass through the dome's ceiling. By evening, a few tenths of an ounce of the rare material accumulated in the crucible. Gingerly using tongs and lead-lined gloves, he moved it to a sealed container. Over the next few days, guided by the shadow, he reset the machine to make mestronium and norstiate, two of the universe's rarest elements. Sage wasn't sure of their purpose.

Then, he reset the alignment sequence to atomic number 73 to make the element tantalum, a crucial component in making smaller, faster electronics. The powdery, lustrous metal would make perfect circuits because of its high level of capacitance, providing volumetric efficiency, even when small in size. This direct method would be much easier than the traditional mining process, having to separate tantalum from niobium and columbite. Now, the technological revolution could really speed ahead. Sage could appreciate all of those things, even though a corner of his thoughts niggled; deploying the Quantronix felt like cheating.

He had been impressed yesterday. Now, that initial reaction was fading.

There was no triumph, no glory in this alchemist's creation of matter. The shadow's activities were not right at a most fundamental level. What was going on here was at best, unwise, and possibly — completely forbidden. It could not end well; there would be a price to pay for this business. Would that price be exacted from him — the unwilling tool — as well as from the pride-drunk entity that wielded it?

Where had that thought come from?

Forbidden by whom?

The Artisan. The Master of the Empyrean.

As the machine spun and spun, Sage lowered his head, beaten and monopolized. There was no escape from his shadow's control. There was no place to hide. He closed his eyes and imagined himself a mole, burrowing to avoid detection.

As the strange stuffs before him formed in the crucible, Sage felt a huge inward exultation that was not of his own emotion; paroxysms of joy so intense he wondered if his mere human body could contain them. It was an artisan-like feeling. And that troubled him deeply. It smacked of mania, delusions of grandeur. Sage chilled. His illness was worsening. He had to keep these emotions contained lest someone — his parents, Dr. Pivantis — decide he must be given drugs or locked away. He forced the euphoria down.

The speaker-phone above the workbench buzzed. His tired arm reached up and flipped the talk switch.

"Do you know it's taken me two hours to track you down?"

Tamara.

For once, Sage would've welcomed a little human contact from the girl he — liked — sometimes — when she wasn't pigheaded — but Tamara was clearly not in any mood to be his confidante.

"What are you doing out at BYSA?" she went on without pausing. "We've got all the product-launch events to finalize, and you're slated to be the star of every show!"

He didn't answer. His shadow-self was watching. If he so much as formed in his mind a mention of the machine, Tamara would instantly find herself cut off.

"Do you do these things just to make my life difficult? Or because you're nothing but a self-involved prima donna?"

He turned to look at the crucible, depositing trace amounts of tantalum. "I do the work that needs to be done."

"The radio-whatsit telescope needed to be fiddled with?" She sighed. "That's not even your hobby. It's your father's!"

"Is there a point to this conversation," he said, "other than your need to spew some bile? Or are you just intent on wasting my time?"

"I'm trying to do my job," she said, "and your absence makes it impossible."

"Look," he said, "It's going to take a while. I'll be back in Porturn in time for the launches. Just assume that I'll go along with whatever foofaraw you cook up."

"You're pre-approving everything?"

Though he hated to admit it, Bristol had been right to hire Tamara. Her work was consistently stellar, and he trusted her. "Yes. Just don't put me out in pink tights or a tutu or something." He flipped the talk switch to the off position.

· Ω ·

Since Sage had arrived at Cos-Ob no one had ventured up the hill. His shadow-self had seen to that. Apparently, Sage had reserved the entire Cos-Ob facility for 'special astronomical observations.' He'd also changed the entry codes, preventing the technicians and astrophysicists from interrupting the Quantronix as it did its magic. They would have to wait for another opportunity to utilize the space telescope. What the great inventor Sage Rojan demanded, he got.

Sage worked for four more days, spinning matter and yet more matter every hour that Sintosy shone on the Tasil Flats. He lived on soup and crackers, and slept on the cot without waking or dreaming. Between sundown and sleep, he loaded the newly-made elements into small, lead-lined boxes, stacking them inside heavy-duty shipping crates, and, using the forklift, piled them behind the closed door of the loading dock. The crates were the same kind used by Bristol Mines to ship product from the refineries to the Bristol Industries warehouse in Porturn City. Each was labeled and accompanied by paperwork indicating it had come from the mining subsidiary. No longer would any of the Bristol technologists complain of a shortage of rare elements for the new products.

On the last day, Sage called for the truck and driver that had brought the components of the Quantronix and together the two of them loaded the crates into the truck. "What's your name?"

"Bix."

"Well, Bix, I need to ask you a favor."

The man smiled self-consciously. "All right."

Sage held out the sheaf of forged paperwork indicating the shipment came from Bristol Mines. Something nudged Sage sideways; the shadow taking control. "Bix, I'm working on a really big deal. Top secret. Every time you do a transport for me, no one but the two of us can know about the paperwork. Here, let me give you a little something in advance." Sage handed Bix a small satchel.

Bix opened the bag, peered inside and lifted out a handful of gold nuggets. His brows lifted in speechless astonishment.

"From a stream in the Kalico Mountains." Sage's voice resonated with smooth confidence. "Inside the satchel is the name of a place where you can redeem them for cash on the private market. Can I count on you?"

Bix stirred the nuggets one last time, and then pulled the strings to tighten the noose of the satchel. "If that's what you say, then that's what I say." He extended his arm and they shook hands. "You got a deal."

Sage nodded and Bix saluted as he climbed into the cab. The truck rolled down the rough road to the space center's main gate and wheeled onto the highway to Porturn City.

Back inside Cos-Ob Sage punched the controls that raised the insulating curtain from the giant space telescope and slowly rotated the turntable— switching the Quantronix with the telescope. From the last remaining crate, he unboxed an immense roll of fabric, attached it to the scissor lift, and slipped the woven covering over the funnel— draping it down the sides of the Quantronix. At the bottom, he tightened a steel cable that ran through titanium grommets and locked the tarpaulin in place.

As he pushed the key into the safety of his pocket, he became aware of the shadow's bold-faced lie painted on the side of the fabric: *Private Telescope— Sage Rojan.*

· Ω ·

Sage spoke to his shadow. "The jet won't be in to pick me up for at least an hour. I'm going to rest."

He lay on the cot and sent himself into a lucid dream state. In moments he found himself striding across the mosaic toward the Library. It was time to do some private investigation into his psychosis.

Suddenly, the shadow was with him.

Sage used the drumming technique, taping his fingertip on the nape of his neck. The sound reverberated through his mind and all through his dreamscape, like rhythmic thunder. A warning that any interference would be resisted. Sage did not know whether resistance would be futile or not; he had used it to blast the leather-winged monster to ashes, but his shadow had not stood in his way since, and had let him use the Library whenever he wanted. Perhaps that had always played into the shadow's plan. Not only was Sage more useful, educated, but Sage had been leaving himself open to the shadow's physical manipulations while he was distracted within the Library's cathedral gates.

The entrance to the Library loomed before him. The shadow was present, watchful, but not threatening. Still, Sage kept up his drumming.

He went straight to the lectern and its directory. Sage knew there were entries in the table of contents that dealt with the "invention of space" and the "invention of time," but he could not remember if there was an entry for the invention of matter. When he checked the great tome's subject index for Quantronix, he was directed to a volume entitled RECYCLIUN that was stored on an upper shelf of the library. He willed the large volume down and laid it on a table of his own conjuring. He dusted it off and read the preface:

> Inhabitants on planets of the inner universe are unable to grasp the true relationship between light and matter. Their view is affected by the brevity of their lives, which only permits vision of an infinitesimal fraction of one recycle of the inner universe.
>
> Each fifteen billion years, matter experiences three episodes in its recycle: CREATION; LOCKUP; and then final ESCAPE.
>
> Residents of a planet are not alive at the start of the cycle to witness the CREATION of matter for their planet. They are born into the middle state, where atoms are in LOCKUP as matter on their planet. They do however occasionally witness ESCAPE when light escapes during combustive events — fire, or lightning — or when matter unravels and becomes light again emitted by nuclear detonation or fusion in stars and suns.
>
> The initial CREATION of matter is the least witnessed event in space-time. Natural CREATION only occurs within the ambit of a black hole, which captures and spins light into matter to create the spheres of the universe. Artificial CREATION can be performed by means of a Quantronix. It should be noted that the use of a Quantronix in space to artificially spin matter from light BREAKS THE PRIME DIRECTIVE OF THE UNIVERSE.

Sage sat back in his conjured chair, frightened. His delusions were deepening. But what he had done — as part of the shadow's plan — was the kind of thing that he'd read about in mythology: where mere mortals, attempted to do what only an artisan or creator was permitted to do. Those stories, he recalled, never had happy endings. His subconscious must be using childhood stories as a scaffold for these delusional experiences. And to create a third personality... the Artisan.

And yet... and yet the internal logic of the world his mind had created compelled him—

He had to make the shadow stop using the Quantronix. It was against the laws of the universe— and the artisan.

But the book — the information — drew him back.

> *Light was in the inner universe first; black holes came after. Light appears to come from stars, but stars are not its true origin. Rather, light is the universe's original substance, used to make the stars. In the beginning, there was only light and it was everywhere. Then, the first black hole appeared which displayed its gravitational power by capturing and spinning gigantic amounts of light around itself to create a stellar body.*
>
> *Once light is spun into matter, it can remain locked inside an atom for billions of years. But eventually it will escape. During the many recycles of the inner universe, no atom of matter has ever stayed spun forever because no black hole, at the center of a moon, planet, or star, has ever been able to keep its hold forever. Spun light, confined within an atom, must always escape its spun state and return to its original straight-line state. Thereafter, for that freed light, there may be a repeat time when it is attracted by a different black hole to be captured and spun once again.*

Before he had witnessed the Quantronix at work, Sage would have scoffed at the notion of the three states of light. Now, he understood. Matter and light energy were interchangeable, recycled back and forth throughout eternity. Neither ever destroyed. He realized that everything, from the tiniest mite to the whole planet Tidon, was a bed of light spun into zillions of atoms of matter. And, someday, it would all unspin back into straight-line light. The heading spelled it out clearly; THE RECYCLING OF LIGHT AND MATTER IS THE FUNDAMENTAL LAW OF THE RECYCLING INNER UNIVERSE (RECYCLIUN).

He read more about light and its unusual properties. It said that in everyday life, the deepest secrets of light were impossible to detect. Its elastic properties allowed it to bend, when near a black hole, at an extreme angle and coil into spun matter. That spun matter formed the exterior body of all moons, planets and stars, with a black hole at their core. Space was defined as the cold emptiness left behind when light spun into orbs. Those orbs, with bodies of light spun into tight matter, occupied a billionth of the area compared to the emptiness of space left behind. And, with that spinning, time was imported into the area of each spun orb and time was defined as the duration through which matter stayed in the form of a spinning atom before eventually escaping and returning back to straight line light. And a star was simply the last and final stage prior to which all that spun light of an orb escaped back to straight line light.

He wished he could bring his father into this place. He'd be able to show him that his doubts about the Bang Theory, trying to explain creation, were well placed. Thaddeus would be overjoyed. Or— no, Thaddeus would be devastated... at the depth of Sage's illness. Was he *able*— able to tell the difference between reality and his delusions?

But Sage's shadow had enlisted — more like enslaved — him to a project that violated the universe's fundamental law. What would the consequences of such a violation be? Could the machine do the cosmic equivalent of tugging on a thread that would cause the warp and weft of space-time to unravel? And, would the shadow care? Or would the destruction of the world and the stars just be another stepping stone on the path to whatever weird end the shadow had in view?

One thing Sage knew: he couldn't be a part of it. And if he could stop it from happening, he would. Even if he couldn't, it was his duty to try.

Unless... the Quantronix didn't exist. He'd been alone for days. Bix had seen nothing but crates... except the gold. So... the machine had to be real... didn't it?

If he wasn't mad enough already, puzzling out this paradox would drive him crazy.

He closed the cover of the huge book and it returned itself to its place on the shelf. He'd been so involved in the discovery of the truth he had not even noticed whether the shadow was with him. Now he felt around with whatever sense it was that registered the entity's presence. And found its absence.

Had the shadow slipped off to use his body again? Or was it lingering somewhere else in his dreamscape?

Sage willed himself back to the mosaic but when he checked on his body it still rested on the cot. Sage tried to send his senses out, to feel where the shadow had gone. The questions that circled his mind needed answers. Perhaps there was more he could press out of the shadow.

There. A flicker of direction. A certain door among the thousands that lined the myriad of corridors across the mosaic from the Library. He sent himself across the great design, squeezed his illusionary body and slid through the separated molecules of the aqua curtain. In a blink he was standing before the door; strangely unmarked as if the catalogue had missed giving it a designation. Drumming on his neck to raise his shamanistic power, he pushed open the door and stepped within.

He didn't know what to expect. Perhaps another record of yet another life on yet another world. But behind this door there was nothing. A gray limbo without form or distance.

And, then, the shadow.

As always, there was nothing to see, no face, no physical form, just a sense of a dark, amorphous presence, at this moment radiating a cold hostility.

Sage cut to the chase. "What are you doing with the Quantronix?"

If he had expected the thing to roil up in anger, he was disappointed. It floated, inert.

"You don't want money, you've made that clear. Through me, you've already got power. We could probably overrule the King if we wanted to. In fact, if I appeared on Bristol Network tomorrow and said I wanted to be king, there'd be a mob storming the palace on my behalf about ten minutes after I finished speaking."

He received no answer. He moved closer to the shadow but it withdrew. He doubted if he could touch it or grapple with it; it never had a body as far as he could tell. "You're not after any appetites of the flesh. You don't have flesh to start with."

The place they were within had no dimension, yet somehow the shadow put distance between them. Drumming harder, Sage willed himself to close the non-space between them.

"What have you got me into?"

He felt no response other than a wave of angry resentment.

"You resent the question?" Sage said. "I resent being made an accomplice in some kind of crime against the fundamental laws of existence!"

Again, no knowledge came his way. The thing hovered, not dead, but not responding.

"At least tell me what I'm part of! The Empyrean— what and where is it? Who are you and how are we connected?" He knew his questions were crazy. There was no Empyrean, beyond the fabrication in his mind. And yet, the delusion was so real—

More anger, more resentment. It was like being growled at out of darkness by some great predatory beast that resonated through his entire cranium.

But Sage held his ground. "Listen. You've made my life a misery. Denied me any kind of normal existence. I've brought great things to the people of Bella Yareo; technology, portable devices, machines that improve workflow and production, more efficient transportation, a broad network of communication opportunities, satellites, digital imaging, freedom from the threat of pirates, and yes they all love me for it but none of that has anything to do with me. Anything I've needed to know, you've put in my head. Any skill, you've put in my hands. I've never tried hard at anything in my life, never achieved the smallest victory. I'm— useless."

His words had no effect on the mist before him.

"Except for the time I backed you down by threatening to kill myself. Well, if the end of this life is going to see me hauled up in front of some kind of judge and made to explain why I was some criminal's henchman, then maybe I'd better just turn myself in now, and hope they go easy on me."

—The gray emptiness disappeared—

He found himself back in reality, lying on his cot in Cos-Ob. What the—? He made to rise.

He had no control over his body. The shadow was close by him, invisible, and full of cold malevolence. Now, his hands came, as if of their own volition, towards his face, fingers spread. What was happening?

They locked themselves around his throat. Did his shadow want him dead? His fingers pressed against his windpipe, tight and growing tighter — the power of a hand forty times stronger than any of its five individual fingers—

He couldn't believe this. His throat hurt. He squirmed.

Their clench exerted full strength. He could not breathe. Panicked, he writhed, tried to twist from his own grip—

Still the pressure increased, cutting off the supply of air to his lungs and the flow of oxygen-bearing blood to his brain. Dackt! He couldn't die this way, never see his mother, father, Tamara—

Veins and tendons in his wrists popped out from exertion. He jerked himself helplessly across the bed, achieving nothing—

Darkness moved in from the edges of his field of vision, until it was as if he was peering down a narrowing tunnel. Then nothing. Silence.

$$\cdot \, \Omega \, \cdot$$

Sage could see again.

But what he saw was his own body lying face-up on the cot, eyes bulging, his hands loose around his throat— loose in death. He'd risen from his own corpse, the shadow beside him.

He looked up and around. Was there some warm light to receive him? No. There was nothing but the Cos-Ob dome, the telescope, and the covered machine.

His own ghostly substance grew thinner, fading. When he grew insubstantial enough, there would be nothing left of him.

Eternal death.

He did not know if he could speak in this form, but he willed a message to pass to the shadow. "You... you, win."

$$\cdot \, \Omega \, \cdot$$

His eyes snapped open and he was drawing in a great ragged breath, filling his lungs with precious oxygen.

He rolled to one side, weak with terror, wishing he had the strength to spring from the cot, flee. But all he could do was tremble.

He dragged himself to a sitting position on the edge of the bed, choking and coughing. "Now what?" His voice was hoarse. Vocal chords damaged.

But the shadow had not stayed to answer.

He staggered to the sink. Washed his face. When he lowered the towel the reflection in the mirror stared at him, whites showing all around his irises, face pallid, mottled bruises on his throat. He raised his hands and flexed his fingers back and forth, fearing their power.

He stared into his own sunken green eyes and hated the fear and helplessness he saw there. He'd thought he'd had some leverage. And now he knew. There was no way out. There would be no tribunal to throw himself before, hoping for mercy. There would be only an end to existence. Nothing beyond.

As he looked closer into the mirror he saw within those green irises, his black pupils momentarily change from round to slits, like those of a cat. From within his mind he heard a growling roar. The shadow, sending him a reminder.

Then his image in the glass darkened, and the reflection of the little sleeping area disappeared. He was looking at a mere silhouette of himself against a gray background.

The dark shape of his head and shoulders faded into the gray, and he was looking at nothingness.

"I get the point. You're the ruler of this body." And he found himself once more staring at the slave called Sage Rojan.

Chapter 14

A MILESTONE had been passed with the creation of the Quantronix, but now whatever patience the shadow had previously shown was gone.

Under Sage's personal supervision — and only his — the Quantronix at Cos-Ob continued to pour out rare elements. These were shipped to the Bristol Industries warehouse in Porturn and distributed to the various divisions that built new technologies.

The shadow drove Sage to work and work, with no say as to what he did or when. Often the impetus came from simple physical pain; a stab behind his eyes, or a blinding agony that enveloped his head. Sometimes the shadow reverted to completely seizing the reins and once again Sage would come out of nowhere to realize he'd lost hours in a day.

Sage was out of control, generating new systems and components to further the development of BYSA's space program as well as furthering his role as a *national hero* with multiple revolutions in communications, transportation, information handling, and social connectivity.

Priority went to the conglomerate's joint ventures with BYSA — which had already crisscrossed Tidon's heavens with communications and surveillance satellites — and the recent orbital missions with test animals that splashed down in the sea off Bella Yareo.

According to plan, it was time for Sage to go 'up!'

Incredibly, Sage's shadow grew anxious, wary and protective of the safety of its host. If the first manned flight into space exploded or burned up in the atmosphere on re-entry, the body in which the shadow resided would be destroyed. *What would happen then? Would the shadow have to start all over again? Could it?* Sage began feeling the shadow's resistance as he went through the training program he himself had devised and passed to BYSA. The shadow was leaning toward denying him the only thing he'd looked forward to in his eighteen years of slavery. Then too, the shadow seemed more impatient, as if time was running out on its grand task. Was that because its nature was that of a spoiled child? Or was it under pressure to get the job done — whatever the job might be — before the law showed up with a warrant and handcuffs?

Sage sought out the shadow in its realm of gray nothingness behind the unmarked door, tempted to put those questions to the shadow, but instead he said, "You can't refuse me the reward of being the first to go up, regardless of the dangers,"

The response that came back was wordless. *I will do as I see fit.*

"It's not just between you and me," Sage said. "Bristol has always sold the space program as a personal priority of mine. 'First in our hearts' and all that. Yank me out of it now, and the whole thing will collapse."

The shadow roiled and blackened like an inky poison.

"You can push me around like a puppet. We both know you can," Sage argued. "But you can't rule hundreds of millions of Bellans. They are already petitioning the government to begin exploring other continents. If we do not act now, the moons will remain unvisited."

The shadow surged and writhed.

"Be as obstinate as you like. I'm their good luck charm, their antidote to all the social toxins created by too much change, too fast. The logical choice for 'first person to leave Tidon soil' has to be me."

The shadow diffused and blotted out any light Sage might have imagined within the realm, but the creature's tantrum came to nothing. Sage waited, and gradually the deep fog thinned to translucent gray.

Sage had won.

He left his shadow's presence, calm joy tickling his gut.

· Ω ·

After finding his way back to the mosaic Sage let his dream draw him towards the Library. He hadn't browsed there much lately;

the knowledge that he might, however unwillingly, be treading on an artisan's toes had put him off.

But now that the first space trip 'up there' was in the offing, he wanted to know as much as he could about the near space surrounding Tidon. He found the appropriate vault.

Tidon, he read, was the second of seven planets circling the rather undistinguished Sintosy star, in the Golden zone where the sun's output allowed liquid water to exist on the planet's surface and carbon-based life was possible. Sage knew, from sampling lives on other worlds, that other chemical recipes could result in self-replicating, and even self-aware, organic materials, but carbon-oxygen-hydrogen life seemed to be the most popular choice.

At one time, he would've wondered at the chances that, out of all the possibilities, he'd come into existence as a blob of protoplasm that could look outward and inward and know that he lived. Now, after all those lives and reading, he knew the universe did not exist through mere happenstance. It was an artifact, and behind it stood the artisan.

He'd seen that all of the sapient species he had visited behind the white doors had some concept of a prime mover, a clockmaker, a kneader of clay, or whittler of wood, who made the world and all that was in it. The shape the artisan took in each culture tended to resemble the creatures that were doing the tale-spinning. To the ten-armed, golden-eyed denizens of the ocean world whose name was unpronounceable except as a sequence of colors, the deity was ten-armed and golden of eye. To the sentient plants of another world, the creator was a tree. Sage therefore doubted that the Artisan, residing in the Empyrean, had four limbs, a head on a torso, and the other bits and pieces that were part of the common design of humanoids.

If the Artisan was a personality that could contain the shadow, Sage wanted to meet… it, even if their meeting might not come under the best of circumstances. If he could only draw its gaze somehow. Then maybe he might stand before some kind of universal law and plead his case. Sage wondered if it would take notice when he entered space for the first time. Surely, Tidon wouldn't have reached this level of advancement without the prodding of Sage's shadow, not at its normal rate of progress.

Not that long ago, Bellans had thought Tidon was the center of the universe. Now they knew it was just another ball of stone orbiting an ordinary sun, part of a smallish solar system, nothing special in the vastness of the Melorius Galaxy.

And Melorius was just one of hundreds of billions of galaxies in a perpetually recycling universe that was not, as the Bang Theory academics had it, just fifteen billion years old. In all its waxings and wanings, its makings, unmaking, and remaking, the inner universe had been around for a much longer period of time. And it would go on indefinitely, one fifteen billion year cycle after another, until it served the purpose for which it had been created.

What that purpose might be, Sage could not imagine. In fact, he'd come to believe he was designed not to be able to imagine it; that it was fundamentally none of his business, any more than it was the business of any of the atoms that formed his body to know how he planned to spend his day.

Which was why it worried him that, willing or not, he was part of a plot whose aim might be to frustrate the grand scheme. Still, maybe if he could break that barrier, get into outer space, if he could do it before the shadow was finished whatever scheme it had in mind, maybe the Artisan would take notice, maybe it wouldn't be too late.

· Ω ·

In his dressing room, somber, Sage brushed his hair with trembling hands. It was the great products launch party to coincide with his nineteenth birthday. Both events on their own would have been enough to draw an audience. Tamara had the brilliant idea to combine the two and he decided he hated her. Butterflies fluttered in the pit of his stomach. How could he have been roped into this circus? Fifty thousand fans in Rolymar Stadium and millions of broadcast viewers would be watching his presentation.

Tamara's poll said the portion of Bellans who approved of Sage's technological inventions was ninety-five per cent. A mere four per cent were undecided, and barely one per cent opposed. But those who opposed him did so bitterly and vocally; this side-show was key to countering their vitriol and furthering Bristol Industries' — and BYSA's — research.

Sage peered into the mirror, stage fright overtaking his flesh and organs, he saw an athletic lad attired in a futuristic purple and green suit. This wasn't him. Not Sage Rojan, but some clown invented by Bristol Industries' PR Department. By Ryze Feldstrum and Tamara Young.

The dressing room door opened — no knock — and Sage turned. Ryze entered, beaming in his white tuxedo, top hat, black bow tie, and prop cane.

Ryze was even more pumped than usual. "Cosimo, it's almost time to dazzle." Ryze grinned and leaned against the door. "Jampacked; sold out. The band is heating them up, getting them juiced."

"And the demonstrators?" Sage tossed the brush on his dressing table. "They must have remembered to show up as well."

"Yeah, but most of them are outside the fence or at the far end." Ryze checked his time piece. "Security has control of them."

"And who has control of security?" Sage poured water into his glass from a cut crystal decanter.

"Come on Sage. It'll be fine." Ryze picked a nonexistent speck of lint from his shoulder. "You'll be super."

A loud rap on the door preceded the magnanimous Duggin Bristol clad in a red tuxedo. He slapped Sage on the back. "Sage, you man tonite. Or, is it Cosimo? The fans love to call you that. Thousands come here. To see only you." He threw an arm around Sage and grinned at Ryze. "Take picture, me and Sage. Here, use new fandangled camera."

Sage put on his best fake smile as the camera's flash momentarily blinded him. Sage quickly broke the embrace.

Ryze waited for the picture to slide out the front of the camera and develop before their eyes. "We've already sold twenty thousand of these babies, they're going like hotcakes. The fans are crazy tonight."

A stage hand appeared at the dressing room door. "It's time."

Sage wanted to get this show over with. He blinked profusely, trying to clear his eyes while he wiped his damp brow, then he stepped out into the popping camera flashes of the narrow corridor.

His mother and father were waiting for him outside his dressing room. His mom patted his cheek. "This is your night. Try to enjoy it."

Further down the hall Tamara waited, smiling encouragement. She had a way of reading him, of knowing just what he needed. His nerves calmed a little. He was glad she was there, even if she was the reason *he* was here. She joined his entourage, holding a hand up against the flashes of light. "I'm doing a five page spread for the Gazette. You'd better be giving us your best."

They rounded the corner to the cavernous back loading dock; open to the night sky and the warm summer wind. "It's just a dumb speech," he yelled against the noise of the band and the crowd. "As soon as it's over I intend to down a bottle of wine and remove myself from this whole mess."

Ahead of them was an underground tunnel, used by football players and referees, which led to the infield where the stage waited. Sage enjoyed the warmth of Tamara's arm around his waist as they walked together. He wished it was that way more often. But, today her closeness was likely an aid to his performance. They reached the stage. "Your 'Youthquake Fans' are eager to hear about your coming inventions in the new product line," Ryze nattered as he passed them in the corridor. "We'll sell or sign up thousands tonight."

From back stage, Sage and Tamara watched as Ryze took the microphone and stilled the maddening crowd. "Now, to introduce you to tonight's hero, the grandest inventor of all time. Some of you know him as Sage Rojan. Many of you call him— Cosimo!"

The audience drowned Ryze in a wave of screams. Sage squeezed Tamara's hand and jogged to the center of the stage, where the spotlights blinded him. The screams crescendoed. This was his moment to shine and Sage decided he'd never wanted any of it after all.

· Ω ·

Ryze joined Tamara in the dark, and the two watched Sage take the stage. "This will skyrocket our sales. Hope he nails the opening."

"It doesn't matter; the fans will love the new inventions. You know that," Tamara said.

Suddenly, the stage plunged into blackness.

"What's going on?" Ryze muttered.

Tamara's panic eased and she pointed upward. From high up above the stage, a large topographical balloon depicting Tidon descended. Light emanating from within highlighted Bella Yareo; then, north and south to the large polar ice caps; gigantic blue oceans with Batakesh to the left of Bella Yareo and Orlandia to the right, like equatorial pillars.

"Welcome to Cosimo world," Sage said, the timbre of his words deeper, more vibrant. "Long have the people of Bella

Yareo wondered what was on the dark side of Tidon. Tonight I give you… Hebron!" The crowd gave a collective gasp as the balloon rotated and the light showed the never-seen side of Tidon. The largest continent, Hebron, lay eight thousand miles from Bellan shores.

"That's not the script!" Ryze, threw his arms in the air. "Where did the balloon come from?"

"I don't know." Tamara was mystified.

"It has a meager population of only twelve million. They are stuck in antiquity, more than a thousand years behind us in progress." Sage's — 'Cosimo's' — voice filled the stadium. "We now know what resides on our planet's surface, but there is still one place no Tidonese has ever explored. Tonight! I will share secrets of the final frontier!"

"He'll bore them. And that's not even Sage's real voice," said Ryze. "What's he trying to do?"

"Space!"

Another balloon lowered, showing a depiction of the seven planets in their solar system revolving around Sintosy.

"Sintosy can reach upwards of ten thousands degrees," the performer — Cosimo, not Sage — continued. "Here, on Tidon, we're safe in a zone that's neither too hot nor too cold to sustain life."

"What the hell is he talking about?" Ryze fumed, pacing.

"Don't have a heart attack. He's out there and there's nothing you can do." But Tamara's stomach curdled. That wasn't Sage. It'd happened before. More frequently lately. And especially if she tried to confront him about his work. Now, the whole population of Bella Yareo was seeing it. And they were eating it up, without realizing its source.

"The people of Tidon are like children with no notion of how a radio or communication satellites work, simply able to crank the control knobs. One might say that the artisan made it idiot-proof, so anyone could partake."

Tamara cringed at the insult; she had hoped he wouldn't make some public statement that would get them all into hot water, but Cosimo didn't give the audience time to object. He pushed on with statistics about light speed and star travel and the distance between galaxies. Other planets. Intelligent life. Crazy numbers; two hundred billion galaxies; 73,000,000,000,000,000,000 quintillion stars in their universe.

"Why is he telling them all this guff?" Ryze rasped, coming forward. "They're here to be dazzled, not—"

"Our planet is on the verge of change," Cosimo stated. "Be assured of that. But to make it all worthwhile, we need to reach out there." He pointed to the rotating balloon that glittered with the pin pricks of a thousand stars.

Ryze halted. "What does he mean by *that*?"

Tamara shook her head slowly.

Cosimo finished to confused but enthusiastic applause that slowly ramped back to cheering as he came off the stage. Ryze grabbed his shoulders briefly. "I guess *I'd* better deliver the goods. The part they *came* for." Then he jogged into the spotlight, his face transforming into an ecstatic grin. "Let's hear it for Cosimo!"

Sage stumbled, as if Ryze had been holding him up.

Tamara caught him. "Sage?" Was this Sage? Or Cosimo? Or maybe... the one she had begun to watch for. "Are you okay?"

"Is the show over already?" It was Sage who responded to her, in a voice so small and helpless it broke her heart. "Did I make my speech?"

"It's over," she whispered, guiding him away from the lights and noise. "You were great."

He stopped, looking about him in the bewildered way she'd seen before. "Tamara..."

She held him while he gathered his thoughts.

"Thank you." He turned to her and in the dim back stage light she saw a gleam of moisture on his cheek. "Without you... I can't tell you how much—"

"Shhh." She covered his lips with her fingers. He mustn't say it. If he had feelings for her, she knew she had to make sure he never voiced them. It hurt her to admit it but it was beyond her purpose to return those feelings. "It's been a stressful few weeks. This circus doesn't help. Hey." She peered into his face. "I'm part of your team. We're all here for you."

Sage's eyes lidded. He swallowed and nodded. "Right. Part of the team." He straightened. "Thanks."

Tamara released his arm and they walked briskly back through the tunnel. As they turned a corner, a deep chanting began to grow in volume and intensity. At the end of the corridor a crowd of protestors were pushing against a line of police.

The trespassers shouted obscenities and waved placards proclaiming: 'Stop polluting our canals,' 'Quit dumping precious metals,' 'Stop technology,' 'Get out of space.'

Sage reached back and grasped Tamara's hand. As they rushed past the protestors, his grip tightened and even though Tamara knew she should break contact with him, she never let him go.

Chapter 15

HE SAT IN AN AIRPLANE, curved steel walls, engine hum, and floor vibrations surrounding him. The door was open to blue sky and wind whistled past the opening. His gloved hands touched a helmet on his head, goggles covering his eyes, and then brown material comprising a one piece suit. He wore a harness holding some type of pack on his back. He dizzily stood up, involuntarily stepped forward—

—and took a final step out into the air.

The shadow! The entity had him in skydiving free-fall. Sage screamed, but no one could hear him. His right arm moved in front of his face, the altimeter on his wrist read 14,000 feet, providing small comfort. Strategically, he flung his arms and legs out into a 'belly to the ground' position to slow himself as the rush of air flapped at his suit.

Then, beyond his control, his body turned, his head pointed toward Tidon, and he accelerated. He knew the numbers. Thirty-two feet per second to a terminal velocity of nearly 120 miles per hour within eight seconds.

His body turned again, tumbling over and around, as the shadow curled him into acrobatic moves; somersaults, back rolls, and side rollovers. As exhilarating as it was, Sage fought to stay alert.

Why was the shadow taking him through this exercise?

He glanced again at his altimeter; eight thousand feet. Head still downward, his tearing eyes recognized the Tasil Desert along the outer foothills of the Kalico Mountains.

Five thousand feet; four thousand; three thousand. The recommended safe-pull region of twenty-six hundred feet.

Time to open the chute! He reached to pull the rip cord. His arm stayed where it was.

Twenty-four hundred feet. He tried the other arm.

Twenty-three.

"Open the parachute!" he yelled.

No answer. Only speed and descent.

Panicked, he imagined flailing his arms, willing them to move. Nothing.

"Why are you doing this?" Sage yelled.

Sixteen hundred feet; fifteen hundred. Sage's heart pounded in his throat, choking him.

The altimeter: thirteen hundred feet.

The dark shadows of tall cactus filled his vision.

Thirteen, twelve, eleven—

Sage's eyes widened — the ground below sped towards him. He was going to die. The shadow was finished with him and he'd missed it somewhere in a dream.

Then, Sage's head moved upwards, arms and legs wide, body level. His right arm freed the rip cord. The small pilot chute flickered skyward, a drogue catching air to pull out the main aerofoil.

Sage's body snapped upward.

A pillowy cushion of air caught him, slowed him. He was safe— safe…

"You bastard."

He felt, rather than heard, the chuckle within.

"You were trying to see how scared I am of dying. I thought you'd already had your fun with this sick test."

It had been a reminder.

"Alright. Congratulations, you proved your point." He drifted, idling under the bright canopy, fighting the nausea of shock. "But I'm a fool for being so gullible. You're not finished yet, you still need me. You won't kill me any more than I'd kill myself."

Sage softly tumbled on the landing. *I will still be the first Tidonese in space. Even if it endangers this precious hideout of yours.*

· Ω ·

"Sage." His office door opened, and Tamara poked her head in, a shimmer of long hair falling from the side of her face making him pause in his work even if he hadn't wanted to. "Oh. Thank goodness you're here." she said, "I thought you might've left for Cos-Ob."

"I'm nearly late already, let's talk as we walk." Sage rolled up his computer, shoved it into his back pocket and grabbed his jacket from the closet.

She closed the door behind her and leaned on it, preventing his departure. "The mission's gone back to the drawing board."

"What?"

"Sit down. You can be an hour late to Cos-Ob. They won't need your input on the heavy-lift rockets before tomorrow."

Sage slumped into his chair and rocked back, grabbing his hair. Dackt, he was tired, but he couldn't just sit here. "What is it this time?"

"Don't snap at me," she flared. "I'm on your side."

He shook the fatigue away. "Sorry. Just— impatient." Was he? Or was it the shadow? "What happened?"

"Today's unmanned flight. On re-entry— slid into the upper atmosphere at too shallow an angle."

He opened his eyes, the shadow alert in his mind. "I programmed those computers—"

Tamara slid onto the couch along the side wall and crossed long legs beneath her. "Well, maybe you did. And maybe you were tired. The capsule ended up more than ninety miles from where it was expected to hit the water."

"Dackt!" Sage rocked his chair forward and leaned his elbows on his desk. "I've been working non-stop to develop every system to its ultimate refinement! The orbiter, the drogue chutes—" *The ceramic heat shield that would prevent the capsule from being incinerated on reentry*, the shadow added.

"There's more," Tamara said. "The orbiter's flotation ring failed to inflate properly. By the time the recovery ship came alongside, the capsule was halfway to the bottom of the sea. We were lucky it was unmanned."

The shadow reared up and Sage fought to maintain control. "Then I guess we'll have to delay the manned flight," Sage heard his own voice, the shadow sending the words, pleased there was a delay. *No!* Sage railed at the thing inside him.

"How long?" she glanced at him, a frown creasing her face.

Until a proper space shuttle is built. The shadow sent its terms. Sage said nothing.

"You realize the whole legitimacy of the space program is tied up with the deadline we've promised the populace. If you don't go, people will start to ask why we're spending all this public money on going into space when there are several continents full of resources that could be developed. If you go, the program can't be questioned."

Exactly. We must go now! Sage cried wordlessly to the shadow. Satellites had been mapping and photographing other continents on Tidon, and the images showed not only dense jungles and vast prairies, but other civilizations: cities built of stone, irrigation works, and food crops like nothing that existed on Bella Yareo. Bellan imaginations had filled with stories of these strange and colorful lands— far more exciting to most than the empty sterility of space. *A delegation has already petitioned the Senate to divert funds from BYSA to build a fleet of ocean-going ships to make contact with Hebron!*

The shadow neither responded to Sage, nor to Tamara's challenge.

She made a show of examining her manicure but Sage got the sense she was watching him intently. "And, this just in, a memo came across my desk a few minutes ago. The military wants more steel-hulled, diesel-powered ships."

The shadow's grip faltered. "Why?" Sage managed.

"To cow Orlandia." She grimaced; Sage wasn't sure if it was directed at a less-than-perfect nail or the situation. "Seems they don't like being a colony with no vote, no choice in trade agreements— their resources for our manufactured goods, etc."

"I can't say as I blame them." Sage said.

"Me neither. But instead of giving them the vote, the High Command wants to send a task force to overawe them. King Ferdason says it's the nation's top priority." She lifted her head. "So. You'd better get those launch and re-entry issues taken care of, or you may find the space program starved for funds, and the country building battleships and aircraft carriers instead."

The emotions that flooded him from the dark place within were revealing: anger and frustration, but also an undercurrent of fear. So, his taskmaster hadn't thought out all the possible outcomes of its great scheme.

Sage smiled. His shadow was fallible.

"What makes you so happy?" Tamara glared at him. "You better be listening to me."

"Nothing, just— you've convinced me. I'll take care of it." Perhaps the shadow was even prone to leaping before it looked. Sage might be able to use that knowledge against it.

She rose from the couch with a feline grace that made his heart race. "You'd better, if you want to be the first man in space." She looked him up and down. "First boy in space." She smiled a very Tamara smile and left the room.

Sage grinned in deep satisfaction, watching the sway of her hips as she left. *Hey*, he said to the shadow, *if you're afraid to go up, you can stay down here. I won't mind going on my own.*

That earned him a stab of pain that felt as if a steel spike had been shoved through his skull but the flicker of annoyance from the shadow was worth it.

Chapter 16

SAGE, STRAPPED into the reclined seat of the orbiter atop a massive three-stage rocket, heard the muffled sound of the seals closing through the isolation of his helmet. He went through the pre-launch routine exactly as he had created it, throwing switches, ramping up, talking with Mission Control. Everything he did and said could have been performed automatically by the on-board computer which was in constant communication with its counterpart at BYSA, but the old-fashioned human touch was part of what kept hundreds of millions of Bellans glued to their communication devices. The launch was scheduled for a week-end afternoon, when Tamara had calculated it would get maximum audience saturation.

The final countdown.

A voice crackled over the communicator, smooth, professional. Inside his helmet the amplified sound of his own breathing was offset by the steady rhythmic thumping of his heart. He was here. He was doing it. He was first. His mother's teary wave flashed across his memory. His dad's proud smile; almost as misty. Tamara, white with fear she didn't know she had. Fear he didn't know she had.

"Ignition."

A rumble vibrated through him, through the capsule, threatening to tear it apart.

And beneath the roar: "We have liftoff!"

The hand of gravity squeezed him into his seat, flattened his face, his chest, pinned his arms and legs helplessly, painfully, against the padding. A deep throated growl filled his ears. He could barely breathe.

Finally, the forces eased and Sage was able to turn his head to look out the view port. The sight of a star-splashed blackness caught the breath from his lungs. He squeezed his eyes shut; waiting for the moment when the Artisan noticed his presence in a place he had no right to be. Surely Tidon's unnatural technological leap would not go ignored; not when Sage was waving it in the Artisan's domain.

But there was nothing. Just silence and the painful beauty of cold space.

The dashing of that small hope hit Sage harder than he expected. He hadn't realized how much he'd been relying on that possibility to push him through the last relentless weeks of work. Part of him had truly thought that if he made it into space something would change.

Sage fought down the urge to shout, to call the Artisan down; mindful of the millions of eyes watching him on the planet below. Instead he took a moment to come to terms with the idea that he was too insignificant for the Artisan to take note of. He'd known this, from all his journeys through past lives, from all the billions of galaxies in the Library's vaults, yet he'd clung to hope regardless. His shadow scoffed. *Do you finally see? You cannot be free of me.*

Sage keyed his microphone; his hand moving at the shadow's command. *Now the real work begins.* "Mission Control, this is Vullantry One. All systems are a 'go'." And Tidon is one big, blue, beautiful jewel."

· Ω ·

Sage's moment of glory as the first man in space ended without incident. As he blinked back to the world, he realized he was standing back in Cos-Ob and the sensation that a great many days had passed without his consent. Someone had buzzed for entrance. His fingers trembled on the security override pad. It took three tries to convince the Cos-Ob computer to open the main entrance door. Suddenly, with a whoosh, the hydraulics kicked in and his dad stood before him. Sage nodded slowly, his throat too dry to speak.

"Sage!" Horror flashed across Thaddeus' face and he dashed forward, grasping Sage's upper arms as though he thought his son might collapse.

"It's okay, dad," Sage whispered. His eyes felt as though they were full of fine grit. "Glad you got here."

"What's happened to you?" The hydraulics whisked the door closed behind them and they were alone in the vast dusky dome of Cos-Ob.

"Nothing. Everything is fine."

Sage realized he was walking like a faulty automaton, his exhausted muscles experiencing waves of shivers. He wasn't sure if it was he or his shadow that made one foot move ahead of the next.

Thaddeus followed, almost stumbling in his concern. "You said to come right away. I thought there was an emergency—"

Sage threw him a smile — perhaps ghoulish, but the best he could muster — over his shoulder. "No emergency. Just—" And suddenly he remembered. He stopped at the Quantronix. "Tremendous excitement."

"How long since you've slept?" Thaddeus paid no attention to the machine or the wondrous contents of its bin. He scrambled about, pulling up a chair. "Sage, you need to see a doctor—"

Sage ignored the irrelevant words. "Two, three, four days. It doesn't matter. Look." From a lead-lined container the size of a shoebox beside the Quantronix, he used tongs to lift out a fine metallic mesh that sparkled in the dim light of the dome.

Thaddeus pressed him into the chair. "First you need food, and then you need sleep."

The shadow did not care. Sage lifted the mesh toward his dad. "Enough of this transuranic substance to make..."

But Thaddeus had bustled off. He returned in a moment with a steaming mug. "The only thing I could find," he apologized, pressing the cup into Sage's hands.

"You see, dad? You see?" Sage carefully returned the precious metal to its container and took the mug. "It can be pressed into the skin on the undersides of the space shuttle's wings and fuselage. Beside it we embed a matching mesh of hair-fine fiber-optic lines."

"Enough of that, Sage. Drink. Get some calories into you." His dad crouched beside him.

When Sage tried to bring the drink to his mouth, he trembled so much, half of it spilled onto his shirtfront, but he didn't care. Or was it the shadow that didn't care? "When laser light of the right frequency passes through the glass fibers, it will activate the transuranic metal. Dad—"

Thaddeus held the mug to his lips and obediently, Sage drank.

"Dad." Sage pushed the cup gently aside. "That great huge shuttle will weigh no more than a recreational glider."

"What?" Thaddeus' fingers stilled on the cup and Sage saw doubt mix with the horror in his father's eyes.

"Anti-gravity," Sage said.

His father stared at him. Then he put the cup on the floor and hoisted Sage up by his arm pits. "We need to get you to bed."

"It's no delusion, Dad. With anti-gravity, the shuttle's engines can be one-eighth the size." Sage laughed, stumbling across the expanse of floor toward the door, leaning on his dad's shoulder.

"Here we go. Just wait while I open the door." His dad placed Sage's forefinger on the print pad.

"We won't even need the big external fuel tank."

The door swished open and Sage blinked at the blinding light. His dad guided him to the newly built apartment attachment.

"That will knock years off the development timetable," he said as his dad poured him into the bed. "It might even be done in a week, maybe two."

Chapter 17

THE ANTI-GRAVITY discovery skyrocketed development of the space program. Shuttles made regular flights into near-Tidon orbit, where BYSA was building a manned space station to house Thaddeus' most prized possession: the space telescope. Technically, the telescope belonged jointly to BYSA and Bristol Space, but Thaddeus had the ultimate say as to who got to use it and onto which part of space it would be aimed.

With the new ease of lifting shuttles into space, BYSA began planning its first manned mission to the moon.

Sage leaned his elbows atop the dividers between the cubicles in BYSA Mission Control, a dozen feet from the bank of huge screens, and let his gaze run idly over Tamara's slim form as she leaned over the shoulder of the technician remotely operating a moon-buggy set up to catch the approach of the first manned shuttle to Tidon's nearest moon. The idea for the remote camera had been Tamara's. Of course. Amazing Tamara. Sage grinned. At twenty she was definitely a woman now, and beautiful. Oh, so beautiful. Right now she was silhouetted against the view from the camera on the vehicle: a black, star-filled sky in which one tiny point of light grew larger and larger. To one side of the image, Tidon loomed, half-lit by Sintosy. It was, Sage had to admit, a magnificent image, like the cover of one of the new science fiction magazines.

BYSA's Mission Control center was packed with scientists, engineers, and dignitaries. King Ferdason himself sat on a gilded chair on the rearmost and highest tier of the horseshoe of workstations that faced the array of oversized view screens. Everyone in Bella Yareo and its new province of Orlandia would be watching this transmission. The center screen was now completely filled with a view of the crater-scarred surface of moon Filus, steadily growing larger.

Tamara laughed at something the technician said. Then she sent Sage a look that said he shouldn't be looking at her. History was being made!

But Sage was too tired to care. Besides, dipping into the myriad of lives stored in the corridors of doors had taught him that a mission to a moon was nothing but a baby step. Out in the billions and billions of galaxies were space-faring civilizations who would look upon Sage's anti-gravity assisted shuttle as not much more than a hollowed-out log. He knew what others could not; Bellans were the new Neanderthals of space travel.

Tamara straightened, apparently satisfied that all was well. She turned and noticed Sage, still watching her. He flicked his eyes up to the screen, but a moment later, she sat beside him. "Nothing to do?"

"My work was complete before take-off." He knew that what she most enjoyed was getting a rise out of him. He refused to engage, but leaned back in his chair, taking in her loveliness.

She turned her attention back to the screen.

The landing would be the biggest broadcast event of the year, if not the decade. Unbeknownst to the hundreds of millions watching in their homes, Bristol Space had sent a robot mission to Filus a few weeks before; a multi-wheeled vehicle equipped with a high-definition camera; now parked within range of the landing site, tracking the shuttle's approach. When the first Bellan set foot on the surface of another world, the robot's feed would be added to the signal coming out of Mission Control and everyone would share in the great moment with multiple camera angles.

"Can we get you in front of a camera after the landing?" she asked Sage. "After the King congratulates the crew? Just to say a few words."

Sage shook his head. "I'm hanging back." He indicated the screen that showed the crew of the shuttle. "This is their day."

"Modesty?" she said. "Is that your latest accomplishment?"

He gestured to where his dad, looking professorial in a sports jacket with chalk-stained cuffs, was outlining the progress of the mission to a group of reporters and interested dignitaries. "My dad's already doing a pretty good job of explaining what's going on. He'll say everything that needs saying."

Thaddeus was telling his listeners how the shuttle, *Canaroc 1*, had gone into orbit five days earlier, orbiting Tidon twice to make sure all systems were in the green, and how it began its leisurely journey across the three hundred thousand miles to Filus. "We could have gone faster," he was saying, "but acceleration and deceleration at such speeds is a tricky business for the body. Too much g-force over sustained periods of time. Better to take more time and have everyone arrive in top condition. Especially considering that one of the crew is no spring chicken." That got a few laughs from his audience.

"Look." Tamara pointed to the screen showing the robot camera's view. Perfectly framed, the modified shuttle descended tail-first toward the surface of Filus, its engines spitting fire. Toy-sized at first, it grew larger until it loomed in the robot camera's view, and then it gracefully set down on a level plain of white dust. The engines cut out and the image switched to a pick-up within the shuttle, where three people in space suits prepared to enter the airlock.

There had been a movement to give the honor of the first landing to Sage — to the concerned twitch of his shadow — but Sage declined, saying he had a more important role to play in making sure the vehicle that went there and back was the best it could be; specially adapted for vertical take-off and landing on the moon.

The feed returned to the external view and every person in the control center — even the King — stood as the hatch opened and a ladder descended. A bulky figure stepped backwards from the opening onto the ladder and ceremoniously climbed, step by step, down to the surface. At the bottom, the figure's booted foot paused midway between rung and dust while the moon buggy's camera zoomed in for a close-up. Then the boot came down, the sole touched rock, and Sage heard the collective sigh fill the control room as every person, including the King, let go the breath they had been holding. The control room erupted in cheers.

An announcer's voice droned in the background and the technicians shushed one another, every eye on the screen. The first man on Filus marched a few paces away from the shuttle, holding two poles in his gloved hands.

Sage turned to Tamara. "Two?" he said.

She gave him a look of a *what-can-you-do?* and turned back to the screen. The first Tidonese on another world laid the poles beside each other on the rocky ground and unclipped a hammer and a long steel spike from his belt. He drove the spike into the surface of Filus, pulled it out, then float-stepped to make a second hole a short distance away. A moment later, he had stuck the two poles in the ground.

In slow motion, he pulled at something wrapped around the top of the first pole and it unfolded into the flag of Bella Yareo. A round of spontaneous applause broke out in the control room. The man in the space suit pulled at the top of the second flag.

"Oh no! He didn't!" said Sage.

Tamara made the helpless face again. "Oh yes. He did."

A second flag unfurled on the surface of Filus: the corporate flag of Bristol Industries, a fist holding several zigzag lightning bolts. The man who'd planted the flags now stepped back and raised his hand in a salute, at the same moment the camera zoomed in on the glass shell of his helmet. Duggin Bristol, first man on Filus.

"Well, he paid for most of it." Tamara shrugged. "So why not?"

Sage hadn't known. No one had known except for Bristol's inner circle.

The grin on Bristol's face looked like it could swallow his whole fist.

Sage shook his head, throat tightening, envious of Bristol, of the men and women around him, cheering and celebrating. What must it be like to take complete and undiluted pleasure in an achievement? Sage might be the Bellan most responsible for this history-making moment, just as it was his inventions that destroyed the pirate scourge, and opened up the world to his fellow citizens. But even as engineers and mission specialists were slapping his back and shaking his hand, he could take no real credit. The shadow had done all of these things. Sage Rojan was merely a puppet on an invisible hand.

The life he might have lived had been replaced. And what small life he did have, when free of the shadow's demands, was tainted by the unnatural knowledge that had been put in his path.

To keep him quiet, he now saw. To keep him from irritating his taskmaster until the work was completed. Even though Sage knew this was knowledge he shouldn't have had, he knew it wouldn't stop his almost-nightly visits to the worlds of the white doors. And that theft — like the shadow's — was profoundly wrong.

He had been corrupted.

He looked at Tamara, happy and complete as she celebrated her part in this great day of achievement. What might their relationship have been, had he not been born under this undeserved curse? They might have been meant for each other, might have lived a joyous shared life together. Instead, she was another continual reminder that his existence was hollow, meaningless. A constant stream of joyless triumphs.

The astronauts had taken the camera off the robot vehicle and were using the buggy to explore, collecting surface samples and drilling down to extract cores. And one of them — Sage was pretty sure which one it would be — was hopping about in the light gravity like a ballet dancer on elastic cords. Now he was swinging a metal club to strike a small white ball he'd positioned on a moon pebble. It arced up and out of view. Bristol tilted back to watch it go, and the announcer told the viewers that the ball was now most probably in orbit.

· Ω ·

Without disturbing Tamara, Sage discretely left the celebrations at Mission Control and rode his motorbike up the hill to Cos-Ob. He did not know what he was going to do when he got there but, as he neared the fenced compound, the shadow directed him toward the outbuildings where the heavy equipment was stored. A series of images appeared in his mind: of himself dismantling the Quantronix and preparing it for transportation to…. Try as he might, he found no image of the destination.

The job was easier, now that he had grown into his adult strength and reach. Since infancy, the shadow had been at work on his body, just as it had on his mind. His muscles were more densely packed with fiber and endowed with more electrochemical efficiency than evolution had ever contrived to make them. "Why are we disassembling the Quantronix?" He opened the shed and started up the forklift.

No answer came.

"You dragged me away from celebrating the moon landing. This exercise must mean something important." He loaded the empty crates and headed for Cos-Ob. "Will it move us closer to the day when you're finished with me?"

Yes.

"Then let's get to work."

Bolts had to be undone, sections lowered by the hydraulic scissors; then the parts had to be crated and taken to the dome's loading dock. It took Sage a day to bring the machine down; less than half the time it had to originally put it up. Half way through the task his phone buzzed where it sat on the work bench.

It was Tamara but the shadow didn't let him reach to pick it up.

A minute later it droned again then beeped as a voice mail was saved. Sage wanted to hear her voice, but the shadow kept his hands focused on the careful packing of the Quantronix's parts. Sage sighed and put it out of his mind, it wasn't like this was the first time he'd failed to answer her calls.

Finally the disassembly was complete. Sage used his phone to send a one-word message. The recipient could not have been far away, because within minutes Sage heard the rumble of a heavy vehicle approaching the dome. When he opened the loading door, he saw a semi-trailer backing up to the dock, and he was not surprised to see that the driver was Bix.

"More hush-hush, huh?" the man said when he stood on the dock and examined the huge crates. He had a partner today and the man climbed down from the passenger side of the cab.

"I'm afraid so," said Sage.

Bix tipped back his peaked cap and looked up at the three moons in the evening sky. One of them was Filus. "We're up there because of you, kid," Bix said. "Just tell me where you want them."

Sage had to wait for the knowledge to come. Then he said, "There's a shuttle prepping for a mission in Hangar B. This goes in the cargo bay. Oh, And here's a little something for your *college fund*."

"You got it." Bix opened the back of his truck to reveal heavy-lift equipment. "Let's get on it, Jastor."

The men were expert at their craft. In less time than Sage would have believed, the crates were loaded, along with the lifters. He said to Bix, "Let me ride along with you."

They traveled down the hill and turned onto the service road that connected to the runways and then, beyond them, to the immense hangars where the shuttles were maintained and serviced between missions. Bix gestured with his thumb over his shoulder. "Mind if I ask what it's for?"

"Science stuff," Sage heard himself say. "It's got to go up to the space station."

Bix nodded, accepting the explanation. "Keep up the good work."

Chapter 18

TWO WEEKS AFTER the mission to the moon was wrapped, and almost everyone's lives had gone back to normal — whatever their normal was — Sage inexplicably found himself exiting the Bristol Towers elevator on the twenty-third floor — heading towards Duggin Bristol's office.

Bristol was in a meeting with his senior staff. Everyone looked up in surprise as Sage came through the door without knocking.

"What?" said Bristol; waving away the secretary who leapt up at Sage's abrupt entrance.

"I want an equal partnership," said Sage, although it wasn't him who said it.

The industrialist blinked twice. "You crazy."

"Either I get half, or I start my own company, invent a lot of stuff that's better than what I've given you. I have the money, and I'll get the contracts."

"I'll sue you into ground."

"You'll sue," said his shadow, "and you'll lose. New patents. Besides, you may have been the first man on a moon, but I'm the most beloved hero the continent has ever seen. Try and find a jury that will side against me."

Bristol turned in his swivel chair, moving his focus out the window and away from the meeting. He waved the other executives from the room. The silence stretched to almost three minutes before the industrialist turned around and begrudgingly said, "All right. Plenty to go round. Forty-sixty."

There was a flash of irritation from the shadow but Sage felt his lips smile, "Fifty-fifty."

Bristol's eyes narrowed.

Sage shrugged, "Take it or leave it."

Bristol took it. And Sage could see he didn't like it.

· Ω ·

One week later, Sage found himself boarding a space shuttle for a rather hastily scheduled re-supply mission. He was there, according to the crew manifest, as a mission specialist in charge of scientific equipment— including the components of the Quantronix. The shadow had been busy.

Sage introduced himself to the pilot, Ashby, the copilot, Ming, and the flight navigator, Grace. Sage smiled to himself. Even though he knew he couldn't get away from his shadow, he felt that the great emptiness of space would be... cleansing.

"Most exciting thing I've ever experienced," said Ashby. "Though don't tell my wife I said so." He grinned back at Sage as his fingers ran over the row of switches between himself and the copilot. "Thanks for getting me in." It was only then that Sage recognized Ashby as the man who'd flown him out to the space center several years earlier.

"Don't mention it."

"All good, here." Ming tapped her checklist into sleep mode. "You know, I sure don't miss the old days."

"What?" Grace inspected the navigation systems in front of her. "When getting 'off-planet' began with a bone-shaking eruption of thunder from a motor as big as a house?"

"Yeah," Ashby joked, snapping his intelligent page to its place beside the console. "Riding on a hundred tons of hyper-explosive fuel, just on the other side of a skinny layer of steel?"

"You guys," Ming laughed, sealing her helmet.

"Those 'old days' weren't so long ago." Ashby's voice came across the radio as the rest of them secured their own flight suits.

The shuttle shook and rumbled as the tractor hauled them onto the apron. Ashby started up the engines and the shuttle rolled under its own power to the end of the runway. Another few minutes passed as they waited for Mission Control's preflight check. Suddenly Sage's personal phone went off. Grace glanced back at him, one eyebrow quirked, and Sage felt a simultaneous flicker of irritation from his shadow. He pulled the phone out of his flight suit and glanced at the face plate. Tamara.

"You're good to go," a voice crackled over the radio. Mission Control.

"All good back there?" the navigator asked.

"Yeah," Sage pocketed his phone and zipped up his suit.

Ashby double checked his settings. "Anti-gravity net?"

Ming's fingers danced over the controls as she monitored outputs on the display. "Ready."

"Mission Control, shuttle ready for takeoff."

"Roger Shuttle One, you are in the green."

With a nod, Ashby and Ming simultaneously pushed the throttles forward. Sage flattened against the padding of his seat as the huge spacecraft leapt forward, rolling down the two miles of runway with a muted growl. A chime sounded, Ashby gently hauled back on the yoke, and the shuttle pointed its nose at the sky.

"Activate anti-gravity net."

"Activated," Ming echoed.

A slight tingle crawled over Sage's body and then the old blast-off changed to bliss-off.

They climbed smoothly through layers of atmosphere. In a brief eight minutes, the twilit sky deepened to black and the stars blossomed from numerous to omnipresent.

"Kill the anti-grav," said the pilot, and the tingle Sage felt disappeared as they curved around the planet. "Life support stable." He removed his helmet and stowed it beneath his seat.

"Orbital Complex Ferdason, this is Shuttle One. We are on approach." Grace shook her short curls free of her helmet; never taking her eyes off the readouts on her screen. "Three hundred yards."

Ashby switched to fine thrusters. Sage preferred to look outside as the wing's leading edge retro thrusters slowed their approach.

Their tasks, drop off supplies for the Orbital Complex space station, then travel to a satellite in LTO — low-Tidon orbit — to make repairs and finally move on to the Rojan Space Telescope for a retrofit. Sage noted the shadow's excitement and he couldn't avoid getting nearly caught up in the eagerness; his father's delight in the Space Telescope was one of the blessings of which Sage reminded himself whenever he got to feeling ill-used by the shadow. It would be a nice change to work on his dad's telescope for a while but he sensed the shadow was waiting for something beyond that.

The docking with the Orbital Complex went smoothly, and they had time for a snack before transferring some of their cargo. The Quantronix remained on board.

Next they disconnected from the station and Ashby used the fine thrusters to maneuver them toward the commercial satellite.

The satellite repair was Ming's first space-walk. She was nervous and tried not to show it as Sage helped her into her EVA suit. The airlock cycled and the woman stepped out into the immensity. First order of business was a radio check, but when Ashby keyed the speaker, the sound coming from the spacewalker was a breathy, "Wow."

Sage grinned. He envied Ming. Not for being in space, but for being able to take pure, unalloyed pleasure in the moment. He remembered his own first moment in space; the naivety that had let him hope that it would somehow free him of his shadow's grip, the disappointment that had eclipsed the beauty of the stars. In some way it felt better to watch someone else experience the joy he had been denied.

Ming let herself float to the outside of the car-sized satellite. It was a commercial unit essential in the global-positioning support for a number of surface systems. Their job was to replace a damaged power converter located under the side access panel. Sage acted as Ming's mission specialist, reading her the step-by-step instructions to remove the nonfunctioning module and replace it with a new one.

Midway, though, Sage found himself becoming edgy, tapping his fingers impatiently on the control board, and wishing the woman would hurry up.

Now where is that coming from?

The shadow. It wanted this routine business completed so it could move on to its own agenda. The Quantronix, still in the cargo bay.

"Calm down," Sage muttered, and only realized he had spoken aloud when Ming said, "Sorry, guess I'm a little jumpy. First-timer syndrome."

"It's all right." Sage forced himself to focus on the electronic pad in his hand. "Take all the time you need."

It took another hour to install the new component then test it in coordination with ground-based technicians. Finally, she came back through the airlock and Sage felt the soft tremor through the floor that told him Ashby had them underway again.

Finally they climbed, circling Tidon at eighteen thousand miles per hour, spiraling upward to four hundred miles above the planet, heading for the Rojan Space Telescope.

The telescope grew larger in the forward viewing screen, and excitement — the shadow's excitement — seethed in Sage's chest.

"Cosimo, this one's all yours." Ashby nodded from his forward seat. "Suit up."

Sage hadn't volunteered for any work on this mission — hadn't even known he was coming along — but he was happy to find his own suit in one of the lockers. Grace helped him suit-up.

Sage lowered the bubble helmet over his head and it snapped shut with the quick-connect ring. He kept his eyes tightly closed as Grace treated the visor with an anti-fog compound to shield his eyes from Sintosy's ultraviolet light. He tested the drinking straw and the oxygen supply, he then keyed the radio. "Vitals?"

Ashby's voice came through the speakers next to his ears: "In the green."

The airlock cycled through its depressurization routine and Sage stepped out into space. He pushed against the bottom lip of the airlock and used the small thrusters of his suit to navigate silently to the orbiting telescope. His mobility was fine, the pressurized suit allowing his joints to maneuver in harmony and the white color of his EVA suit made it easy for him to be seen against the darkness of space. His tether line — which Sage compared to the umbilical cord which, he had been told, he held onto when being born — followed as he attached himself to the great instrument. The assignment would take a few hours: Sage had to add another directional gyroscope to the seven such devices that already allowed the telescope to orient itself to any point of the vast blackness.

The work was engrossing. It also had to be performed to a high degree of precision. But Sage could feel his inner shadow nudging him to speed things up. *Hey. You signed me up for this mission. I'm going to do the job right.*

Sage felt a surge of anger and for a moment lost control of his hand. *Listen.* He released the handhold on the outside of the telescope and let himself float loose of the machine. Sage whispered, "If you don't stop bothering me, I'm going to tell Mission Control that I'm burned out and need a month's stay in a stress-relief facility. They'll put me away, and the more you throw tantrums and generally make me look like the nut job I am, the longer it will be before they let me out. Now, cooperate."

"Sage?" Ashby's voice over the radio.

"Fine. Lost my grip." *It is fine, isn't it?* His shadow didn't like being outfoxed. It was the main reason Sage occasionally played such cards. But the entity withdrew, grumbling and promising dire retribution, and he was left alone to hang in space and work on his father's beloved telescope.

Sage adjusted the new component. How wondrous it would be if his life stopped right then and there. If the cooling system in his suit failed, if the heat from Sintosy boiled him to death. Or maybe it would be better if some micro-meteoroid, not much bigger than a grain of sand, came hurtling at him at twenty thousand miles an hour and holed his supposedly impervious suit, exposing him to an unpressurized vacuum; his body would immediately swell to twice its size or more, and he would be gone in an instant.

What would you do then? He asked the shadow, and felt the chill of its anger deep inside him.

When he re-entered the shuttle, Ashby was wrapping up a conversation with BYSA Mission Control. He turned to Sage. "They want us to stay with the satellite for a while."

"How come?" Sage peeled off the suit with Grace's help.

The pilot shook his head "Not sure. They'll update us. In the meantime we'll just have to sit it out."

The unexpected delay sent the shadow to the brink of a full tantrum. For Sage, it felt as if a rope had suddenly tightened around his brain. His field of vision went red but for a narrow tunnel. He fumbled for the next handhold as he floated to his seat.

"You all right?" Ming asked, glancing back from her co-pilot's chair as Sage pressed against his forehead in agony.

Sage couldn't control himself well enough to answer. He could feel words boiling up from where the entity was forcing them into his mind and he had to fight to clamp his jaw shut, or else hear himself cursing the concerned shuttle crew.

Stop it! he begged the shadow.

Images flooded his mind: murdering the crew, taking the controls, flying off by himself.

Do that and it all ends now. Hero of the nation or not, they'll throw away the key.

The shadow shook violently, then like a gust of wind dying, subsided.

His vision cleared. Ming and Grace were eyeing him with wary concern. Ashby said, "What was that all about?"

"Just a headache." Sage strapped himself back into his seat.

· Ω ·

As the crew whiled away the delay, Sage gazed out his port, brooding over the scintillation of stars and pushing back the lingering pain in his head.

"Those incoming galaxies, shown by the space telescope, are amazing." Ashby lounged into a corner of his chair, sucking on a packaged energy drink.

"There's a ton of new ones." Ming toyed with a mindless game on her pad while Grace lay back in her seat, eyes closed. "Last week Dr. Rojan discovered a Quasar 8.4 billion light years away."

"Yeah," Ashby agreed. "The doc's on a roll. Stephan's Quintet, Messier 82."

"Don't forget the Carina Nebula," Ming added. "That galaxy is over nine quintillion miles away."

"Nine quintillion…" Ashby whistled, "You ever wonder that we could be out there someday?" His voice faded as Sage drifted to sleep.

Sage woke when his seat began to vibrate around him. The shuttle was decelerating. Someone had taken the time to strap on his safety harness.

"Good morning, sleepy head," said Ashby, grinning widely from the pilot seat. "Mission Control gave us the green. We just finished climbing to seven hundred miles and we're about ready to kick her out. You ready to go?"

What?

The answer came in a burst of information. Apparently Sage had used his new partnership status to demand the construction of his own private space station. There had been a detailed report, signed by Sage of course, that had enumerated the cost-benefits of the project— on the grounds that highly valuable and completely indispensable materials could be manufactured in its weight-less environment. Bristol's number-crunchers had authorized the expense without a quibble. Bristol had had no say in the matter.

Ah. Sage nodded.

"Good. Then Sage. Ming." Ashby was out of his seat, float-ing toward the lockers. "You're on this. I've got backup. Grace, mind the farm."

"Got it." Grace slipped up front.

While Sage and Ming helped each other suit up, Ashby reclaimed the cargo bay atmosphere. Next, Sage and Ming crawled through the internal airlock, opened the wide hatch on the shuttle's side, and began unstrapping the cargo. First they moved the individual station sections — made of strong, lightweight fiber — out into space.

Tethered to the spacecraft, and moving around by way of small jets of compressed air, the two assembled the modules in the prescribed order— it was all clear in Sage's mind now. The moment the seams of the components were lined up, a powerful adhesive activated itself and made an airtight joint stronger than welded titanium. It took less than two hours for them to construct the dumbbell-shaped station; two spherical domes connected by an air-locked conduit wide enough for a man to pass along.

One of the spheres held all the usual accoutrements of a space station — accommodation, life support, communications, tools — while the other was empty, nothing but a space with a magnetic floor, and a chair that faced a small square hatch open to space.

They ferried over air and supplies and started up the recycling systems. The place became livable, by BYSA standards at least. And Sage knew what would come next.

"This goes into the empty dome," he told Ming, indicating the Quantronix— the only thing left in the shuttle's cargo bay.

"I've been wondering what it was." Ming's voice crackled in his ear. She helped him wrestle the large pieces toward the airlock.

"New kind of telescope," Sage lied, grappling with the other side of the apparatus. Although it was virtually weightless in space, it still had mass. To get it moving required overcoming considerable inertia, and stopping it meant defeating that same momentum.

They eased the mechanism out of the shuttle and across the short distance to the new station, carefully orienting the funnel shaped object so, in the end, its control panel matched up precisely with the open hatch in the empty dome. Immediately, the same adhesive that had sealed the station's components together, welded the machine to the orbiter.

Ming floated back and looked at the contraption. "What's next?"

"I'll have to do the next part on my own," he told the co-pilot. "Internal hookups."

"Better take a break. We've been up for over fifteen hours."

Sage realized he was exhausted. *I need to rest and resupply,* he told the shadow.

But he could feel the excitement radiating from within, like heat from a blaze, and he knew the shadow must be getting close to completing its secret mission.

"I'll stay out and finish this," Sage informed them.

"Buddy," Ashby's voice came over the radio, "you're already way over your time limit. I can't let you stay out any longer. Come back to the shuttle and we'll all get some shut eye. We can start again fresh in a few hours."

"The work needs to get done and the sooner the better."

"You can't go it alone." Ming double checked his fastenings. "One of us has got to be on the com, in case anything happens. And we're all beat."

Sage could sense that the shadow would kill them without a qualm if they frustrated him now. He might black out for a moment, and then find himself standing over their corpses.

"I'll be fine. Besides, I'm the only one who knows what needs to happen next, what's the point of holding everyone else up if I can just do the work now and get it done? The orbiter's life support is fully operational, you can spot me till I'm in, then I'll finish what I have to do and sleep there."

They didn't like it, but nobody ever argued with Sage Rojan— except for one particular young woman who wasn't present at that moment. They watched him enter the life-support module. A moment later, he radioed that he was safely inside, all systems were green and they could tuck themselves in for a weightless sleep.

"Take it easy, kid," Ashby said, before signing off. "I mean it."

· Ω ·

Sage crawled through the connecting tube to the module housing the Quantronix, barren but for a single chair and swivel-mounted control panel. As Sage sat in the chair and reached for the console, a shiver of anticipation — not his — went up his spine. His fingers hovered over the controls. "What are we doing here?"

A burst of information filled his mind: the waiting was nearly over. The shadow's project was almost ready. Sage's mind filled with the sensation of a realm made entirely of light and power. An *empyreal* place. Sage felt the shadow's yearning to be in that place, to stand before an entity of all encompassing power, and display its masterpiece. There was a fleeting glimpse of a schematic Sage recognized— Tidon circled by four moons. Just like in the fairytale from his dad's study. *Lunar Four*, the story of Tidon's fourth moon.

"You want to make a moon?" He withdrew his fingers from the control panel. "What's the point of that? We've only just begun to explore the three we've got." *Work*, commanded the shadow.

"I want to know why. I have a right to know why."

The shadow seemed to laugh at him. He was a worm, a brute, nothing but a tool designed and built to do a job. He would never understand the glory of true creation, was not worthy of the knowledge he could not, in any case, encompass.

"Try me."

The answer came back, a growl. Either Sage could assist consciously, or the shadow would seize control of his body and work him to exhaustion.

Sage sighed and let the shadow set him to the task of completing the Quantronix's integration with the orbiter.

Moments later, a flutter of triumph from his shadow. The Quantronix was ready.

The big machine hummed as Sage flipped the switch to divert power from the orbiter's main solar captures. The lights in the module flickered; the life-support monitor blipping alarm then subsiding.

Excitement and elation pulsed from the shadow; it was like having a downstairs tenant throwing a party beneath the floor-boards.

The shadow fed him new instructions. The collection area for the matter of the new moon would need to form in the freedom of space in a field all its own. But first they would have to create that field.

The shadow directed him to set the Quantronix to start collecting the rays of light coming from Sintosy. Sage was kept busy using controls he'd never touched before, balancing and adjusting the Quantronix's output, so the new-spun elements related to each other in some complex, shadow-only-knew arrangement. After an hour, he keyed the sensor that let him see what was accumulating in the crucible. At this point, the results were noticeable only through inference, as the sensors detected minute changes in the field that filled the receptacle. The shadow had him open a separate panel that had been built into the side of the console and activate a series of switches. The machine on the other side of the orbiter's wall vibrated the entire space station as it shifted. Sensors reported that the field contained by the crucible had been everted from the machine; an image formed on the screen of a small globe of energy keeping pace with the orbiting station.

"Now what?" Sage asked, his hands once again poised over the controls.

Now we begin.

Then Sage was engrossed in scaling the controls back and forth through a range of settings as the spinning of different substances began. He surmised that the shadow meant the new-made moon to be composed of a vast array of elements but after five hours, the sensors reported only a miniscule quantity of matter in the field. *It would take millions of years to make a moon at this pace.*

Sage was instructed to wait, to make sure the arrangement was stable and self-sustaining. Then it let him know that his work here was finished— for now. The machine could be left to operate on its own, spinning new matter out of Sintosy's light, except for the short period when the space station's orbit put the dark bulk of Tidon between the star and the Quantronix's receptacle; an eclipse of a mere dozen minutes. When the process reached a certain point, he would have to return to change the settings on the machine. Sage rose from the chair and stretched, his back muscles stiff. He checked the Quantronix's chronometer. He only had another three hours before the shuttle crew would radio him to return to planet side. At last he was free to sleep.

Sage strapped himself to the bunk in the life-support module. He didn't bother with the lucid-dreaming technique, but let his mind wander through the events of the past twenty-four hours. His thoughts turned to the realm of light and power. The *Empyrean*. The place where the spirits resided, but also the place where the shadow was from?

The entity the shadow wanted to parade before could be the Artisan, but Sage wasn't sure. He didn't want to believe that his slave driver had access to the ear of the Artisan; surely no such omnipotent being would condone the shadow's methods. Yet the shadow seemed confident that it could win the entity's favor regardless of its abuses. The thought troubled Sage.

He glanced out the viewport to the cloud spun world beneath him. Suddenly he felt very alone.

Chapter 19

THEY CAME BACK DOWN to Tidon in the early evening. Sage let the crew handle the debriefing, and he headed to Cos-Ob. There he used the workshop controls to gently bring the large radio telescope directly under the widening aperture of the dome. He aborted the instrument's regular standby program and entered the coordinates that would lock onto the new space station. A moment later, a strong signal came down from the Quantronix — orbiting in the western sky, seven hundred miles up. He could feel the shadow at his elbow, eager.

He transmitted a coded message to the Quantronix and received an immediate answer: the device was functioning as programmed. Sage felt a buzz of self-satisfaction from the bottom of his mind and a flush of renewed energy as if the shadow had decided to share some of its inflating ego.

Next the shadow moved Sage to the main computer. It ignored the one blinking message symbol and accessed, through a remote link, the robotic production line in Porturn City. The interface appeared requesting a production schematic. The shadow began drawing something that Sage didn't recognize.

Sage didn't interfere, sensing that if it wanted to, the shadow could send him away as it had while designing the Quantronix. Perhaps Sage had earned some trust with his recent good behavior or perhaps the shadow's eagerness had made it forgetful, Sage didn't really care. He quietly mulled it over, his hand flying across the drawing tablet without his input, when suddenly the shadow paused. His hand stilled. Sage felt an inside frustration surge. On the screen was a half-designed... something.

A rage as black as the ones Sage had known in his child-hood balled his hands into fists. Sage winced as he remembered the scattered glass of slides; his father's precious microscope, cracked and dented, on the tile floor. But instead of putting his fist through the screen, Sage felt the shadow withdraw.

Sage was left sitting in his chair feeling empty and sick. His hands shook as he saved the project and exited the interface. He wasn't sure what had made the shadow stop, but based on the frustration that still lingered somewhere deep inside him, perhaps the shadow had forgotten something. Perhaps it was looking through the Library right now for its answer.

He wondered what it had been making. He reopened the file and stared at it but no new insights surfaced. It looked like some kind of platform— disc shaped, with a ring of what looked like small emitters around its base. Sage sighed and turned off the screen.

He shifted his focus back to the radio telescope. It was still receiving the Quantronix's signal. Sage set it to return to its default program and listened for a few moments just in case some alien civilization was broadcasting its version of, "Hello, we're here. Are you there?" When the shadow didn't return and he heard nothing but the background static of the universe, he decided it was time to get some long delayed sleep.

· Ω ·

Sage appeared in his dream state, as always, above the great mosaic. The Library's gates were tiny in the distance. He extended his senses, expecting to feel the shadow amidst the secrets of the Empyrean, but he was surprised when the tug of sensation came from the opposite direction, from beyond the aqua curtain. Sage debated taking the time to explore the Empyrean while the shadow was busy but a niggling thought urged him to discover what the shadow was doing. It was rare that he could sense the shadow's location within his dreamscape but this time the draw of it was like a lighthouse beacon. He sent himself skimming across the vast design to the room of white doors and squeezed himself through the aqua barrier. In a blink he stood before a door on the highest floor.

67-213. Like all the rest, the door was indistinct apart from its number, yet Sage could sense that it was somehow more significant for the shadow.

Sage stepped through the door, familiar with the sensation of sliding into its contained other-life. When the vision materialized, Sage found himself watching a lone figure wander down a crumbling city street. Buildings slouched, worn and empty, around him. The sky overhead cast a deeper blue even though Sage instantly understood it was midday in what passed for high summer on this world. In the same instant Sage knew he was the last— last of his kind, but not living; an artificial life, an android amidst a world silenced by biological warfare. Sage watched the figure sift through the husks of automated machines and the small crumpled heaps of other civilian models. He wondered if the android had seen the end of this world or if it had been created after its passing; but when he moved to rewind the vision nothing happened. He tried to speed forward but again nothing happened. Then all of a sudden the scene jumped and the android was standing in a golden field holding a digging implement; at its feet was a large trench. Its face was impassive as it stared at the tangle of artificial limbs in the bottom of the hole. It had dug this grave though it didn't understand its reason for doing so. It recognized none of the civilian models it had buried and yet it felt... pain. The scene jumped forward again but this time with an angry abruptness and Sage sensed his shadow at the controls.

The android was returning from the trench, fresh loam dusting its hands and streaking its face. It stopped in the center of field and a shimmer of rainbow colors rose from around its feet. The android materialized on a platform in a room with arching metal walls and dim orange lights. Sage understood that it had reached its home; an orbiting space station high above the planet's devastation. The shadow-led vision focused on the platform as the android stepped away from it and the scene jumped forward again. A shimmer of color and the android was stepping off a smaller model of the platform in the center of a large crumbling building. It was looking for raw materials for some kind of repair but Sage found himself more interested in the disc the android had been using. Or was that the shadow's interest.

So that's what the shadow was building. Some kind of instant transportation platform.

The android returned to the space station with a handful of gutted parts and immediately opened a panel in the large platform to begin diagnostics and repairs. Sage felt his shadow's sharpening attention as the guts of the machine were exposed.

Sage looked for something he recognized to lead him through how the platform functioned but the vision skipped ahead before he could make sense of it.

The next flash was of the android sitting at a table beneath a large viewport that gazed down at a brownish world, small metallic pieces and parts lay scattered across the table where it worked. One of the smaller disc models was being dismantled and rebuilt. The shadow focused closer, its distant impatience subsiding as it found what it was looking for.

The space station shook as if from an impact. The android didn't react as pieces and components jumped across the table. Sage felt his shadow growl, and when he blinked the pieces were back where they had been a moment before. There was another quake but there was no alarm and once again the android remained unmoved. His shadow's irritation rose. Sage glanced at the walls and felt a splash of vertigo as he realized he could see straight through to the stars. *What?* The vision was dissolving, no, his dreamscape was dissolving.

Sage found himself in a uniform gray mist. His shadow was gone. And there was a new pounding in his head— a sensation from the waking world.

He blinked awake lying on the cot in the observatory. Someone was rapping hard knuckles against his forehead.

Tamara looked down at him, her blue eyes snapping fire. "Sage Cosimo Rojan you'd better be in there."

Sage batted her hand away and squinted at her. "What... Tamara?"

"Yes it's me. What, did you forget that I exist or something?" She straightened with her hands on her hips, "You know I've been trying to get a hold of you for the past three weeks? A *month* Sage."

Sage scrubbed his face with both hands, feeling five day's worth of stubble and a profound exhaustion. He sat up; intending to swing his legs over the side of the cot then thinking better of it when he remembered he'd stripped down to his underwear for sleep.

Tamara threw her arms in the air. "You don't even answer your voicemail. Why do I even bother?"

"Uh, good morning?"

She held up a finger, "Oh no, you do not get to 'good morning' me mister. It's five in the afternoon. Bristol's in a fit over something. And he wouldn't even tell me what it was. I *hate* being out of the loop Sage."

"Oh."

"Oh?"

He winced; he supposed he should have guessed that. After all she was still Vice President Corporate Communications. He glanced around the small room for his pants and found them in a much too distant corner.

"Sage. Even your parents have been getting worried. What have you been doing?" Somewhere along the way she'd picked up the habit of creasing the line between her eyebrows like his mother did when she was stern or worried.

"I've been busy," he hedged. Somewhere inside he felt the stirring of the shadow. Sage wrapped the sheets around his waist and got up to retrieve his pants. He collected them and shuffled to the bathroom. He caught a glimpse of her look just before he closed the door and mentally cursed. She was going to want a better answer than that. Sage pulled on his pants and spoke through the door, "Bristol's got me working around the clock. You know how that is." He shoved a toothbrush in his mouth.

"What did you do to set him off?"

He paused his brushing, "Oh you know," he spat into the sink, "asked for equal partnership."

He opened the door. She was sitting cross-legged and serene on his bed. "You did what?" she asked. She looked him up and down; from his bare feet to his bare chest to his mussed hair. She frowned, "You need a shave and a haircut. You're practically skin and bones! Do you ever actually *eat* anything?"

"Sometimes."

"You're impossible!"

Chapter 20

THE PARALLEL LINES across the runway flashed by faster and faster in Sage's peripheral vision as the shuttle accelerated down the long strip of concrete. This was his first solo flight in one of the big birds, and it was good, phenomenally good, to be on his own— or as much on his own as he could be.

Sage pulled back on the yoke and the shuttle's nose rose into the air. The thrum of the big tires on the hard surface ceased. He was airborne. He kicked in the engines' full power and his body slammed against the pilot's seat, his eyes driven into their sockets.

A moment later he activated the anti-grav. The display indicating the strength of the anti-gravity field registered maximum, a fact confirmed by the tingle in his muscles.

Shuttle Fortitude tore through billows of clouds, effortlessly higher with constantly accelerating speed through the ever-thinning tropo- strato- meso- and exo-spheres. And then, into the cold, dark emptiness of space. Sage cut the anti-gravity drive, throttled back the engines, and set the automatic pilot to locate his small space station.

There wasn't another person on the planet who could walk into BYSA and say, "I need a shuttle for a private mission." Even Duggin Bristol would've received an argument. But all Sage Rojan had to tell Mission Control was that he needed to check on his experiment at the seven hundred-mile-high orbiter, and schedules were rearranged.

"What you got cooking up there?" the head controller had asked. "Another world-changer?"

"Something like that."

"Can't wait to see it."

This day was no errand run. Sage was not interested in the Ferdason complex or the satellites at two hundred miles up, or the larger BYSA-Bristol space station at three hundred miles, or even the Rojan Space Telescope at four hundred miles above the surface.

The coordinates of the private space station and its Quantronix were already programmed into the shuttle's computer. Sage let the spacecraft take the con as he enjoyed the view of the beautiful blue Tidon. He felt big compared to the humans who were less than infinitesimal dots somewhere back on the surface. *Perhaps this was how the shadow has always viewed human life.*

The shuttle continued to climb, orbiting Tidon in a widening spiral. Even as he checked the spacecraft's altitude, he saw the burst of flame from the leading edges of the wings— meaning that the shuttle was decelerating. He'd been out of his pilot's chair — floating — and although he couldn't feel much of the slowing, he bumped gently against the far wall. Worse, he also felt the shadow's impatience with him as he pushed off, sending him back toward the controls.

In the days since he'd activated the Quantronix, Sage had regularly checked its output, by way of a deeply encrypted data feed on his computer in the Cos-Ob dome. The scale the Quantronix's sensors used meant nothing to Sage; the information was solely for the shadow's use.

One thing he was sure of, the Quantronix's rate of production did not satisfy Sage's master — it was easy to think of his second personality in those terms — and Sage had come under irrepressible pressure to arrange this expedition. Even now, as the shuttle completed its twelfth orbit and aligned itself to match the station's path and speed, Sage felt a testy prod to get the job done.

"Lay off," he said aloud. "I'm cutting the autopilot now to bring her in by hand. If you make me screw it up, your precious Quantronix might be damaged."

The shadow receded, but did not disappear.

Sage guided the big spacecraft close to the small space station, working the micro-controls to regulate the shuttle's position. When he had the two orbiting objects exactly aligned, he looked more closely at the station and its bolted-on matter-spinner.

The Quantronix's light-gatherer was fully extended. Outside of the station, a ball of dark matter spun within the containment field. It looked to be a good twelve feet in diameter, though Sage could distinguish nothing more about it than its size, its spherical shape, and the fact that its deep blacker-than-black surface did not reflect light.

Sage did not really know anything about how the Quantronix worked. It spun matter from light, and it was presently set at a slow speed. To have created that much matter from photons in the time since Sage had built it, struck him as impressive.

But the shadow was nowhere near happy. Sage realized he was here to reset the machine for faster production. But that would require moving the station to a higher orbit, so as not to endanger Tidon.

"Wait a minute," Sage said. "What kind of danger?"

The shadow writhed serenity: Sage was not to worry about it. Everything was in hand. And the shadow did not have time to explain every detail to— Sage got an impression of a clumsy neophyte.

Sage gritted his teeth. "What kind of danger?"

Frustration and impatience snapped back across the serenity. *None of your concern.*

"If what we're doing is a danger to the planet and the millions of people on it, I'm pretty sure it *is* of my concern."

His hands and arms ceased to be under his control. One palm came up, giving him a hard slap across the face.

The shadow's derision was plain to feel. *Fight me if you want. We can leave the Quantronix where it is. But you can't stop me from setting it for faster production. Help move it or let's see what happens when I don't.*

"All right," he said, his heart fluttering uneasily in his chest. "Just show me what to do."

The image was clear: tie the space station and its Quantronix to the shuttle, then haul them higher into space. And keep well clear of the new-spun matter.

Cabling the space station was not too difficult although Sage did not like the idea of working outside the shuttle with no one aboard to help him if anything went wrong. He decided to depressurize the cargo bay and leave the spacecraft via its hatch rather than go out via the personnel airlock. Airlocks had been known to malfunction, and if Sage was going to find himself stranded in space, he wanted the tools in the cargo bay to be available.

He began the process of depressurization, and the shadow nudged him angrily. *Go out the smaller airlock to save time.*

"It's a matter of minutes," Sage told it, then painted a picture of himself stuck outside the shuttle, waiting to die when his air ran out. The entity's response — a blast of rage — surprised him.

But the sudden flare of anger was not the surprising part. Sage was taken aback by the realization that the shadow had brought him up here, all on his own, without considering the possibility that, in the unforgiving non-environment called space, he might easily die— and leave the great work uncompleted.

"Do you not consider the consequences of your actions? Are you in that much of a hurry to make a moon?" Sage's impressions of his shadow lowered.

The response was a stab of pain from one end of his skull to the other.

"Dackt!" He blew out a breath when the agony faded.

The shadow swirled inside him, furious at Sage's resistance and the loss of minutes the punishment had produced.

"Do that at the wrong time out here, and you'll find yourself looking for a new beast of burden."

The shadow churned, but held itself in check.

Sage exited the spacecraft without incident, air-jetting to the space station with a cable of braided microfilament unrolling behind him. He rigged the tow-line, attaching it to a cleat on the end of the station, then hauled himself hand-over-hand back to the shuttle. He made it back inside, buttoned up the airlock and removed his suit.

Sage reseated himself in the pilot's chair and oh-so-slowly brought the engines back on line. They were weightless at this height, but the space station, the Quantronix, and most especially, the new ball of matter in its containment field, had the same mass and inertia as they would've had on Tidon. Sage didn't want to test the tow cable by a sudden jerk and find it wanting.

Hurry it up! The words sounded in his head.

"Dackt it! I know you think I have no brain, but that's a lot of mass out there. Or hadn't you considered that? You want me to have to go out and splice the cable, when it breaks? Take up extra time making unnecessary repairs?"

The response was as much a growl, as anything. *Just get us up to speed,* came the answer.

"We'll take it slowly, and speed up as we build momentum."

The shadow gave off more frustration and impatience the way stars gave off heat and light.

Sage gently adjusted the shuttle's speed.

"There. Twelve miles an hour over the previous orbital velocity. By the way, you haven't told me how high we're going."

Sage got no answer. He eased the throttle up a little more. "Even a smallish moon is a lot bigger than a one-man space station. We're less than a thousand miles out. Nothing compared to the moons: Filus is three hundred and fifty thousand miles out, Sotus is four hundred and twenty thousand, and Milus four hundred and fifty thousand."

No answer.

"I figure you'll want to go even farther out than Milus, because what's the point of making a new moon if it just crashes into one of the old ones? So I'm figuring five hundred thousand miles at least. And, even when we get up to a decent speed, that's going to take a while. Days."

The dark mood thickened. It was like being in a house with a basement filling up with foul, black water. Sage didn't need to see it to know it was there.

Still, Sage was interested to know if he could exploit what he was beginning to see as a fatal flaw in the shadow's character. It was grossly impatient. It rushed things, and rushing things created errors.

He put the shuttle on auto and caught a shift of sleep. When he woke, the shuttle was passing Milus. He was now well beyond the furthest that any human had ever been from Tidon. He'd seen plenty of pictures of the scarred moon — there had even been a couple of unmanned landings — but it was different to see it close-up and personal. Milus had had a long-past history of volcanism; the cones and lava fields were plain to see. So were the pit-marks of impact craters, uneroded in that airless, water-less place.

Sage recalled again the fairytale book — *Lunar Four,* that his dad had shown him as a child — where Tidon had once had a fourth moon; which exploded when its first powerful Pimple Burst volcano split the entire rock. It was destroyed in that cataclysm during the early years of the solar system. Most of the remnants of the broken moon had crashed onto Tidon or been swept up by the other three circling moons, which accounted for the huge spread of craters on the face of moon Milus.

Tidon had been named because of the gravitational effect its three moons had upon its tides, particularity when the moons — which all orbited in the same direction — rode in the same part of the sky. What effect would a fourth moon have on the three bodies' interrelated trajectories?

He shook his head to rid himself of the swirl of thoughts, and turned back to the porthole. Behind Milus sat Tidon, a blue orb hanging against the speckled blackness. How beautiful. And how wrong for someone to mess with its beauty.

He did not begrudge all the improvements and advances that his captor, through him, had brought to Tidon. But the planet was inhabited by an intelligent species; in time, they would've invented all the wondrous things they'd been force-fed. And none of the inventions had been for the benefit of the Tidonese. That was just a side effect of the shadow's overweening ambition. If it could have achieved its ends by making Sage's people miserable, it would have done so without a qualm.

Moon Milus faded into the distance. Sage kept the speed constant at five thousand miles an hour. *At least another day to go,* he ate and slept. He used the lucid dreaming techniques twice, trying to track down the shadow, wherever it lurked in his skull, but it avoided him and this time there was no sensory beacon to tell him where to go. It could hide behind any of the doors, and the odds of Sage just stumbling into it were effectively nil. He decided that the next chance he got he would use the time in his dreamscape to consult the Library instead, and hopefully learn something useful about artificial moons.

Sage was at the shuttle's controls. He felt the shadow. Awake, examining the readouts through his eyes, checking up on their progress. "What happens after? When you produce the new moon?"

No answer came.

"Does someone give you a promotion? Extra marks for showing initiative?"

The head pain came, like a shard of ice-cold steel transfixing his skull. Sage rocked in the pilot's seat, and his hand slammed against the controls. The engines roared and the ship lurched forward. The pain instantly faded, and his hands reached independently, easing the throttle back.

"Idiot! Slowing the ship doesn't slow the tow."

The shadow released his hand — why? Was it uncertain? Did it want Sage to explain himself?

"If that mass hits our engines, we could be up here forever."

The shadow withdrew. Not happily.

The shuttle blipped as it registered the station barreling towards them under its own momentum. Sage nudged the throttle to match the station's new speed and decided he would worry about slowing it back down when they reached their destination.

Five days after departing home, the shuttle and its payload reached six hundred thousand miles. It took some careful maneuvering of the auxiliary thrusters to let the space station pass the shuttle without tearing the cable. Sage matched its speed once the station was visible out the front viewport then slowly eased the reverse thrusters until the tow line was taut and the station began to shed momentum. Finally they established a stable, geosynchronous orbit above Tidon.

Again, Sage, alone, had to get into his spacesuit unaided, and again he went out through the cargo bay hatch.

Solo in his spacewalk, Sage pulled himself along the tow-line until he reached the space station. It checked out, so he turned his attention to the Quantronix and the newly created matter. The stuff was blacker-than-black, standing out against the glitter-spangled darkness of space. He had a moment of the vertiginous perspective shift that could happen in space: he suddenly felt as if he were looking down into a bottomless black pit. An object this black, he knew, must be composed of something that absorbed all the wave lengths of light — which was odd, when he thought about it, since it was matter created from light itself.

A flashlight was clipped to his belt harness. He pulled it free and shone its beam toward the ball of matter. *Mistake*. Even before the shaft of light was centered on the dark object, the beam narrowed laser-thin and he felt a sudden pull on the flashlight, as if he was holding a magnet beside a strong magnetic field. His hand holding the flashlight pulled toward the object. He locked the fingers of his free hand around the cleat at the end of the space station and jerked himself back.

The flashlight was still caught in the invisible grip of the dark sphere. As he pulled back, trying to free it, the beam of light *bent* towards the mass, curving like a fishing line when the angler hooked a big one.

His flesh chilled, even in the heated suit. *Dackt, there's only one thing that could be doing this.*

The matter accumulating at the end of the Quantronix was not ordinary matter.

It was dark matter, the seed of a black hole.

Sage could not free the flashlight beam from the dark matter's grip. Let it go? Sage had no idea what would happen if the flashlight's mass encountered the newly created dark matter. He feared to think.

Turn it off.

Of course. Sage pulled back his thumb and flicked the switch of the flashlight's barrel. The effect was like cutting a taut fishing line. His arm jerked back and the torch would have gone flying if it hadn't been tethered to his glove. *Dackt.*

Stunned, Sage worked his way down to the space station's airlock and let himself into the life-support module. Its systems came to life and in a few minutes he was able to shuck his helmet. Water dripped from his suit— his own sweat, not yet recycled by the internal systems. Sintosy had nearly boiled Sage inside the suit, despite the near-absolute-zero temperature of the vacuum that had surrounded him. He toweled off, drying away the sweat before it had the chance to become airborne.

He crawled along the conduit that led to the module housing the Quantronix's control panel and checked the Quantronix's data feed.

The shadow took control of Sage's limbs. It reset the dials and indicators on the Quantronix, cranking it up to its highest possible speed. Sage felt the hairs on the back of his neck prickle. The shadow didn't have to say anything for Sage to feel the illicit risk involved in the action.

The shadow disappeared and Sage felt the sudden heaviness of sleep. He pushed himself to the life-support module and strapped himself into the harness. He decided it was time to learn what he could from the Library about the thing he had spent the last days dragging up here. Sage drew one even breath then another and the dreamscape rose to meet him.

Chapter 21

SAGE SAT CROSS-LEGGED on the Library floor with his back against the lectern. The Empyrean Directory was lying open on his lap and a small mountain of books surrounded him on all sides.

He'd remembered reading something about the creation of planets in the Library a long time ago. When he ran his finger down the page, the word that leaped out at him was *Recycliun*. The directory led him to a volume on the shelves, a dusty tome with a ragged cover and only a number on its spine.

— RECYCLING LIGHT UNIVERSE — RECYCLIUN —

Yes, this was information he'd encountered before but had not been able to retain.

And now it came to him that there was a reason why he could never hold on to what he read in the secrets of the Empyrean: the shadow had never allowed it.

Sage opened the book. And when his dreamscape didn't come crashing down around his ears, he began reading.

The book was divided into sixty-seven sections. The same number as there were tiers of vaults and floors in the room of white doors. That could not be a coincidence.

He scanned the first section, *Cycle One*. It covered a fifteen-billion-year history of the universe. *Cycle Two* contained the history of the next fifteen-billion-year period. The implication was obvious: each mention of the universe lasted for fifteen billion years then seemingly recycled to move on into the next cycle. He did a quick calculation — sixty-seven times fifteen billion — and came up with a smidgen over a trillion years.

That would come as a shock to Bellans. They were just getting used to the idea that the cosmos might be billions of years old. He read on.

Each cycle of the universe saw it double in size and mass, with twice as many stars and galaxies. The natural mechanism by which light was spun into matter, and which the Quantronix simulated, was a black hole— a generator of moons and planets. Each planet was born with a black hole at its core. If it survived long enough, it had the capacity to expand into a hot sun. Ultimately, after billions of years, some of those suns grew to be so gigantic the fires in their interior core lost control of their contents. When they could no longer sustain the forces that fired them, they went Supernova, in a devastating explosion that destroyed entire solar systems. Out of that destruction came the doubling of the universe. The book went on to explain that the power released in a Supernova was large enough to ripple the fabric of space and split the black hole at its core. The energy wave, as it expanded, would destroy all celestial bodies in its path, thereby doubling the black holes that had been at the centers of those destroyed suns, planets, and moons. This phenomenon accounted for the doubling of the universe's total matter at each recycling.

His fingers took him to the final section of the book — *Cycle 67* — then traced down the page to where it read: *Star Population 73,786,976,294,838,206,464.* More than seventy-three quintillion stars at the universe's trillionth birthday. He flipped back through the pages to *Cycle 66.* Thirty-six quintillion stars. Then he flipped back all the way to *Cycle 1.* The star population in that first iteration numbered exactly two.

"Numbers," Sage's math teacher had once told the accelerated group, "can run away on you, if you don't keep an eye on them."

Sage was sure his dad would be happy that his son was once again trashing the Bang Theory. *It was ridiculous to accept that a big bang had flung the contents of the universe out into space where the smaller balls of hot matter cooled and hardened on their out-* sides into moons and planets while more colossal orbs *fought off the cold of space and stayed hot as suns and stars.* Now he was seeing how the universe really became so large, growing from infancy, expanding in fifteen billion year cycles, doubling with each go around. That is, if he wasn't crazy.

Flinging off the circular arguments, Sage's mind now turned toward the lives behind the doors. Each of the sixty-seven levels contained scores of hundreds and thousands of past lives. Each level must correspond to one of the sixty-seven cycles of the universe. The question that had long troubled Sage was: to whom did those lives belong? Were they his alters? Could a person diagnosed with Dissociative Identity Disorder have *millions* of alters? Or was he someone who'd actually lived all those lives? But if so, how was that possible? And where did the shadow fit in to that?

Frustrated, Sage gave up trying to puzzle out his mental state and focused instead on what he did know.

Sage thought back to his sessions behind the doors. He recollected the orderliness of the numbers that marked them. At the top level was a door with the highest number: *67-888* in bold black letters.

He realized now why the tiers formed an upside-down pyramid: the lowest level was Cycle One, back at the cosmic genesis, small and narrow, with only a few lives living there.

He had wondered why the highest level broke the pattern of the reversed pyramid, why it was narrower than level sixty-six just below it. Now he knew why. Cycle Sixty-Six was over, its fifteen-billion-year lifespan completed with its thousands of doors. But the Sixty-Seventh Cycle was still in existence right at this very moment, probably on millions of planets scattered through the galaxies. There were still additions that would occur before the recycle was complete.

There would be more lives, probably many more, to be catalogued and stored behind the white doors of the highest level.

What would he find on the other side of that last door?

Sage closed his eyes and imagined himself standing in the grand foyer. When he opened his eyes he was there. He willed himself to rise up, past the lower and middle levels, ascending as the levels widened, more and more lives at each tier. Sage progressed horizontally along level sixty-seven, the number on each door moving up in sequence — *67-882, 67-883,* — until he stopped at the last door, number *67-888*. The white panel looked like all the others; nothing distinguished it. He put his fingers to the smooth surface and pushed. Instantly, as always, he was drawn within, and 'the show,' as he had come to think of the life records, began to play.

A sick feeling crept into his stomach.

I should have known.

The life was his. First as a baby; then in school; meeting Bristol; building the war planes; rocketing into space; creating the Quantronix. He sent the story spinning forward—

But the action stopped, and he was looking at himself, sleeping in the harness in the space station, six hundred thousand miles above Tidon.

He took an inward breath.

So. Not dead. No... no horror revealed.

Not yet.

But what did it mean? The last in a sequence of lives. So. All the other previous existences behind all those doors on all those levels were his earlier instances of life? Reincarnations? Or were they all just byproducts of his delusions?

He stepped out into the corridor and went to the second last door, *67-887.*

A disembodied point of view: in this montage he walked the streets of a city. Unlike any of the other lives he had sampled, this one's surroundings looked familiar; cobbled streets, horse-drawn carriages, and a clock tower at one end of a civic square.

Porturn City.

But the people walking about wore fashions from the olden days, and there were no cars in sight. As always, it was easy to tell who was the central figure, the 'owner', of this life: a middle-aged man, at this moment sitting on a bench in a shady part of the square, writing. There was a newspaper lying beside him.

Sage zeroed in on the top of the page; the date— twenty years before he was born. The title at the top of the man's page looked familiar. A heading he had read in a book once. Then he remembered. Sage stared at the page.

Was it possible? Was this the man who had written *Lunar Four*?

He pushed the life-record roll forward, faster, to see when and how this one ended. But it didn't end. It was as if the reel had been cut. The action simply froze.

Why? Every other life, behind every other door he'd visited — and there had been thousands of them — ended in the central figure's death. Was this man still alive as well? But no, Sage had read the author's bio. The man had died of a heart arrest, no surviving relatives... Sage rewound and fast forwarded but nothing changed. The recording simply stopped as if the camera watching had suddenly disappeared.

Out in the corridor, he stared at the last panel, reading again its label: *67-887*. The 887th life lived by someone during the sixty-seventh iteration of the trillion-year-old recycling universe. He touched his fingers to the numbers, as if he might absorb some knowledge through their tips.

Above the digits was another row of symbols—

▲▼178♦✿. They appeared above every number on every door. Sage's eyes glossed over them, as they always did. But—

He touched the fingers of one hand to the nape of his neck and began drumming. He looked again at the meaningless symbols. He had never really focused on them before.

And why not? He knew the answer to that one: because the shadow didn't want him to.

He drummed harder.

The symbols didn't change. The obvious solution came to him: the numbers on the doors such as 67-253 changed because the lives changed; the other symbols above didn't change because the entity living those successive lives was constant.

So ▲▼178♦✿ was either an identifier of the being who was now Sage Rojan, or it was the identifier, the name, of the shadow.

Fear — his own fear — swirled in him. He had figured it out. These lives, these memories, they belonged to the shadow. Sage was the one who did not belong.

A moment later, he was zooming back across the figured floor, toward the cathedral gates.

Standing at the lectern, drumming relentlessly, Sage willed ▲▼178♦✿ to appear in the directory. The response was slow in coming, as if the Library was reluctant to inform him, but finally he was directed to the shelves labeled Empyrean and Firmament. He opened the designated volume.

The book began with an overview. The Empyrean was the highest level of existence. It was outside the phenomenal inner universe of planets, stars, and galaxies, outside of space and time, and was inhabited by noncorporeal entities — 'spirits' was the only word that fit — of the highest rank. Highest, that was, except for the Artisan, the actual creator of the universe, who existed in a realm above and beyond even that of the Empyrean.

The Firmament stood below the Empyrean. It was the working level, where spirits toiled, preparing and recording visitations — that seemed to be the technical term for incarnations — down to the inner universe. The beings that lived those lives — humans, animals, aliens — were of a lower rank than the bureaucrats who archived visitations in the vaults of the Empyrean.

Sage was pretty sure his shadow was neither an upper spirit of the Empyrean nor one of the bureaucrats who operated the system. He knew little of either, but holders of high office tended to sustain a system's rules and rarely acted to subvert them.

"Names, names… where do I find its name?" His eye fell on a section entitled *Firmament Nomenclature*, pages of alphabetical and numerical listings which seemed to be the names of spirits. None matched the symbols on the white doors.

He went back to the table of contents and scanned further. Another heading popped out: *Trillionists*. The term resonated in his mind: sixty-seven iterations of fifteen billion years. He turned to that section, rapidly scanning the information.

▲▼178✦✿.

There.

The identifier had a catalogue number beside it. It must have its own volume in a separate section of the library.

Sage skimmed down the aisles, heart pumping, breath short, eyes tracking the numbers on the spines of the books, looking for section ▲▼. And there it was. On a lower shelf, he knelt to pull the book free. The cover bore, in large and boldfaced red ink, the symbols ▲▼178✦✿.

On the first page, a heading: *Spirit* ▲▼ — *Trillionist*. Beneath it was a block of print:

> *One of the early spirits in the inaugural universe cycle, Genesis. Number of splinter visitations into the inner universe:* **178✦✿**.

Sage didn't know what ▲▼ or ✦✿ meant. His first idea was that the first two symbols might be a title, followed by some multiplication factor — **178** — and perhaps ✿ was a factorial power of some kind. Perhaps the ✦ at the end meant some kind of continuation. Under ▲▼ there were more statistics: 76,499 spirit splinters down into mainstream organics; 11,834,652 tiny splinter visitations related into lesser, though still complex, organisms, which seemed to refer to higher animals; and 6,593,275,543 microscopic splinters into vegetation, insects, bacteria, and viruses.

He had no idea what to do with the information. He'd wanted, at some level, for all of this to be about him, his existence. *But how could it be? The fact that the shadow was so protective of this information said this information was about it. The shadow, not Sage.*

Sage was no more than a puppet, up against an entity that had existed since the dawn of the inner universe, a trillion years of experiences Sage could not even imagine. What was it like to be a spider, a germ, a tiny assemblage of viral protoplasm so small that a bacterium loomed the size of a battleship? What did millions of such experiences do to an immortal being that had split itself in so many ways?

And how could a lowly hand puppet hope to stand against the — power — all that knowledge must convey?

There were folk tales on Bella Yareo about people who'd been possessed by sorcerers. Sage had grown up thinking such notions came from the age of ignorance, before Bellans had discovered reason and science. Now he was not so sure. The being he could now identify by the unpronounceable symbols ▲▼178♦✿, fit the definition of sorcerer: a malevolent, criminal spirit that seized hold of a person to work its selfish will upon the world. He cringed at the thought that he might be teammates with a demon.

Demons! A corner of his mind recognized that his delusion had got out of hand. The depth and complexity of his psychosis was truly frightening. He should assert the tiny fragment of his sanity that remained. And yet... and yet, he couldn't dismiss the awful truth of his shadow.

The Trillionist is a spirit. I need to know more about spirits. He mentally marked the ▲▼ section for future reference then went looking for a wider scope of information. The directory led him to a section labeled *Spirit World*. His hand flew across the shelves, finding books, scanning their covers and contents, until he found what he searched for.

He read the introduction: *A spirit assigned a visitation into an organic form on a planet in the inner universe leaves behind its primary Firmament entity and departs as a splinter of that entity. At the Firmament clearing gates, its memories are expunged; ergo it can start the new life within an organic form as a new experience. Each*

action and sensation experienced within the organic state is recorded, and the record transmitted to the Firmament via the tether that connects the splinter to the upper realm, so that upon the spirit's return to the Firmament at the end of that organic life, its experiences are added into its personal grand archive.

That raised a question. If the Firmament's clearing gates were supposed to wipe away all memory, sending the splinter down as a blank, then why was his life filled with knowledge from the Empyrean, the Firmament, and past lives?

He looked up and around him, at the shelves, and all the aisles of shelves surrounding him. *Illicit.* He remembered, when he first walked into the Empyrean, the sensation he had of treading over something sacred, wrongfully taken. Perhaps the shadow had found a way to slip through the Firmament without losing its memories. He thought back to the second last recording, how it just ended without cause. Perhaps—

The floor rattled under his feet. Heavy pounding thrummed in the distance, growing ominously closer. Sage got to his feet, gripping the shelf in front of him. It became semi-transparent. His hand sank through the wood as if through mist.

What?

The thick book became pale ash in his hands, page after page, until he was left with only the empty binding.

A puff of air blew the ash into his eyes, nose, and mouth, and it reeked of old char.

The shadow?

He didn't sense it near, but it must be behind the loss.

He spoke to the air of his dreamscape. "I won't quit. I'll find a way to get rid of you."

Silence reverberated around him. Emptiness.

Sage left the Library, out onto the mosaic. But something had changed; he no longer hovered over the great design, flying where his dreaming mind willed himself to go. Instead, his feet were touching its surface.

All right.

He peered into the murky limits of the great expanse, dread falling through his stomach.

The surface beneath one foot gave way and a piece of the mosaic dropped into darkness. Sage leaped and landed just beyond the falling segment, but the place beneath him now divided, a long crack running away into the distance, widening as it went.

He willed himself to run, faster and faster, toward the opposite side, where the portal to the corridors of past lives waited.

Sage performed the drum tap on the base of his neck, even as he threw himself forward.

His dreamscape resounded to the thunder of drums. His legs became a blur, his feet barely touching the pattern, as he sped toward the aqua curtain. In a blinding burst of speed and precision, he leaped from one subsiding piece to another. The aqua curtain was only five long bounds away, then four, now three, two—

He rammed his shoulder against the blue water, now turning to ice—

It resisted— then became the molecules of hydrogen and oxygen which separated, and he poured through.

The last fragment of mosaic collapsed and fell, dwindling, into a well of black infinity.

Still drumming, he dropped down to the floor of the foyer and waited for the molecular version of the aqua to crystallize.

Through the blue shimmering wall, the mosaic, last seen crashing in fragments into an abyss, was back, whole and intact. *I have to remember. This is still my dreamscape. Not every sight I see here is to be trusted.*

The great design was a representation of the shadow's most useful tool — a tool named Sage Rojan — there was no way the entity would destroy such a valuable instrument. The previous falling away of the mosaic was an illusion. A nightmare. Sage was coming too close to understanding things the shadow did not want him to know.

Sage pushed against the curtain, intent on returning to the Library, but this time the wall stayed solid. He tapped harder on his skull and willed the aqua to let him through but the barrier remained cold against his hand. It seemed the shadow wasn't going to let him go.

Sage turned around to scan the sixty-seven tiers. There. A flash of darkness disappearing into one of the doors on the second level. Had the shadow been watching him?

Sage rose to open the door, his hand hesitating on its handle. Was it wise to pursue the spirit into its lair?

Then all at once, he was in total darkness. He stopped, stood listening, hearing nothing but the blood rushing in his ears. He could see nothing; there was neither light, nor anything to see.

The shadow was near— was *there*, and not far distant. Had it called down darkness to hide itself?

He took a step toward it, and felt himself falling through a threshold. The door! The shadow had drawn him through the door. There was solid ground beneath his feet but the darkness remained. When no show began to play, he put out his hands and felt forward. "What are you trying to do?" he asked. He could sense the shadow before him, just out of reach.

The words were fading in his own hearing when he bumped into something soft that yielded, as if stretching, before him.

The soft resistance suddenly became taut, then hard. It tightened and he had the sense of being jerked upright, his feet losing contact with the floor. Panic. He struggled, but every effort he made caused the constriction to grow tighter. He gasped for air and forced himself to calm. He was captured, cocooned, as if in a spider's web, wrapped, still living, in silk, to wait until the captor came to feed. But this was still his dreamscape.

I'll just wake up and end this.

You're trapped Sage. You've pursued me this far, but no farther.

Sage twisted. He couldn't see the shadow. He couldn't see anything. He became lost in inky blackness.

· Ω ·

Darkness evaporated and Sage realized he was in the cargo bay of the shuttle. The shadow had once again taken control of his body. But this was different, he had no volition. In a weird double sensation he felt himself still hanging in the silk trap of his nightmare. Yet, he could see the waking world as if he was watching a screen hanging in the blackness that otherwise surrounded him.

"And so," Sage heard his captor's voice say aloud, "a new phase begins. I have your body. I don't particularly need *you* anymore."

Sage was caught. He had walked straight into the trap like a simple minded rodent— a rat in a maze. What had he done?

Mom. Dad. Would he never hold them again? Would he ever tell them he loved them? The shadow wouldn't. He might never get another chance to flirt with Tamara — because, he realized, that was what his argumentativeness had been—

His eyes had filled with tears. The screen blurred—

—wait! How could that be?

The shadow's control of his body did not extend to the autonomic nervous system?

Stop that! The voice rolled through the blackness. *I've left you your feelings, but I don't have to.*

Sage fought to control his emotions. The thought of the shadow playing his feelings gave him an image of some multi-legged creature at the tiered keyboard of some vast musical instrument. The sight brought him disgust, then anger.

That's better, said the voice from the darkness. *Anger gives you energy.*

His anger was directed at himself as much as at his captor. All these years, it let him explore past lives and discover the secrets of the Empyrean; thinking he was gaining some freedom, positioning himself for the day when he would have the strength to revolt and break his chains. But in fact the shadow had been single-minded. It had followed its plan, and waited until its goal was in sight. Only then did it spring its trap. And Sage had fallen directly into its hands.

That this *thing*, spirit entity, demon, whatever it was, would be walking around with his skin...

Sage struggled against his prison. He hammered at the webbing that held him; a dark frustration rising that he knew was his own. But the webbing didn't give. A part of his mind understood that in this realm he could not get tired, he would continue to fight against his ropes for an eternity and nothing would change except his rising anger.

Sage drew his emotions under control; searching for that calm that allowed him to slip into lucid sleep. He would wait. He would watch. If this was a game of patience then at least Sage still had a chance.

The shadow went about its business, unfastening a small cargo container that was secured to the bulkhead of the cargo bay. The shadow disengaged the clasps and pushed the container toward the Shuttle's airlock. The label on the container showed that it had been consigned from Cos-Ob and his own signature was in the authorization box.

The shadow unsealed the container and pulled out two large grey discs.

They were made of a material Sage did not recognize, neither metal nor plastic nor organic. The shadow pushed one of the discs through the airlock and into the shuttle's cabin, where it adhered to the wall that acted as a floor.

A moment later, he took the second grey disc and, working along the cable line, bore it to the station. He went through the airlock and attached this disc to the floor of the life-support module.

Then he disconnected the tether from the station and returned to the shuttle. The shadow didn't bother to release the monofilament cable from the spacecraft itself until Sage reminded it.

Back inside the shuttle, the shadow yanked off the space suit. Instead of returning the gear to the locker, it carelessly left the suit floating about weightlessly.

Sloppy, said Sage and the shadow sent a message of strong indifference.

The shadow set the autopilot to land the Shuttle Fortitude spacecraft back at the BYSA space center on Tidon. It would take several days to return to BYSA but Sage had a feeling they weren't going to be on the flight. When the green light flashed to signal that the on-board computer was set, the shadow floated over to the disc and adhered Sage's feet to its glimmering surface.

It grasped a control module in one hand. The shadow looked down to where the shimmering colors were now enveloping Sage's feet and flowing up his legs. The rainbow beam moved ever upwards, soon encompassing his whole body. His view of the shuttle's cabin faded behind the swirl of colors and Sage saw his thumb flip a switch on the controller.

Sage expected to feel the sensation of molecules in his body disassembling, disintegrating, and melting away— only to reassemble at their destination. But instead the cabin simply disappeared behind the shimmering colors. Then the colors dispersed, and Sage found himself looking at the walls inside of Cos-Ob.

Outside, he could hear a distant truck engine and, nearby, a bird twittering from a high-up nesting point on the observatory dome. Ghostly smoke, liquid nitrogen used to cool the telescope's instruments, hung in the air.

He had traveled six hundred thousand miles back to Tidon in virtually an instant.

The shadow stepped from an identical disc waiting on the floor of the Cos-Ob and checked limbs and torso to make sure Sage's body had come through intact. It had. *So, no more shuttle trips up there to check on your little project? If that wasn't quantum teleportation, what was it?*

"Something better. Now, be quiet. I'm busy." The shadow repositioned the large telescope and set it to the new location of the Quantronix. The view was much smaller now and it waivered with atmosphere distortion. The shadow sprayed the scope's large mirrors with carbon dioxide to remove residual dust blurring the view. It sat Sage at the Cos-Ob computer to receive the encrypted data feed that began streaming in.

Then, immersed in numbers, it remained there for two days, only rising to respond to bodily necessities.

At one point, apparently dissatisfied with what it was seeing, it returned to the grey disc. The shimmering colors came again, fluttering upwards over his body; then instantly he was back inside the space station orbiting six hundred thousand miles up. They sat for half an hour at the control panel in the empty module, the shadow making minute adjustments and readjustments. The device now spun matter in such quantities, it might take only years to make a new moon for Tidon. Would that pace satisfy the shadow's impatience? Sage knew better than to ask. The entity stepped back onto the disc and they were instantly back in Sage's Cos-Ob dome.

Upon their return, Sage heard a voice coming from the all-frequency radio monitor mounted on the wall beside the workstation. "BYSA control calling Shuttle Fortitude. Do you hear us?"

Fortitude was the spacecraft making its way home on autopilot, with nobody on board. Sage tried to respond, but his movements were locked in. The shadow didn't care.

"BYSA calling Fortitude. Come in."

You should answer that.

The shadow paid no attention. Its focus was on the new data from the Quantronix.

A different voice came over the speaker. "Sage. Dad here! We see the shuttle coming back on autopilot. Are you all right?"

Hearing his dad's voice tore at Sage's heart.

The shadow grunted in satisfaction at the new information on the readout.

How could this thing keep working? If protocol wasn't followed someone would get suspicious. *And if I don't answer a lot of people are going to be worried.*

The shadow did not even bother to shrug.

"Sage?"

They'll find out what you're doing. They'll start watching where you go and soon they'll know about the dark matter, the risks you're taking with it. You think my pestering questions are annoying, try explaining what you're doing to the rest of the world!

The shadow hissed in sudden anger.

"We're worried about you. Sage?"

It vaulted for the grey disc.

The shimmering flooded up over him again, and then he was in the crew cabin of the Shuttle Fortitude. The shadow keyed a com switch, and said, around a convincing yawn, "Sorry, Dad, I've been dead to the world for hours. Too much work."

The voice was Sage's, but there was something different about it: a lower resonance, almost monotone.

"Are you all right, son?" Thaddeus's voice came back. "You seem a little down."

Dad! Dad! I'm in here, locked inside—

Oh, come on, the shadow sneered. *Your dad can't hear you. You best get used to being locked away. As long as I'm out here, you're in there.*

No! No—

"I'm fine," the shadow said.

"You don't sound it. Maybe it's time you took that vacation we used to talk about."

Now, rage bubbled up in the shadow, and Sage felt it struggle to maintain control. "I just need a little quiet time," it said. "I'll put in a few days at my place at Cos-Ob after I get back."

"I don't know, son—"

"Cosimo out." The shadow turned off the com.

Chapter 22

THE SHADOW MOVED through the world masquerading as Sage Rojan. In some ways, the experience was similar to Sage's encounter with past lives. But there was no fast-forwarding here. He saw through his own eyes whatever the shadow looked at and heard every sound that came through his own ears. If he chose, he could feel whatever his hands would touch, the warmth of the sun on his face, or the ruffle of the breeze through his hair. He supposed he would even taste what his mouth ate, although the shadow had so far not bothered to eat anything, instead running Sage's body on stored reserves.

The connection remained open twenty-eight hours of the Tidonese day. Sage could think of no reason for the continuous show, unless the shadow enjoyed taunting him.

After landing the shuttle, there was an announcement for Sage to go to the Operations room. Sage could sense that the shadow enjoyed his body's superb capabilities; flexing each muscle group independently, adding an extra swagger to his steps. Perhaps this was why it had worked to modify and improve his muscles and coordination from the first days of his infancy. They entered the room with its wide wall of monitors and projection equipment and the long conference table at its center. Sage's parents occupied one side of the table while BYSA's Director Brantford sat at its head. His parents stood as Sage entered the room, their faces clearing of the worry they had been holding between them.

"Sage—" his mother began. She approached with her arms wide to embrace him but the shadow brushed past her as if she didn't exist. The shadow took the seat at the furthest end of the conference table and folded Sage's hands across its glossy top. Trapped inside his own mind, Sage saw the hurt in his mother's eyes and watched her struggle to hide it from the rest of the room as she and Thaddeus retook their seats.

The sharp eyes of Director Brantford drilled into him from across the table. The shadow seemed unconcerned.

"Sage Rojan. You have violated protocol. Protocol you yourself put into place. Without scheduling in advance and without proper support crew, you took a shuttle past the pre-authorized orbiting height." Brantford leaned forward and pressed his fingers together, "Given the unauthorized use of BYSA property I am well within my rights to request a full explanation."

"What's going on, son?" his dad said.

The shadow smiled. "I believe I already submitted a full report outlining my intentions."

"Your report outlined the cost-benefits of producing highly valuable and completely indispensable materials in the weightlessness of space but it did not specify the need for that station to be situated at, what was it?" Brantford referenced his notes, "Six hundred thousand miles."

The shadow shrugged, "A minor change in plans. It was unavoidable."

"And yet you failed to carry out proper procedure. You have shown very poor judgment in the past week and it is my responsibility to inform you that you have been grounded in accordance with BYSA Mission Control Policies."

There was a flash of heat from his shadow.

His dad cleared his throat, "Son, I think it's time to take that vacation. You can take your motorcycle; get out of the city for a few days."

"Enough! I will not take time away from my work just to feed your silly whims."

His father's lips parted in shock. Genosa paled and shared a glance with her husband.

"My research is critical to the future of the space program. If it wasn't for me there wouldn't even *be* a space program."

"Did something happen out there in space?" his dad asked, "When you were out of contact for so long?"

The shadow ignored the question and stood. It leaned across the table towards the Director, "Let me make this clear. Bristol Industries supplies all of your funding. All I have to do is cancel your contract. Your resources will dry up in a matter of weeks and then we'll see who needs whose permission."

The Director sat back in his chair.

The shadow was right; there was nothing BYSA could do to stop Sage Rojan from doing what he wanted, not with the power of Bristol Industries behind him.

"I believe we're done here," the shadow said.

Brantford rubbed his forehead and sighed. "It seems we are." He closed the folder in front of him and stood.

Helpless, Sage watched the shock and distress on his mother's face as his dad put an arm around her and led her away.

· Ω ·

Sage struggled. The pain in his parent's eyes had renewed his will. He couldn't let the shadow ruin everything he cared about. He pounded at the webbing that held him frozen to the mockery of life that he could see but couldn't change. The net stretched around his blows, absorbing the energy of his fists and never quite loosening its hold.

Sage grabbed two handfuls of the stuff in front of his chest and pulled. The threads stretched to their capacity and Sage gritted his teeth, pulling harder, feeling the strain on limbs that weren't real.

After a long moment the confining web began to yield, then to tear, no longer impervious. Its fabric slowly parted and Sage's head squeezed through the rent. He reached his arms through the gap, and pulled it wider. Then suddenly his shoulders were going through, followed by his whole body, and he had time to wonder if this place still had a floor or if he would fall into an abyss.

Sage found himself lying on a hard surface in the dark. Good. He took a metaphorical breath and called upon the nameless sense which allowed him to know where things were in the landscape of his mind. The exit was *this way,* and not far. He stood and began walking on imaginary feet.

Outside the confines of his dreamscape, the shadow was returning to the Cos-Ob. Sage felt its attentions draw inward. Distantly, Sage felt his lips curl up. He may have freed himself from the net but the shadow was unconcerned. Sage stumbled through the dark, following his senses until his hands found the door through which he'd passed into this prison. He set his fingers to the back of his neck and drummed up his strength. He pressed against the portal. Nothing happened. He pressed harder, this time willing the door to open. Still nothing.

He backed off a step then swung an emblematic kick. His heel struck the hard surface with bone crushing force, the jolt of it sent a shock through his entire form.

The door did not yield.

He was still a prisoner. His body's ears brought him the sound of a low chuckle, coming from his own throat.

The shadow mocked him. "Why would I let you go anywhere? There's nothing you can do but watch."

· Ω ·

For ten days the shadow flaunted its control over Sage's body. Working long consecutive hours for whatever goal was next on its list; building more transporter discs, minutely adjusting the Quantronix, setting the robotic assembly line to build more of the matter-converting machines. Forgetting to eat. Flatly refusing all of Tamara's attempts to talk to him.

At first Sage had thought the shadow's earlier penchant for not letting him rest or eat had been a result of the spirit's lack of connection with the physical needs of his body but now he understood that the shadow just didn't care. It was too impatient to care. Sage felt himself lose weight even from within the confines of his inner mind. Whenever he caught a glance of the bathroom mirror he was troubled to see his eyes sunk deeper into his skull. He was pallid and the lack of life in his skin echoed the lack of life that stared out of his eyes.

Whenever he could, Sage tried to contact the outside world. If his parents or Tamara were present, he'd try to squeeze the optic nerves of his eyes, hoping to make his body shed tears which they might notice. He'd yell and scream, "Help me, it's Sage; I'm trapped in here." But the screamed words never left his actual mouth.

And the shadow had a way of cutting such episodes short, turning his body, using his feet to walk away. Then afterwards, reprimanding him, like a jailer yelling at an inmate, "Stay quiet in there. Nobody's going to hear your screams for help. Shut up. You're giving me a migraine."

Oh, a headache, Sage sneered. *You gave me splitting headaches for years. See how it feels to get back your own medicine.*

· Ω ·

A week later Tamara walked into Sage's office at Bristol Industries. Tamara leaned both hands on Sage's desk. "All right that's it," she said, "We need to talk about this."

"Go away. I'm busy." The shadow barely looked up from Sage's desk where he was adjusting a new quantum teleporter.

"Actually I don't think I will."

"You're just another employee. You'll do as you're told."

Tamara turned the screen away from Sage's field of view. "I'm not *just* another employee."

Sage watched from his blackness as the shadow readjusted its gaze to the young woman. In recent weeks, Sage had seen successful executives look away when the shadow stared at them. He wondered what they saw in that gaze.

Madness, of course. Whatever it was, Tamara was not afraid of it. In fact, Sage wondered if he caught a flash of conceit in her eyes. "What's going on with you? I mean, you've always been weird, but lately you're setting new standards."

"Mind your own business."

"You *are* my business." She straightened. "I'm the one responsible for getting you here, the one who built your future; the one who knows your past."

Sage heard the shadow grunt.

She crossed her arms. "Oh, yes. You killed the pirates and went into space. But that was yesterday. What have you done to make people love you lately?"

"I've got more important things to think about." He turned the computer screen back.

She leaned in and put her hand on his arm. "No, you don't. You may get to do whatever you want but that's only because people loved you once."

The shadow reclined back in his chair and laughed. It didn't sound like Sage's laugh, and it stopped Tamara cold.

She colored at his derision. "Listen, Sage... No, you know what? Never mind." She took a step away from his desk, a conflict warring in her eyes. "You used to be a quiet, modest genius," she whispered, "Now you don't seem to care about anything but yourself. Something's happened to you. Something's changed."

Sage felt a flutter of unease from his master.

The shadow narrowed his eyes, "You don't know what you're talking about."

Tamara shook her head. "You know I do." She turned and walked to the door, then stopped, her fingers on the handle. "When I look you in the eye, I don't see Sage Rojan looking back at me."

· Ω ·

When she was gone, the shadow locked the lab door and placed the modified quantum teleportation disc on the floor. He stood on it and a moment later stepped off the disc in the private Cos-Ob dome at BYSA, where it went immediately to check the data feed from the Quantronix.

For the first time, Sage felt a shock go through the entity. Something was not right with the data. He sensed the spirit's mind racing through scenarios faster than Sage could follow.

What's wrong? Sage said. *Another outcome you didn't plan for?*

"I can make you feel pain," said the shadow.

Won't change the situation. What's gone wrong?

Instead of answering, the shadow stepped onto the disc and instantly ascended to the space station. It went to the observation port and took a direct look at the accumulating dark matter outside the module.

It'd only been a few days since the shadow had last adjusted the rate of spin. But the black object obscuring the view of Tidon was gigantic.

It's growing too fast, isn't it?

The shadow stared at the black mass; Sage could feel the entity's anxiety swelling. Sage realized with a shock what the shadow had already detected: the newly spun matter was no longer held by the Quantronix's containment field. Instead, it had broken free and now accompanied the space station in a synchronous orbit, spinning ferociously of its own accord.

Each spin adding to its strength as it whetted its insatiable desire for more light.

You've done it, haven't you? You've overreached, and now you've let it get out of hand.

"Silence!" The shadow worked with Sage's hands, trying to use the Quantronix to slow the spin of the matter. But within moments Sage knew, from the spirit's spike in anxiety, the effort was futile.

The shadow's distress lessened its control. Now, for the first time, Sage not only felt echoes of the shadow's emotions but could see the shadow's goal fully formed in his mind. Making a moon was to have been ▲▼178✦✿'s demonstration of its abilities as an artisan. Impulsive and impatient by nature, it had chafed under the Empyrean's rules and restrictions. Whatever the process for working its way up to artisan might have been, ▲▼178✦✿ decided it would skip the preliminaries and go straight to the head of the line.

But, true to its nature, it had done a rush job.

Still, the shadow was self-confident. Sage felt it fight down its anxiety and begin looking for a way to solve the problem. And it was sure that the way would be found.

The shadow made an adjustment to the Quantronix's controls, looked out of the port, and then made another change. But a moment later, it was in confusion as some calculation failed to deliver the desired solution.

They traveled back to the planet, to Porturn City, to the lab. The shadow threw itself into a frenzy of investigation, much of it spent in the mental Library consulting the masses of shelved volumes.

I think the idea is that you master this stuff before you try your first prototype.

That won Sage stabbing pains that left him gasping. But it seemed to him that his only hope of loosening the shadow's control and escaping his prison was to keep the spirit off balance. What a ball of hungry dark matter growing six hundred thousand miles away might mean for Tidon, he didn't want to think about.

Chapter 23

SAGE BEGAN RECEIVING more and more of the shadow's thoughts as its level of anxiety rose. Sage now knew the spirit feared the possibility that the dark matter, grown large enough, would begin to suck light from the sun— would, in fact, ultimately destroy Sintosy. The hungry mass was growing rapidly, lengthening and expanding with each minute. The shadow's concern, however, was not for the destruction of lives on Tidon; but that the loss of a star would attract attention from the Empyrean.

The spirit mined its own memories; not the ones behind the white doors, but ones from past the Firmament, amidst the realm of power and light. Sage caught images of the shadow in the upper halls of the heavenly bureaucracy, studying blueprints, graphics, and texts pertaining to the formation of stars. Along with direct memories came other impressions: the spirit had been a minor functionary — a glorified clerk of the Empyrean — that had wangled its way into a region of the upper realm to which it had no right of access.

It had not studied the arts of the artisans. It's exposure to those complex disciplines was more like that of a messenger whose rounds took it through the offices of engineers and architects. It had learned "just enough to be dangerous."

But nowhere in the shadow's repertoire of remembered drawers and compartments was there a how-to manual that told what to do about a Quantronix gone rogue. Sage knew the spirit believed the problem had been a miscalculation of the rate of spin that had somehow engaged every newly created atom onto a synchronous, aligned vortex axis. The longer the thing spun, the less there was a chance of reversing the process. The renegade force was operating under its own rules; unstoppable once set in motion.

Sage expected this realization would concentrate the spirit's mind. Instead, its thoughts turned to what Sage could only call a daydream: the spirit proudly accepting congratulations, showing off the newly created moon to an admiring Empyrean bureaucracy.

How could an entity that had lived millions of lives, at every level over a span of a trillion years, have the emotional maturity of an adolescent? Something must have gone wrong somewhere along the line, unless the spirit had been created flawed in the first place. One thing was certain: no well-run universe could afford to allow this spirit to come anywhere near its operating machinery.

And there was no way the spirit, encased in visions of grand success in a discipline where it hadn't even mastered the basics, was going to solve this problem. In that moment Sage knew it would ultimately come down to him.

· Ω ·

The shadow stepped off the teleportation disc into the main room of Cos-Ob and froze as it took in its surroundings.

Tamara, leaning across Sage's workbench, her fingers flying over the computer's keys, jerked up as she realized he was suddenly standing behind her. She glanced at the door, surprise painting her face.

"What are you doing?" the shadow snapped. The darkness around Sage seethed with the flash of the shadow's anger. "How did you get in here?"

Tamara straightened and met his glare. "Give me a break; you're combination codes haven't changed since high school!" Her surprise had melted away leaving behind an equally heated anger. "And just for the record, whatever you're up to, it's about to come crashing down on your noggin."

The shadow's level of anxiety spiked.

It shoved her away from the workstation and took her place at the keys. "How dare you interfere with my—" It looked at the screen and froze. Every file on dark matter and the Quantronix was open across the display and a program bar was filling to completion in the corner.

Send All - Complete, flashed across the screen.

It rounded on Tamara with a growl. "What have you done?"

Tamara didn't back down. "What you should have done days ago! Now BYSA, the Bristol board, the government, the military... they all know what you've got growing up there."

Sage felt the shadow's anger rise to a boil. The darkness of Sage's inner prison flickered.

"They're convening a meeting. You've got three hours to decide what you're going to say to explain how you let a ball of dark matter get out of hand at the edge of Tidon's gravity well."

"It's under control." The shadow growled. But Sage was barely listening. The confines of his prison had changed. With each angry surge of the shadow's emotions the darkness sputtered like a reverse candle. Sage glanced down at his imaginary hands and realized he could see his fingers. The shadow's will was weakening, draining elsewhere. Sage went looking for the door.

Outside his dreamscape, Tamara shook her head, "You are seriously that arrogant that you would risk the ruination of an entire planet. Sage I promised never to call you crazy, but I take that back, you're out of your mind if you think you can get away with this." She raised her chin, blue eyes hard chips of ice, "You're way out of your league."

"That's a lie! This is my destiny." It prowled forward, muscles coiling and tensing. "How dare you assume—"

Her eyes narrowed, "I've been watching you. You're not everybody's favorite any more. I could show you the numbers." She ticked them off her fingers, "You've made no public appearances in months, you haven't invented anything since who knows how long, and the few times you do go outside, you act like a conceited jerk."

The door of his prison was solid under Sage's hands but this time, when he pushed, he felt it shift. He backed up a pace, preparing to draw his will around him.

The shadow had reached Tamara, its roiling black anger focusing with laser intensity. With a jolt Sage saw its intention.

No. Sage threw himself against the door. It shuddered but held. *No!*

Sage's hand under the shadow's control struck Tamara across the face. She stumbled and the shadow pursued her across the floor, fingers coiling into fists.

Sage hit the door with all his strength. It split down the middle with a solid *pop*. Light began spilling through the crack. Sage felt the rush of his own will returning to him and he threw his senses wide. *Stop!* He commanded.

Sage's body stilled. Sage felt the flush of surprise from the shadow. The shadow struggled.

You! What did you do? Let go!

Tamara regained her feet and pressed a hand to her cheek. Her eyes blazed undaunted. "That's it; you're on your own." She stalked to the door and punched the access pad; then abruptly she turned back. "You're going to be at that meeting or they're going to come and get you. And if they have to put you in a cage to get you there, I'll pick the size myself."

She left and the door slammed closed behind her.

Sage's body remained locked in the center of the room. He tightened his grip against the shadow's struggles to free itself. *I will not let you go.*

No? the shadow lashed out at him.

Sage stumbled and for a moment he seemed to be back in his body; feeling the dry air on his face, the sweat on his back, the complete control of his limbs. Then his vision darkened, tunneling inward, and he was falling.

· Ω ·

Dark. He was back in his mental body, standing before the cracked door.

An attack was coming. That was all that Sage knew.

The light pouring through the fissures in the door wavered as something moved on the other side. Sage backed away from the threat he could feel seeping towards him.

The door flung open. In the glare of the light stabbing in from the foyer beyond stood ▲▼178♦✿. It was now humanoid in shape, glowing with cool radiance, it wore no clothing and showed no signs of either gender or age. Its head tilted; a blank radiant disc with no eyes and no mouth.

The ovoid shape where a face should have been, passed through visage after visage. Tidonese faces, monkey faces, strange arrangements of hair and horns and scales, compound eyes and jagged mandibles, saucer-eyed, rubber-skinned faces, beaks surrounded by tentacles, scaly snouts full of teeth, yellow, slit-pupiled eyes, bird faces, fish faces—

Sage braced; there was nowhere to run. He would have to fight. The shadow stalked him, a nightmare creature confident and deliberate. Sage drew his will around him.

The shadow spread its arms wide, "This is my domain. You have no power here." Solidity grew from the floor, grasping Sage's feet.

He couldn't move. His feet were encased, as if in concrete—

Cool sweat flashed up Sage's neck. "Poor, stupid Sage." The shadow stood over him. Inscrutable expressions came and went in the blink of an eye. "Want to know how it was supposed to go? What your piddling life would have amounted to before I came along? Before, that is, you go away for good?" The shadow's voice preened. "You would've been an engineer— quite a good one." The shadow walked behind him, forcing Sage to twist in his imprisonment. "You would've gone into the airplane industry and ended up a grand old man with a half-dozen kids to your name."

"An engineer?" Sage pushed back the clammy fear.

"Oh, and you would have married that annoying Tamara Young and produced a passel of brats."

Life. Love. Achievement. Horror welled up inside him, and a yearning so powerful it drew tears to his eyes. "You denied me... *everything*."

"Everything?" The shadow tilted its ever-changing head, mildly puzzled. "I made you a national hero, famous from one end of Bella Yareo to the other."

"You're the one who wanted to be famous." The irony was a bitter stone in his mouth. "I only ever wanted to be happy."

"It's academic now," said the shadow, "because this is the part of the story where you fall off the edge of the world. Afterwards, I'll keep this body going for a while. It doesn't bother me to extinguish you. I used a body on Tidon to do a practice run decades ago. That human vanished just like you're going to. I'm not afraid to die. I've done it thousands of times. But you should be, with just one life to live."

The shadow looked up into the darkness above. "I believe your executioner is here." It raised a hand toward the invisible ceiling, and the distant beating of wings preceded a savage cry of hunger.

Sage recognized that sound. A memory from long ago: the thing with the leather wings. The thing that had chased Sage from the foyer of past lives the first time he'd wandered here.

"And its mate," said the spirit, "who's even bigger. I've given them enough of my power to extinguish your spirit."

"Spirit?" Sage stiffened, a spark of anger kindling in his chest. "You're saying I'm a spirit. That this was supposed to be *my* life?"

The shadow sneered. "You've done a poor job of connecting the dots— how else could your life have been different without me? You're a splinter, a visiting spirit. Brand new and still wet around the ears. And don't you dare think, for even a moment, that all those lives behind the doors are yours. Those are mine!" It snarled. "My memories which you have been snooping through for decades."

Sage clenched his fists. "This life was meant for me. You— stole my life."

"Finally you're starting to get it." Disdain flashed across the ever-changing face. Sage glared back at it and the multitude of expressions changed to cruel satisfaction. "I slipped past the Firmament Clearing Chambers and slid down your tether. I inserted myself into this human's body along with your newly created spirit, making its first visitation from the Firmament down into an organic. I chose you *because* you were brand new. Destined for a world I wanted to revisit. One *they* didn't want me to return to."

The shadow continued, "With you running this body, I was invisible, a second spirit, in this body, free to do what I wished. The Empyrean won't care that a first-time splinter on a nondescript planet runs a little faster or knows more than it should."

Sage struggled against the bindings around his ankles. "How could they not notice all the changes you've made to Tidon? All the leaps in technology that can't be explained?"

"Who cares what you think?" the shadow whirled. "When I head back up to the Firmament, I'll depart this body. The record of this life will go with me and get added into my main entity in the Firmament. And you'll get nothing because there won't be a spirit with the designation ❖❖1 in the Empyrean anymore."

❖❖1 *was that Sage's designation?*

"Your first splinter will be mine forever."

The full import of what the shadow had told him sank in.

For the past years, he'd harbored the thought that he could be a reincarnation rather than a lunatic, but he'd only ever thought of himself as a shadow of the shadow— a splinter, temporarily thrown off, only to be reabsorbed.

But now...

He wasn't a splinter of the shadow, he was his own spirit.

This may be my first visitation, but I am in the body I was meant to inhabit.

The legitimacy of that realization struck Sage. The shadow was the interloper. It was the one who didn't belong! Rage reared up in him. *His* rage, not the shadow's. Different. Potent.

A rush of wings whistled through the air above.

The shadow laughed again; low and ugly, "Here they come."

Sage looked up. He remembered defeating this monster once, back when the shadow had only intended to scare him into submission. A new level of confidence resonated within him.

Sage put his hand to the nape of his neck and began to drum, the sound echoed, rebounding in the darkness.

His drumming amplified, deeper, and filled him with an ominous power. He gathered his will beneath him.

The shadow cocked its multi-visaged head. "Oh, it thinks it has claws?"

Sage shook his head in disgust. "Each and every time. You never seem to figure it out, but every single time, you underestimate what you're up against. I may be in your domain but *you* are the one in *my* mind."

The glowing figure took a half step back.

Sage crouched, spotting the diving beasts. Energy pulsed, white hot, throbbing to the shaman's beat. He brought his fury up through the floor — through *his* floor — flooding through *his* dreamscape body. He channeled all that anger through his free arm, and towards his outstretched finger tips.

A rush of coruscating energy — the lightning to his drummed-up thunder — erupted from his finger tips. But this time the power was not directed at the monsters stooping from the darkness to seize him.

He directed all of it at his shadow.

The blast smashed the shadow backwards. It tumbled end over end, then struck the wall beside the open door, slumping to the floor— inert.

The flying monsters burst into flame and the pressure around Sage's ankles released. He was free.

He flung his head back, arms raised, greeting the fine drift of ash that floated down from the darkness.

But—

No time. He crept quickly but cautiously toward the shadow which lay on its side, glowing but unmoving, the front of its head still a parade of faces.

It wasn't dead. It gave off a kind of life force that Sage could sense— but it seemed to have lost its ability to act.

It's in shock.

Once the shadow returned to its senses, Sage wasn't sure what would happen, he wasn't sure he wanted to know. But for now he had some time.

Pearlescent grayness surrounded him. The door to the prison lay open. He made his way through the mist towards the exit, towards freedom. "Time," he said aloud, "to wake up."

Chapter 24

SAGE WOKE ON the floor of the Cos-Ob. His hands probed the torso of his body in an effort to confirm that it was really him.

A wave of relief washed over him. It was followed by the slow flush of dread. He didn't have much time.

He jumped up from the floor and dashed out the door, flicking his phone open as he ran. He had to get to Mission Control, pull the team together.

"Rojan here." Dad's voice.

"Dad. I don't know how long I have to talk, so just listen. I've been held hostage by my shadow— I'll explain later. It's done something—" The motorcycle was across the compound. He sprinted.

"Hold on, your what—"

"The shadow can take over any minute, Dad. Just get your team together at Mission Control. Right now. I'm on my way from Cos-Ob." He pressed the phone against his shoulder and pulled the bike off its kick stand. "The shadow was using technology, a machine, to spin dark matter and it's out of control—"

"Wait a minute! I can't—"

Sage pumping the starter hard. The engine caught.

"Dark matter—"

"Just do it, Dad, please! It's me. I need you."

"Okay. See you when you get here."

"Sage out." He slipped the phone in his pocket.

He twisted the throttle and the wheels squeeled as the bike hurdled down the hill towards BYSA. He leaned into each curve on the pavement. Freedom felt good, the summer breeze blew by, fresh against his cheeks. Gravel flew off the shoulder of the curve as Sage dropped the motorcycle into a sweeping turn. The toe of his boot tapped the pavement. Rubber bit asphalt and he hung on at the edge of the tires' adhesion. He felt the machine's power growing as he revved the bike.

Tamara!

There she was, walking down the long hill after she'd left Cos-ob. Sage saw her look back over her shoulder, scowling at the roar of the bike. He had to tell her, make her understand, get her to help.

Suddenly, the shadow was there.

Sage's right hand crushed the brake lever. The front tire ground to an instant stop, and the motorcycle bucked. Sage lost his grip on the handlebars and flew forward, catapulted from the seat. He landed in the thick brushwood as the motorbike crashed, tumbled, flipped, and rolled over him.

Fire raced across Sage's shoulders, neck, and head. Blue sky whirled overhead. There was a chugging mechanical cough, then— silence of wind in the scrub.

"Sage?" A distant voice. Tamara.

Sage's eyes blinked rapidly, trying to stay focused. He gasped for air. The shadow pushed at his control, squeezing him out.

Then Tamara was at his side. "Are you alright?" she asked.

"Tamara." His voice: constricted. Sage's right hand drove an already bloodied fist at Tamara's face, barely missing as she ducked to the side. Sage's left hand came up and grabbed her long hair, yanking her sideways. He tried to call out but the shadow had locked his throat.

Tamara screamed and seized Sage's maverick wrists with power far beyond her size. Her nails dug into the wrist of the hand that held her hair, until the grip released.

She pinned Sage to the ground, her weight on his chest. "Sage!" Tamara shouted. "What are you doing? Stop it!"

He couldn't breathe. He gasped, panic shooting adrenaline through him as he writhed on the gravel-spewed rock, pressed to the ground, feet kicking.

Inside, the shadow thrashed through his mind. Sage felt it like a hot whip flaying the inside of his skull.

The world faded.

"Sage!" Tamara yelled again. Then suddenly her lips were on his. Like a shock of cold water the storm inside froze. He blinked, his vision spinning, growing dark at the edges. Her lips were soft and cool against the burning of his skin. Sage's feelings for Tamara boiled unbridled to the surface as his pain was immediately forgotten. Sage lost the battle to stay conscious.

· Ω ·

If this was a dream, it was unlike any other Sage had ever experienced.

He was in a white world, without sky or ground.

Diffuse light surrounded him, but he could see that he had no actual body. In this place he was everywhere and nowhere at once but he was also not alone. Two figures met in the center of this world. Both glowed with an inner light, both were nondescript; featureless and yet unique. He thought he recognized one of them, perhaps by the sharp angle of its shoulders or the arrogant bend of its spine. The calm presence of one met the angry swirl of the other and suddenly Sage remembered.

The shadow... the spirit that was his shadow.

"▲▼178♦✿." The calm spirit spoke and the voice echoed like the silver chime of bells, "I am Assistant Supervisor of Visitations, ✛✛63✿✿. I have been monitoring your actions as per Empyrean direction."

The shadow flared then paled.

"I have been instructed not to intervene but I have come to my own decision." The spirit rose to its full height as if taking a large breath. "As Assistant Supervisor I am forcing you to relive your entire Visitation Archive in sequence."

"No!"

The calm spirit ignored ▲▼178♦✿'s outburst. "You are to fully re-experience each visitation to learn the lessons that you lack."

Anger and disgust radiated off the spirit, "You may, of course, try to speed the revision process. Learn as you go."

"You can't!"

"Only after you have completed every review from beginning to end for every splinter in your existence will my discipline be considered complete. Only then may you regain this conscious form."

▲▼178♦✿ lunged forward with a roar. The calm spirit held up its hand and the shadow stopped midstride as if held by invisible bonds. "Be careful ▲▼178♦✿, you have already threatened my vessel twice, it would be unwise to do so again now that you know who I am." Then with a snap of the spirit's hand the shadow blinked out of the glowing white world.

· Ω ·

Sage woke in the medical bay at BYSA. His head ached and his muscles, which had protected his bones by absorbing the worst of the crash, screamed in protest as he glanced around the room. His thoughts were fuzzy and he felt for a moment like he was wading through mud to remember anything other than the crash itself. Then he saw Tamara curled on the chair next to his bed and everything rushed forward. He gasped, suddenly out of breath.

"Tamara!"

She opened one eye and glared at him. "You should be sleeping." She shifted deeper into the hard plastic chair.

"But the shadow! The dark matter. Where's my dad? I have to tell him!" Sage scrambled against the tangle of the sheets.

"Calm down. He knows. The team received everything I sent to them."

"No you don't understand. The shadow! The shadow—"

"Yes?" she quirked an eyebrow. But Sage had turned his attention inward, to the emptiness inside himself, the sudden *roominess* of his mental interior. He stared at his hands, flexing his fingers one after the other. He waited but there was no resistance. He relaxed just a bit, and when the shadow didn't rise up to take control of his limbs, he breathed out in sudden wonder. "Am I free?"

"It's only temporary."

Sage glanced at Tamara, another memory tickling. Of a white world and two spirits instead of one. "You did this?"

She smiled, "Yes. And it felt good. I'd already decided to intervene but I was waiting for the right moment. But like I said this isn't permanent. ▲▼178♦✿ will be back once it finishes the task I set it to."

"Why? How? I don't understand."

She nodded then shrugged, "It's what I could manage under the circumstances. I'll explain it all to you soon. For now we have time to clean up his mess."

"So you're a spirit, like my shadow. Like... me. And everything I've experienced, all my life, is real?"

Her brows drew together in surprise. "You didn't know?"

"No." He could barely squeeze the word past his constricted throat. "I thought... I thought..."

She waited; comprehension and pity creeping into her face.

"When I was a child," he managed, "I was diagnosed with Dissociative Identity Disorder."

"Oh, Sage."

"I always thought—" he swallowed, determined to say his piece. "—that I was mad. Crazy. For a very long time I thought it was *me*, doing these things, that I was responsible—"

"Oh, Sage, no." She reached a tentative hand across the space between them. "You, your spirit, went through the cleansing chambers normally. How could you know anything of the Firmament and the Empyrean?" She cocked her head. "But you *do* know. Don't you?"

Sage averted his gaze to look out the medical bay window. "I thought everything, absolutely everything, was a complex, convoluted delusion—"

"Sage, it's real. The Firmament is real. The Empyrean is real. I'm here, from there."

"The shadow brought down all the secrets of the Empyrean and stored them in my mind. But it never really studied them. It doesn't really know what it's doing."

Tamara frowned, "So that's what it did and consequently how you already know so much about it. You stumbled into the Library that ▲▼178♦✿ was keeping in your mind."

They were silent for moment, both lost in their respective thoughts.

"Tamara, if the cleansing chambers are supposed to strip a spirit of its memories than how are you here?"

"What ▲▼ did to slide through the Firmament cleansing chambers was pretty sneaky. The Empyrean functionaries took a while to figure out its game. Till now, no one in the Empyrean had ever thought a spirit could cheat its way into the inner universe with all of its memories intact. I'm surprised it managed to get the entire contents of the Library as well."

"So even the Artisan was caught by surprise?" Sage asked.

"No." Tamara snorted. "Although I'm sure ▲▼178♦✿ would like to think so. As soon as it became clear that something had happened, the supervisors decided to send someone else down to keep an eye on the transgressor. I was sent as the spirit of Tamara Young. Unlike all spirits before me — except for ▲▼178◆✿ — I have my memories too. I'm the Assistant Supervisor, Visitations, for this galaxy," Tamara said gently. "My job is to monitor the situation."

"Monitor? But aren't you doing more than that already?"

Tamara glanced away. "That's a bit more complicated. And unfortunately we have more pressing things to attend to right now." Tamara stood. "Provided you're feeling up to it, we should join the others in the conference room. If anyone is going to get us out of this mess, it's going to be you."

· Ω ·

With Tamara's help Sage got out of bed, cleaned himself up, and ate a hearty breakfast. By the time he was ready for the postponed meeting Thaddeus had arranged, the senior military command, BYSA's top scientific staff, the best minds from Bristol Industries — including his mother — and the highest officials from the King's advisory council were assembled and waiting impatiently in the conference room.

The assembled experts viewed Sage with a variety of reactions. They had always seen him as their hero; now the cracks in his armor were clear to all as he moved stiffly into the room with Tamara's aid.

He and Tamara had agreed they couldn't reveal the secrets of the Empyrean to those attending. Such information would be impossible for most people to comprehend, and might send them into a panic— or precipitate catastrophic leaks to the media. Sage had no choice. He had to personally accept the blame for what the shadow had done. He had to stand, beet red, and face these men and women. Admit to over-stepping his boundaries; to going behind the backs of BYSA's officials.

Inarticulate with shame, Sage described erecting the new satellite. He assumed responsibility for inadvertently creating the maverick dark matter spinning light of its own powerful free will.

The president, as head of King Ferdason's advisory council, was the ranking official in the room. "Why? What drove you to make these decisions?"

Sage's throat constricted and his mouth went dry. "Hubris."

"Hubris!" the president choked. "Hubris? That's it? Not only did you put our lives at risk but you did it merely out of hubris?"

He bit down on his lip, trying to contain his wrath. "Let me understand this, Sage. Once the dark matter unleashes it cannibalistic appetite on Sintosy, there's no turning back. Am I right?"

Sage hung his head. "Yes."

"Eventually Sintosy will destabilize and explode." The president was red with fury. "That's what you said, wasn't it?"

"Yes, sir."

"And with that, obliteration occurs for the entire solar system. Have I got this right?"

Sage swallowed. He nodded, unable to speak.

"Sorry, Sage, I didn't hear you."

"Yes, Sir." Sage lifted his face to the ring of shocked experts. "Explain."

"When Sintosy is destroyed, it will create two new black holes, split from its core," Sage said. "The supernova, or the resulting blast from the explosion, will destroy every celestial body in its path and there will be two smaller black holes produced from each planet and each substantial moon in its wake."

"So, if I follow your explanation," Thaddeus said, "Each black hole will devour all the escaping light it can from its exploding neighbors. The explosive forces combined will push the black holes away from one another, which eventually act as seeds for new solar systems."

"Yes."

"But you said a star's death was *normally* a very slow process," The president went on without waiting for a reply. "Almost undetectable. But you sped it up by creating this light hungry dark matter. Now, unless we can get this dark matter under control, everyone on Tidon will die."

Sage lowered his head once more, and shakily slid into his seat.

The president threw his hands up in disgust and sat down.

"There's more," Thaddeus said, "I've been watching this thing through the space telescope. There's already a filament of light streaming into it from Sintosy. The phenomenon is not yet visible to the naked eye, but it will be soon. We may not have much time left."

"Sir. I can confirm that." A thin young man raised his hand.

"Selai?" Brantford nodded.

The solar astronomer, stood. "Sintosy's photosphere shows a rising number of high solar flares, firing outward past its outermost corona." the astronomer consulted his notes. "Its diameter has been a little less than 1,187,000 miles for many years, but in the past few weeks that has increased to almost 1,225,000 miles, a measurable 38,000-mile expansion."

"That's bad?" said the President.

"Yes," Sage said. "It means the dark matter is loosening atoms deep within our sun." He ran a hand over his face. "The star is already unraveling."

The dire mood in the room was palpable.

Brantford, director of BYSA, stood. "What's done is done," he said neutrally. "The courts can assign blame and punishment later."

"If there is a 'later'," the president growled.

Brantford acknowledged the point with a single nod. "But right now, we need to do what we can to avert this disaster. This is a job for the scientists."

"Please." The president waved a hand in Brantford's direction. "It's all yours."

"Dark matter," Brantford mused. "Until now, it was nothing but a theoretical concept. We need data. We need to know more about it. We need to calculate its mass and rate of growth. We need more information on its internal structure and composition."

"Right," Thaddeus said. "But first, we should turn off the Quantronix. We can have a team up there within days."

"That won't do any good," Sage said quietly. "It's already growing without the machine's direct input."

Several more ideas were thrown onto the table: Physically towing the black hole farther from the sun; building a screen in space to prevent Sintosy's light from reaching the black hole, someone even suggested trying to blow it up with the new bombs in production—

Wait, what if they could get it over to the planet's dark side? Put it in an orbit permanently in Tidon's shadow!

"I have a suggestion." Sage interrupted the debate on the potential effectiveness of bombs on something that fed off light energy.

The voices at the table instantly silenced.

"Well. Let's hear it," Brantford said.

"I originally placed the Quantronix into a geostationary orbit so it was in a permanent stationary spot right above BYSA and the Cos-Ob. It rotates in the same direction and at the same speed — with consideration for tangential velocity relative to Tidon — so that it could be observed every minute of each day from Cos-Ob."

"We saw that," Thaddeus said.

"What if we change its orbital position and speed so, in reality it stays hidden in permanent darkness behind Tidon."

"We'd have to be precise," Thaddeus said. "But... cutting off the light source should keep it from growing."

Brantford steepled his fingers, "The problem becomes, how do we go about moving it? It's spinning far too fast to even attach a cable."

A deep seated tug, the flicker of a lost memory, and suddenly Sage knew he already had the answer. The shadow had designed a tractor beam; it was already sitting on the assembly line.

· Ω ·

It was the middle of the night at BYSA control center. Sage listened on his headset to the voices of the two astronauts, Ashby and Grace, who had volunteered to execute the mission, "Reverse orbit." The big screen monitor was sectioned into multiple views: input from the shuttle Fortitude in front of Ashby and Grace, a camera trained on their faces, and two outside the shuttle, one facing forward, the other, aft. On the forward view, the stars were blotted out by a long, narrow area of absolute blackness.

Sage, Tamara and Thaddeus, along with the BYSA staff, listened and watched.

Six hundred thousand miles above Tidon, the shuttle man-euvered into position.

"BYSA." Grace's voice crackled over the headsets. "Requesting permission to activate beam."

Brantford, as chief of BYSA, hesitated, responded. "Permission granted. Careful, these are uncharted waters!"

Thaddeus touched Brantford's arm, but Sage was too far back to hear what his father said.

Brantford opened his channel. "Grace. Maybe you and Ashby should take an hour to de-stress. Stretch out. Defocus your minds. Eat."

"Negative, Sir," Ashby replied. "We'd just as soon get this baby to bed. Besides, there's no way we can keep this thing off our minds. Permission to move to tractor beam."

"Go ahead, Fortitude."

Sage leaned forward, studying the multiple screens as Ashby activated the mechanism.

A hand slipped into Sage's. He looked at Tamara, her face drawn and tense in the reflected flicker of the screen.

She didn't acknowledge his glance. Every ounce of her attention was focused on the screen, he wasn't even sure she knew she'd gripped his hand.

The beam's emitter hummed over the com as Ashby slowly upped its intensity. He had the targeting system pointed square at the heart of the dark matter.

Sage had made sure the particles it was emitting were as close to the containment field particles that the Quantronix had used initially, but his own experience with the matter's insatiability for light energy made his knees weak. If he had made even the slightest error in his calculations...

The ground crew let out a collective sigh as the beam locked on successfully. The faint glimmer of energy snaked ahead of the shuttle and disappeared in the void that was the nascent moon.

"Fortitude, good work." Brantford's voice was calm with suppressed elation.

"Thank you, sir." Relief was evident in Grace's voice, and the screen showed the two astronaut's faces reflecting their cautious optimism.

"Let's haul this baby around," Ashby activated the reverse thrusters with a delicate tap.

The tractor beam on the forward screen seemed to go taught as the shuttle began to pull away from the dark matter. The beam brightened slightly as if compressing under the new strain.

Tamara's hand tightened in Sage's.

"Wait," Thaddeus leaped forward. "That's not looking good—"

Grace drew in a sharp breath; her hands flying across her readouts and displays.

"BYSA?" Ashby's voice was tense over the crackle of the radio. "We're experiencing—"

The tractor beam, visible in the forward screen, pulsed, brilliantly rigid between the shuttle and the dark matter. The radio crackled.

"BYSA to Fortitude." Brantford stood, hand on the microphone hovering before his lips. "Ashby, what's going on there?

"Sir the tractor beam—"

"Disengage now!" Grace screamed. "Disengage!"

Agony in Ashby's voice. "We're being pulled—"

The black void suddenly loomed in the forward screen and numbers on the readouts flickered in astronomical ascension—

The screen went black.

No. This wasn't supposed to happen!

"What happened?" Tamara whispered. "Where are they?"

"BYSA to Fortitude." Brantford's voice droned in the silence. "BYSA to—"

"No feed." The communication technician's voice was low, choked.

"Get them back on line!" Brantford roared. "Right now, do you hear me? Get them back—"

"Sir, there's no feed." The technician's face lifted into the ghastly light of the monitor. "They're not transmitting."

"Get them—"

"Sir." A new voice. Selai, the solar astronomer. "Tracking from our satellites confirms. Fortitude is no longer out there."

· Ω ·

The photos Tamara spread on Sage's desk at BYSA Mission Control showed the night sky over Bella Yareo. Arcing from the western horizon, a thin stream of light terminated invisibly at a point.

"The hole's pulling more light from Sintosy," Tamara said. "It's visible with the naked eye now. These photos aren't enhanced. Anybody who looks up into the night sky can see what's happening. We told the people of Bella Yareo that it's a harmless experiment, six hundred thousand miles away. But with the weather changing so fast..." She took a cleansing breath. "The BYSA information desk is flooded with calls."

"What are we telling them?"

"Not the truth," she said. "There'd be mass panic. We're putting out a story that it's all part of some new wonder that Sage Rojan is dreaming up, to make their lives better than ever."

"Sage Rojan. Hero," he said bitterly, shuffling the photos back into a pile.

Chapter 25

AFTER THE LOSS of Ashby and Grace, Sage buried himself in his mental library, searching for a new solution to the ball of dark matter that was siphoning off the sun. He'd already spent what felt like a lifetime amongst the shelves. And yet nothing was giving him answers. It seemed that once the Recycliun process was started, there was no known way to stop it. Frustrated, Sage left the Library and took his efforts to the tiers of white doors.

Tamara had told him not to open or enter any of them. Somewhere amongst the thousands of them, his shadow was racing through its memories, struggling to return. But Sage couldn't help but consider that the answer he needed was somewhere buried in the shadow's past lives.

Sage wandered the levels. Trying to remember which life each door held behind its numbered face. The shadow had been right, he'd spent decades snooping through them; he should be able to remember if there had been something—

—door 67-213.

The teleportation discs... Inside that life, the shadow had been an android, the planet's last sentient being; every other living sentient had been destroyed. The world it inhabited had been scattered with discs, most of them still operational. Was it possible, even though the shadow had lived that life generations ago, that the discs could still be there? Sage wouldn't know unless he tried to get there using one of the discs the shadow had built here.

He knew the discs could travel a nearly limitless distance. But they needed coordinates.

Sage stared at the door. Coordinates hadn't been on his mind when he'd stumbled through this door the first time. He knew he'd watched the android enter some but he couldn't remember what they were. He would have to check but that meant going through the door...

The idea of going against Tamara's warning made him uneasy. If the shadow was anywhere near this memory Sage might inadvertently release it. But this was the only idea that Sage had stumbled on.

Sage reached for the handle and bit his lip. With a deep breath he walked through the door.

His world tipped as he sank into the recorded past life. Things reshuffled and suddenly he was right way up again and the memory began to play.

The vision opened with the android on its space station home, filling its satchel with supplies. *Perfect.* It was already preparing to make a trip down to the surface. Sage snuck a peek over the shadow's shoulder as the android entered coordinates and transferred down to the planet. He took a moment to memorize the coordinates he'd read. Elated by the speed of his discovery, Sage scurried the player to the end, to see if the world had repopulated in the android's lifetime. But the android had only survived a few hundred years more, its parts rusting away. The world had still been empty at its death. The room went black.

Sage needed to get back to his waking life. He had to tell Tamara.

He left door 67-213, turning around one last time to see the ▲▼178♦✿ insignia. A shiver travelled down his spine.

Sage had nearly been the shadow's latest victim. But, after all this time of exploring the spirit's past lives, Sage had come to realize one thing: nowhere in the sixty-seven recycles and trillion year history of the inner universe did any species survive from one cycle to the next. Each and every species was along for only a short terminal ride.

· Ω ·

"Sage. Sage!"

Sage swam up from his dreamscape, prodded by the shrill note in Tamara's voice. He surfaced, and opened his eyes. Searing light streamed through the low window over his cot at Cos-Ob, silhouetting the young woman's upper torso as she shook him. He lifted a hand. "I'm awake."

He sat up, feet on the warm tiles, as he shook the layers of sleep away. He ran a hand through his hair and squinted at her. "What's up?"

She slid the window curtains back. "Look."

Sintosy was slowly falling below the western horizon, burning in a flawless half-dark sky. Streams of fiery gas stretched out from its corona and disappeared into an inky blackness higher in the sky. It had been six days and even in this blink of astronomical time, the heat wave that struck the planet with the acceleration of the sun's outpoured radiation was beginning to shrink bodies of water, moisture feeding into swirling winds. Three hurricanes had already smashed on Bella Yareo's shores.

Bristol had kept Tamara working to the point of dropping, spinning the news, but rumors and hysteria bypassed Bristol's propaganda and his iron fist on the public media. Derogatory posters blaming Sage had begun showing up on every billboard and post, depicting him as a monster. "Rojan has no solution, except to say, 'Burn, baby, burn.'"

"Down there." Tamara nodded to something out of his line of sight.

Sage stood on legs that still ached from his bike accident and shuffled to the window. Below the hillock where the desert observatory had been built, a mob — an army — of people surrounded the barb-wire-topped fences of BYSA. Bristol's private security forces manned the pitifully few towers interspersed along the fence. More men with body armor and shields lined the inside of the complex. Sage sighed, too tired to form a reaction. It had all been building to this.

"It's not just us." Tamara let the curtains drop. "Bristol Industries' in Porturn is under siege too."

Tamara bit her lip. "Sage... the house you grew up in... it was torched last night—"

Sage lifted his head in alarm. "Mom and dad? Were they—"

"Your dad's fine. They're both in a guarded unit at the hospital."

"Hospital?" Fear gripped Sage's throat and he slipped into a chair.

"Your mom was hit by a rock in the back of the head as they were trying to escape. Sage. She's in a coma." Tamara sat in the chair opposite the small table and took his hand. "The doctors have every reason to believe she's going to recover. The early signs are good."

Dackt! Why had Sage let the shadow control him all those years? He should have fought harder, found a way to get rid of it. *The shadow. This was its fault. This—*

Sage stood up. He had to get to Porturn.

"What are you doing?"

"I have to get to the city. I have to see them."

"You can't get out of here. Didn't you see that mob? They'll tear you to pieces."

Sage turned, and grabbed her hand. "Yes I can. And you can too."

Tamara looked at him in disbelief.

Sage told her about the planet where the shadow had lived a past life during 67-213, how it had used a transportation disc to instantly travel between planets, and how the shadow had already built and used the discs.

"And," he added, "through the android's eyes I saw a biosphere which might be close enough to Tidon's for our survival. If the pads still exists— we can move our population there."

Tamara drew a hand impulsively to her face. "You can't physically move over two hundred million Bellanese to another planet in the time we have left. And how will you convince the people? Now that they hate you? Then too, what about the people on the other continents? What becomes of them?"

He rubbed a hand across his face. "I know! I know! But it's the best we've got right now. We need to at least try."

She blinked and nodded. "If we could build more transit discs— Our industrial complex might be converted to ramp production—"

"Then you agree?" He took her hands in his. "This is our best chance. After this, all we've got left is begging the Artisan for a miracle."

She glanced away from him. "We should give this a try."

· Ω ·

"It's a long shot." Sage regarded the conference table surrounded by the dubious — and in some cases, hostile — faces of Bristol's top engineers in the BYSA conference room. "In fact, it's a way-to-hell-and-gone long shot, but it's the only one we've got."

He gestured to the grey disc he'd placed on the floor at one end of the big room, and then to the second at the other end. If he was to have any chance at saving even a fraction of the people of Bella Yareo, he had to convince these engineers. Now. "Watch."

Sage stepped onto the first disc and entered the coordinates on his hand console. Shimmering colors danced over him moving from his feet and he was gone. Instantly, he was the object of wide eyes and the cause of some open mouths as he reappeared, standing on the other disc. "Instant transit," he said, "and it works over any distance. In fact, it operates in a realm where distance doesn't actually exist."

BYSA Director Brantford put his hands up to squash the swell of hushed whispering. "Leave aside how it works!" he snapped at the group. "Time for that later." He turned to Sage. "And where will the evacuees go?"

"To another planet," said Sage.

"Another planet!" the president exploded. "Is it safe? What do we know about it? How will we—"

"I've been there," Sage said into the stunned silence. "Hopeland is different from Tidon. No moons. A different solar system in a different arm in this galaxy. Hopeland will have its challenges, that's for sure— weather, shorter days, a colder climate. It will take work to make it our own, but it's safe and uninhabited and if we start now, we can make it."

"This isn't rescue, it's a jail sentence!" the president cried. He pointed a finger. "You did this!"

Brantford stood. "If you don't want to go, give up your privileged place at the front of the line," he snapped. He turned to Sage. "Can we transport everyone?"

"We need to try."

The president passed his hand across his face. "Another planet," he said.

"Mr. President, we have a lot to do before Tidon becomes too hot to support life," Sage said. "May I continue?"

The president nodded, subsiding into his own world.

Sage pointed to the graphics displayed on the digitized wall. "The coordinates of the receivers have to be precisely inputted so there is no cross-transit interference. Our first explorers can take half of the first run of new discs with them to Hopeland. Thereby doubling our transit capacity with each production run. The other half of the discs get set up here at BYSA Mission Control. We'll organize all evacuation procedures from here. Then we can start moving people and equipment."

"Look." Tamara activated recorded footage on the wall. "We already sent a camera there and back: coordinates 542:4:6295:2 — Galaxy Melorius 542 — Hesdum Spiral Arm 4, next arm to ours — Star Terrance 6295 — Planet Hopeland."

A scene appeared: a blue sky with white clouds and a yellow sun, above a gently rolling landscape of prairie with a row of trees along a stream. The camera's audio pick-up played sounds resembling flying insects and the far-off calls of birds.

"After the camera," Sage paused, looking around to catch the eyes of everyone around the table. "I went and took a look." He heard a gasp and saw his father staring at him in horror. "I'm back; and I'm fine."

The gravity on the new world was less than Tidon's. The grass had not cut his legs open, the sun had not blinded him with ultraviolet emissions, and he had not fainted from lack of oxygen. He'd walked a few minutes in a straight line, turned ninety degrees and explored in another direction, then angled back to the disc.

"The foliage is different, but not terribly so. I could see a big lake or an ocean off in the distance. I saw no sign of cities or settlements of any kind. I heard no electromagnetic communications on any frequency. This is our best shot."

Tamara turned away from the screen to address the assembly. "We'll set up solar power installations, bring in light vehicles for our reconnaissance patrols to find promising sites for settlements. Flashlights, hammers, nails, tents; crops to plant and animals to stock."

It would be the greatest collective undertaking in Bellan history.

"In fifty years, a hundred at the most," Sage summed up, "Hopeland could be about as technologically advanced as we are today."

· Ω ·

By morning, Bristol, the King, Tamara, and the various bureaucrats were consulted in their respective bastions via secure link, and the permissions were given. With Sage's help, Thaddeus' team re-scaled the assembly line and production of the discs began. But with the riots — and without the freedom to easily move goods from location to location — Sage's team had their hands tied. Producing new discs required raw materials.

Sage went on the air, trying to quell the upheaval and explain what had happened. He took the blame, reduced to saying that the dark matter was the result of an unforeseen accident and that everything that could be done was being done. He brought up the word 'evacuation.'

The prospect of evacuation panicked the people. Some beat on the doors at Bristol Industries, BYSA, even the King's palace, demanding their place in line. Mistrust sabotaged an evacuation lottery, with thefts and murders for precious low-numbered tickets. Others simply burned and looted, seeing nothing but hopelessness through their fury. A stream of armed helicopters brought Thaddeus a trickle of raw materials, and slowly, the first transit discs were cranked out and tested.

· Ω ·

Sage materialized in his office in Porturn exhausted and weary. They were as far along as they could be with production; the material shortages had once again ground them to a halt.

Sage made his way to his father's lab. Thaddeus, still overwrought by Genosa's condition, barely grunted his greeting, his eyes as dark and as shadowed as Sage had ever seen them. When he failed to respond to Sage's prompting to get some rest, Sage decided to leave his dad to his work and return to his own offices. But there was nothing to do there either, so he sat at his desk and leaned back in his chair. A broadcast droned quietly just within his view. Tamara joined him shortly after and pulled up a chair to sit quietly beside him. Together they watched Duggin Bristol on the late news, a clip of the billionaire's helicopter departing its truncated pyramid and landing on the courthouse roof, followed by an interview outside the judge's chambers. The big man, surrounded by his bootlickers, gleefully waved a sheaf of papers.

"Sir," the reporter was saying. "There are those who say your case was shaky, and the judge only ruled in your favor because of your position and wealth."

"No!" Bristol cried, raising a fist. "King Ferdason appoints only wise men to be judge."

"...or that the judge took the opportunity to err on the side of public opinion." The reporter thrust his microphone back in Bristol's face.

"Again, I say. King Ferdason appoints only wise men to be judge."

"There, you have it, folks." The reporter turned his harried good looks toward the camera. "His Honor, Judge Thatcher, today ruled that the contract between Duggin Bristol and Sage Rojan, giving half of the industrialist's massive empire to the rising young genius has been declared void. Bristol keeps control of Bristol Industries, and the young man who is being labeled 'the destructor of Tidon', has been expunged from the company."

"Of course," Bristol grabbed the microphone from the reporter, "means nothing if world ends. Me, Duggin Bristol, man of principle."

Tamara reached across his desk and turned off the monitor. "I guess you're fired," she said with a wry smile. "I guess that means your parents too huh? Along with me, since you *were* my job."

"Petty vindictiveness."

She shrugged, "I bet he's just angling to be the first man off the planet."

· Ω ·

Bristol arrived at BYSA via helicopter in a less-than-amiable mood. The mob gathered outside of the Bristol Industries headquarters in Porturn had smashed their way past a police blockade and trashed the place. BYSA was the only protected place he could go.

Sage and Tamara were sitting down to a working dinner when Bristol barged into the office, arguing lawyers in tow. "I wish see this new world," Bristol said. "Be first man on new Hopeland."

"Sage has already been there." Tamara said, exchanging I-told-you-so looks with Sage.

Bristol signaled for a flunky to bring him a plate. "Then I be first settler."

"And stake out the first land claims?" Tamara teased.

Bristol didn't react to the sarcasm. "I am businessman," he said. "I go, I do business."

"I thought we were no longer partners." Sage said sarcastically. "You took back my shares of the business and fired me. Tamara's too."

Bristol shoved Sage's work aside and leaned on the table. "You use my money, my men, my equipment. I go first."

"Then you'd better shred that court order," Sage said.

Tamara held up her hands. "Whoa, you two. We don't have time for this macho one-upmanship. We still all need each other here."

Bristol pursed his lips and then blew air from his mouth. "If I shred court order, then I go to new home first? OK. Why make big deal over small piece of paper. You keep half of what we now got. I keep one hundred percent of what I find on Hopeland."

"Okay, but we're sending a military reconnaissance team first," Sage said. "We need to set-up properly before anyone else goes."

Bristol's face darkened. Tamara kicked Sage under the table.

"But you can be the first civilian!" he said.

The lawyers looked at each other. One of the Bristol's men said, "You would have to sign a waiver, Sir. In case..."

"I sign waiver to walk on moon. Bring me paper."

"Here," Tamara said, she produced a piece of paper and pen out of her bag. She indicated to the men standing behind Bristol. "All these wonderful lawyers can be witnesses."

Bristol pulled his glasses from his pocket and looked at the single page suspiciously. "It says I refute judge's order. All previous documents enumerating Sage Rojan as half owner stand in place."

"That was fast," Sage murmured to Tamara.

"I was pretty sure this would happen," she replied.

With a flourish of his pen, Bristol signed, and threw the paper in Sage's face.

· Ω ·

By midnight, the first ten-man recon team was scheduled to go to Hopeland. They went armed, just in case something had changed, or they met predatory beasts, but their instructions in the event of meeting intelligent beings was to offer peaceful greetings.

The first three soldiers went through, one after another. Each carried weapons, gear, supplies, and two pebbles: one white, one black. The first soldier sent back a white pebble. All clear. The second went through and sent back his white pebble, then the third.

"I go now," said Bristol.

"My orders are—" said the colonel leading the mission.

"Irrelevant," said the billionaire, stepping onto the disc.

Sage leaned over to whisper to the colonel. "We've always found it's best to just let him have his way."

The military man shrugged and pressed the switch. The industrialist disappeared and the next soldier moved onto the disc. He underwent transit and moments later white pebbles signaled their safe arrival onto Hopeland.

Two more soldiers went through, white pebbles received. But then the seventh member of the recon mission disappeared with no pebble sent back.

"Wait," said the colonel.

The next man who was to go through stopped at the edge of the disc. They waited, but nothing came through.

"Is it functioning?" the colonel asked Sage.

Sage consulted the readouts. "It seems to be. May I?" Sage took the control from the officer and pressed the sequence of buttons that would transmit back to BYSA whatever was on the other disc.

Still no pebble. But the disc was now covered by a fine white ash.

"What is that?" said the colonel, stooping to run a finger through the stuff. He rubbed it between finger and thumb. "It's greasy."

Sage turned to the soldier about to go through. "Your surveillance gear. Your camera."

The soldier touched one of his pockets. "Yes, sir."

"Put it on the disc and set it to begin taking pictures in ten seconds, one frame per second. Wide angle panoramic shots."

Sage crossed the room to where a model of the solar system had been carelessly pushed aside to make space. He gutted it of its turn base and set it on the disc in the center of the room.

The soldier looked to the colonel, and at the latter's nod, he placed the camera on the disc. "Set for panoramic sweep, one frame per second. Timer's on."

He stepped back and Sage spun the turn base. He sent the camera to the other world. Fifty seconds later he brought the camera back. It returned, smeared with more of the white ash, still taking pictures. The soldier recovered the device.

"Let's see what it saw," the colonel ordered.

He and Sage shared the camera's display. The sky was still blue, the trees along the stream were still there, but the gentle, grassy slope leading down was now charred.

"Wild fire?" asked the colonel. "The disc set off a fire and they ran?"

But then the display showed the next picture, from a different angle as the camera rotated fifteen degrees. More charred grass. Close to the camera was a dark object, slightly out of focus.

"Can you fix the focus on that?" asked Sage.

Tamara took the camera and worked its controls to enhance the close-up of a human head, lying face-up. The profile was recognizable, despite the seared skin.

"Duggin Bristol," Sage whispered.

Pale with shock, Tamara turned the camera display to the next image: charred clothing with burned flesh protruding from cuffs and collars.

The camera continued to show its contents. The last image was taken facing up the slope from the grey disc.

A multi-legged walking vehicle, resembling a metal centipede, with a long tube extending from its front, clearly scanning for more intruders. The contorted bodies of the soldiers lay scattered before it.

From the tube's open end a few wisps of grey smoke drifted skyward. Beside it were several four-legged figures in jointed armor, each with two arms carrying long-barreled weapons.

"Can they use the disc to transport here?" the colonel whispered urgently.

"Yes. But I can make it non-functional."

"Hurry. Do it! Now."

Deep inside Sage's mind he thought he detected the sound of laughter.

Chapter 26

"I WAS HOPING it wouldn't come to this. I'm not sure how sympathetic the Artisan will be." On the mattress at Cos-Ob Tamara held Sage's hands as they sat cross-legged facing one another. Since noon, the air conditioning had been cut back to save the emergency generators, and since midnight, it had been off. The room was sweltering, and desert winds raged outside.

"How could it not care that millions of people are going to die?"

"You don't understand Sage. This is the Artisan. The great creator, who has been here through every recycle of the universe. A billion people are just a few grains of salt in the ocean. Trust me, this isn't going to be easy."

"But we have to try."

Tamara sighed. "I know."

Sage took a deep breath. "Okay so, how do we do this?"

She dropped her gaze. "I can't be of much help to you for the first part. You're going to have to find the tether that connects you to the Firmament on your own. Then it's a matter of climbing. Don't worry, I'll be making my own journey. I'll be waiting in the Firmament when you arrive."

"And ▲▼178◆✿? Is it still busy reliving its past lives?"

"That's the tricky part. It's close to being finished by now. And once done ▲▼178◆✿ may decide to either regain the use of your body in an attempt to find out what we've accomplished. Or, and this is more likely, it will travel up the tether to seek an audience with the Artisan and argue its case. If that happens, you'll have to make it to the Firmament first."

Sage tightened his grip on her fingers. "So it's a race."

"Yeah." She nodded. "Ready?"

"Ready as I'll ever be." With that he closed his eyes, summoned up his lucid dreaming technique and in moments he was striding across the vast mosaic of his mind toward the aqua curtain that led into the foyer of past lives.

Sage stood in the foyer, looking at the tiers of corridors with their myriad of doors. The tether would be here, but he would have to find it. He glanced around, wondering when his shadow would materialize. Surely it wouldn't take long for Tamara to find her own tether — she probably already knew where it was.

That was what troubled Sage. The shadow knew this realm better than he did. If all the shadow needed to do was beat Sage to the top of the tether then it wouldn't even need to attack him straight on. It could be climbing the tether right now.

Sage squeezed his eyes shut to think.

Behind the doors were only memories. Whatever capabilities the spirit possessed, it could not edit one iota of what it had already lived and recorded. The Library, too, was only a memory. And the great mosaic was simply a schematic of Sage's mental powers, laid out in a format that allowed the spirit to tinker and augment Sage's abilities. But there was one place where the shadow clearly had the capacity to create new facts; where it had built the prison that had held Sage. The realm of grey mist and darkness.

Although the room was behind one of the white doors, it did not contain any record of a visitation. The room had been created by the spirit, and disguised to look like a past life, because it was the one place where the errant spirit was vulnerable.

Sage opened that door.

Somewhere inside, hidden by nebulous vapors, was the end of the singular tether that tied the shadow and Sage to the Firmament. Sage had only to find it. And so he groped and wandered through what seemed to be an endless mist, his outstretched hands meeting nothing. All the while, he was aware of the time slipping through his grasp.

Nothing.

How much time had passed? How many Tidonese had died from the soaring heat, horrific storms, and civil chaos? As the infrastructure in Bella Yareo failed, what would happen to his mother, clinging to life through fragile, technological support?

You'll never fiiinnnddit. The shadow's singsong words were a hint of a whisper, surrounding Sage, emanating from every direction at once, dissipating into the gloom.

Sage waited.

Time stretched.

He took a step forward, but then stopped himself. This would be just what the shadow wanted; Sage to walk willingly into another trap.

Suddenly, Sage was struck hard, sending him sprawling. The glowing spirit rushed past him, disappearing into the mist.

Sage was on his feet in a moment, ready to race after the spirit, but again he stopped himself. He would not play the shadow's game. Not this time. The flash of the shadow's burning form blazed momentarily through the fog, then another flash from a different direction. And another. Sage felt himself lose all sense of direction but he stayed where he was, sensing the shadow's growing frustration when he didn't move. It must be close. Or else why would the shadow be trying so hard to draw him away. The shadow blazed passed him and this time he saw what he wanted. The tether. Illuminated by the shadow's own glow. It gleamed like a shining ladder of tightly braided silk rope; rising through the mist and attached seamlessly to the floor.

Sage leapt for the highest rung he could reach, his feet scrambling onto lower supports. The ladder trembled. But far above, the shadow was already climbing. Ascending at phenomenal speed up through the mist.

Sage concentrated on the rungs under his own hands. Climbing as fast as he could go. It took no more than a dozen rungs to bring him out of the mist and into a place where the air — not air, metaphorical air — seemed as clear as purest crystal.

Far above him, the shadow scrambled higher. The spirit was a glowing spot on the grey ribbon that soared impossibly high into the sky that was not a sky. Above them was nothing, no cloud, no blue, no sun, moons or stars — just the swaying rope ladder rising into infinity, dwindling to a thread, then to a gossamer, before being lost in the immensity.

And all around him, too, Sage saw thousands, millions of tethers. He knew these ties belonged to those still on Tidon. Most were empty, but on many he could see motion; splinters of spirits descending to take up the duties of a new life; others ascending after death. He wondered which one of them was Tamara.

He couldn't tell. All he knew for certain was that he was climbing and so was the shadow, and that he'd better climb faster.

Out of the corner of his eye, Sage noticed a nearby humanoid spirit ascending its tether without the necessity of moving arms and legs; floating up as if toed by an invisible line. The ladder was no more than a metaphor— it was not his phantom limbs that performed the climb; it was his will.

He took one hand off the rung it had been grasping, and began tapping the back of his neck. The drumming sounded.

Climb, he told his body, *climb fast, soar up this tether.*

He slid smoothly up the gray silk, the drumbeats urging him higher, the hand that gripped the ladder's side rope slipping upwards without friction. He willed his speed to increase. He would have felt an onrush of air against his upturned face, if there had been any air to push through.

Another thought: Sage willed himself to simply disappear, and appear directly to the top of the tether. But apparently that was beyond his capabilities.

The shadow's form glanced back and it seemed surprised at Sage's approach. It turned back to the ladder above it and put on a new burst of speed.

Sage drummed harder, so that the clear ether around him echoed with his beat.

The shadow strained to rise faster but again Sage slowly gained. *Faster. Higher.* He would soon be within touching distance of the creature that had twisted and tormented his life.

He dug deep within himself for power, for life force, for any source of vigor that would let him eclipse the figure above him.

It was strange; to be trying hard. It felt good.

All his short life, accomplishments had sprung from his head and hands without effort. He'd lost very few contests so his victories had had no real meaning. But this time a triumph over his lifelong taskmaster and adversary would mean everything.

The thought gave him power. Time passed, measured only in the sound of his own shamanistic heartbeats that echoed all around him. He gained on the shadow, closing fast.

And then—

Beyond his adversary, there was an end to this great climb.

All the tethers disappeared into a layer of mist, like a worldwide overcast of purest white. Unlike the others Sage saw ascending, he and the shadow approached the ceiling with rocketing speed.

Sage could almost reach out and touch the shadow. They entered the mist, and Sage was surrounded by a cool glow.

He looked up his tether —

And the shadow's foot filled his field of view.

Sage ducked, as the kick scraped across the top of his head and down his shoulder. There was no pain, nor any real shock of impact, only a burning sensation where the spirit's foot had grazed him.

He stopped dead, clinging to the tether by one hand.

The shadow drew up its leg again for a second kick.

I don't think so. Sage seized the ankle of the shadow's cocked leg with his free hand, and yanked. It kicked nothing but ether.

A gleam flashed in the shadow's hand.

A knife.

A knife?

In an instant, the spirit had wrapped the tether around its legs and inverted itself, sawing the threads between itself and Sage —

No!

Was there gravity here? Would he fall? Would he return to his sleeping body in Cos-Ob and wake? Or would he die in his sleep?

With immense effort, Sage threw a hand over his head and gripped the shadow's wrist, arresting the sawing blade.

The shadow snarled. *You will not speak to the Artisan!*

Sage grasped the ladder above the knife with his other hand. The shadow pushed with its knife hand, forcing the blade against Sage's strength and across the ropes.

Strings popped and sprung. The tether groaned. One more slice; that's all it would take. The shadow jerked its arm but this time Sage pulled over and down. The momentum of the shadow's thrust was thrown into the not-air over Sage's shoulder.

The shadow lost its grip with its legs and it tumbled past Sage, yanking its arm from its socket, swinging like a dead weight from Sage's hand.

The shadow glared up at him. *Now's your chance. Let go. You want to. You've always wanted to.*

Sage clutched at the rung of the ladder. *You're coming with me. To face the Artisan*. He willed himself upward, into the mist, dragging his burden.

No! The shadow flicked its wrist, twisting its arm out of Sage's grip. In an instant, it was gone, fallen. Mist swirled about Sage, as he clung to the ladder.

Sage stared below in shock. There was no cry, no sound of the shadow striking— anything.

Had he killed his shadow? His one constant companion since birth. Hated enemy, but teacher, too. The one who knew his every thought, every feeling...

Sage lifted his face to the mist. He could not hang here on this tether for eternity. There were millions of people on Tidon who were counting on him. His mother. His father. Tamara would be waiting for him. Slowly, he willed himself to rise.

He did not know how long he ascended through the mist. All sense of speed, or even of motion, gone. He could see nothing, hear nothing, feel nothing but the sense that the tether was still there under his hands.

The mist thinned above him, or at least the omnipresent glow brightened. *I've made it*, he thought.

Higher, he told himself. *Finish it.*

A tremor on the tether was his only warning.

A roar of anger rose from below him, and the red-hot hand of the spirit closed around Sage's ankle. Rage blasting him like a blazing furnace.

The shadow yanked at him with such force, that Sage was almost pulled from the tether.

Terror jolted Sage to action.

He wrapped his arms through the rungs, and raised his free leg to kick at the unseen adversary. His foot struck something, hard. The grip on his ankle loosened, and he kicked again at the same spot.

But this time the shadow seized Sage's other ankle and held on. To Sage, it felt as if iron fetters, still hot from the forge, had been clapped about his ankles.

No! Sage shouted into the mist. *I was free!*

Since infancy, this selfish, arrogant creature had ridden him, oppressed him, and used him like a slave and a beast of burden. His life had been twisted and perverted to this cor-rupted spirit's purpose, and that purpose had turned out to be a foolish, destructive act of pride. And now, when relief was finally within reach, the spirit meant to pull him from this tether and cast him back down into his body, to seal him there until the sun exploded.

Sage could feel the entity's grip dragging him down. He had outmaneuvered it before, but if this was a contest of strength,

Sage knew he would lose. How could he compete with a being that had lived a trillion years?

The light above his head was brighter. *Maybe, if I can just get my head out of the mist-barrier, I can—*

Call for help? the shadow's laugh was vile.

Sage shut everything from his mind but the image of himself rising; the need to pull himself up.

The spirit tugged at his ankles, trying to knock him from the ladder. But Sage drove even the thought of such a defeat from his mind, pushing himself to the purpose. *I will rise. I will climb another rung, and then another; and nothing will hold me back.*

He reached up and pulled. Hand over hand. Had he been in his own body, his muscles would have strained and his joints would have popped as he strove to lift his own weight and the shadow's. But this was another realm, and if there was any place in creation where purity ought to count, this must be it.

He reached and climbed, reached and climbed. The light above him was brighter than ever. *I am these hands. I am these arms. I will make it.*

Beneath him the rage intensified beyond anything Sage could have imagined. How could an entity contain such anger and not burst apart? Another furious tug at his ankles, the spirit was hanging from Sage's legs, swinging itself back and forth like a pendulum, trying to tear them both loose from the tether.

I am these arms. I am these hands. I will not fall. He reached, pulled, reached, pulled, reached again—

And his hand disappeared into light.

He felt around for the next rung. And found nothing.

Desperate, he held fast to the topmost rung and searched with his hand in a circle. There must be something to grasp. The spirit's weight seemed to increase with every swing of its mass. Then his hand gripping the ladder began to unclench. He struggled to pour force into his fingers, but the strain was too much. From below, he heard the cruel bark of the shadow's laugh.

Then a cool strong grip clenched Sage's searching hand.

He rose smoothly and easily into the light. The weight on his ankles disappeared.

A tall, glowing figure in long robes stood upon the floor of the Firmament, its faceless head tilted down at him in puzzlement. ❖ ❖ **1**, *you're rather heavy for a first-timer.*

Sage breathed in relief and nodded at the tallspirit. That's because I'm not alone. The shadow had not yet come out of the mist to this place of light. Sage pointed downward.

Oh, said the spirit. It waved a hand and a part of the floor became transparent. Through the gap, Sage could see his tether, descending to the inner universe beneath. And on that tether, crawling quickly down, was a shape he recognized.

The tall spirit made a circular motion with one finger and immediately the ladder that Sage had so arduously climbed began to roll up, far faster than the shadow could descend it. In a moment, the shadow was pulled onto the floor of the Firmament.

The tall spirit looked from Sage to the shadow and back again. *Two spirits on one tether?*

I can explain everything. The shadow lifted itself majestically to its full height, serene and kingly. Where once, Sage had seen the shadow as a naked, multi-faced humanoid, now, like the other spirit, it cast itself in long, white robes, its head a hairless, faceless, flesh-toned ovoid.

You can try, said another voice.

Sage turned.

Another spirit approached, taller than the one that had helped him, but also faceless and wreathed in glowing robes. *I am Tamara, ✚✚63✧✧ Assistant—*

The shadow shucked its affectation and bolted.

Sage sprang after it, and executed a flying tackle that brought the spirit down with a satisfying *thump.*

The tall spirit turned. *Nice tackle ✧✧1. Now, you were saying ✚✚63✧✧.*

I am Assistant Supervisor of Visitations for this galaxy, the spirit that was Tamara said. *This is ▲▼178♦✿, who has committed more crimes than I have time to list.*

· Ω ·

Sage felt new.

He was at home in his new skin as spirit ✧✧1. Tamara had taken the time to point out that in his spirit form he could shed the image of his splinter body and appear as whatever he wished but he'd only ever lived one life so he had decided he would look like Sage Rojan for as long as he intended to return to his body.

He entered a domed amphitheater. It was a dish-like depression akin to a perfectly symmetrical valley. Its immensity made the Cos-Ob look like a pimple.

Around him, through a restless expanse of drifting vapors, walls rose, row on row, to fuse seamlessly with a hemispherical ceiling or sky. Light infused the mist, seeping up from beneath him, emanating from the walls, interlacing a tapestry of halos above with a dazzling, sun-like source directly overhead. He knew unquestioningly that the mists around him were spirits like himself, some small and newborn, as he was, others larger and as old as the universe. The blinding light streaming in the center of the dome was something omnipresent, perhaps even the Artisan itself.

A heraldic voice reverberated within Sage's skull. *Your Highest Artisan, Members of the Archangel Empyrean Assembly. This special Tribunal has been summoned to determine a course of action in regard to an improper visitation by one Trillionist ▲▼ designation ▲▼178✦✿.*

The shadow, in the form of a glowing ovoid, materialized in the paddock area of the dome.

Charges are as follows: improper clearing process; failure to use the tether recorder; unauthorized appropriation of spiritual knowledge; interference in the speed of technological advancement of a sentient species; attempted construction of an unnecessary and unbalancing celestial body.

With that comment, the illumination of the dome intensified to dazzling brilliance. On the ceiling and all of the curved walls inside of the spherical dome, like a three-dimensional moving picture augmented with sensory detail, streamed thoughts and emotions from hundreds, thousands, and millions of simultaneous points of view. Sage's life. Or, more correctly, the shadow's visitation, flashed in a rapid series of events for all to perceive.

Done, the illumination dimmed to its previous level.

The heraldic voice echoed within Sage's mind again. *The events are factual, and not under debate. The question to be resolved is: were the laws of the Empyrean breached? The respondent may speak in its defense.*

Sage listened with relief. There was no question as to the shadow's guilt.

The shadow drew itself in a circle, the center of attention. *The function of a spirit,* it said in a reverberating, oratorical voice, *through millions of visitations, is to grow in knowledge and wisdom.*

Listening silence greeted its words. Surely the spirits would not believe anything the shadow had to say, however eloquent.

My aim, it continued, *was to exalt myself in order to participate in the ongoing creation of the ever-expanding universe. These actions, displayed before you here, are evidence of my achievement of those Empyrean goals. My intent was to display talent, not to destroy previous works of art. As for any destruction caused — as minimal as it may be — I apologize.*

Murmurs of approval greeted these words.

In the millions of lives I have lived over a trillion years, the loss of one solar system is a trifle in comparison to the development of a new, primary creative force. I have displayed initiative, persistence, intelligence, ability, planning, and creativity, the shadow declared. *I have improved sentient lives on the planet Tidon through accelerating their technological revolution. Yes, I miscalculated a crucial component of the project, but is it not the Empyrean way to learn by experiencing?* The shadow's voice rose at the end, carrying clearly to even the farthest reaches of the dome.

Sage listened with growing amazement at the quiet attention of both the spirits and the great presence overhead. Was it possible the shadow's rationalization would be taken seriously?

If there were any Empyrean laws broken through my actions, they would lie in my use of the Library of Spiritual Knowledge. But that too was in pursuit of the Artisan's goals!

Silence pulsed through the tribunal. The mist that was the bodiless accumulation of the spirits undulated with eternal patience. But Sage was anything but patient. He could sense engagement, the minds of the spirits and the Artisan weighing the evidence. How would the Tribunal rule?

The answer came forward as a conception; a voiceless, engulfing rumble which quaked from and through every piece of the dome. *This lowly spirit* ▲▼178♦✿*'s apology is accepted. It may have been overzealous, but its reasoning reaches beyond petty rule, to conceive the larger aims of the universe—*

No!

The explosion of Sage's outrage catapulted him from the sea of spirits.

What is this disturbance? the herald cried.

Impertinence! A shock of voices cried from above and below. *Interrupting the Artisan!*

Then, Tamara rose from the multitude. *Listen!* She spread her intent far and wide. *This is the spirit who was wronged by* ▲▼178♦✿*'s actions.*

A newborn spirit? With the gall to come here before the Artisan? the herald scoffed.

Its nomenclature is ❖❖1, Tamara corrected. *This spirit was the rightful owner of the visitation to the human Sage. It was his visitation that* ▲▼178♦✿ *misappropriated. He has a right to be heard at this Tribunal!*

He has done nothing to earn rights. ▲▼178♦✿ sneered. Sage's vision blazed hard into ▲▼178♦✿.

And the people of Tidon? More than two hundred million of them? Do they also have no rights? Sage challenged. He appealed to the pulsing beam above. *Most High Artisan. You have seen the facts. You have heard one interpretation only. In the name of justice, listen to a differing view.*

The Artisan's vast rumble permeated the tribunal, silencing all competing thought. *What are the rights of millions of bacteria in the construction of a monument of learning?*

Hear him! Tamara cried. *Rule against him if you must, but hear his words!*

It's no use, Tamara, Sage said. ▲▼178♦✿*'s right. Who am I? A first-time spirit. I know nothing of this place and its laws.*

Sage! Tamara implored, her thoughts were close, intimate, only for him. *You can't give up now! Not after all this. Think of your father — all the work he has done. Think of your mother. All those people. They're depending on you.*

Tamara was right. He had no right to give up. He had allowed his planet to fall under a danger of his own making. If he ever wished to atone for his actions he could never stop fighting to save it.

Artisan — Sage lifted his head and appealed to the omnipotent being above him, *please I beg you, spare the people of Tidon. Do what you will with the spirit that has broken your law but spare the innocent lives. They, like the spirits that reside here, are sentient creatures. They have loves and hopes and dreams —*

Sentimental rubbish, ▲▼178♦✿ scorned, and to Sage's growing dismay, there was a resonance of agreement around them.

When they die, their lives have merely to return here. The deep voice echoed. *All will start again.*

But the lives they had will be gone!

It is of no consequence. The Inner Universe will move forward without them. The Artisan seemed puzzled by Sage's persistence. Sage felt its scrutiny.

Tell me! What good is wisdom if it hath no feeling?

The question appeared to catch the amphitheater off guard. Even the Artisan paused.

Feeling has no place amidst progress! ▲▼178♦✿ snapped, angry that it had lost control of its audience.

Do you seek to build a monument of learning or do you close your doors to differing views?

How could you, as new and inexperienced as you are, teach us anything? ▲▼178♦✿ sneered.

Silence! The Artisan boomed. The light around Sage intensified. *Speak,* it rumbled.

Sage took a breath. *There are no inconsequentials. Even a single atom, though small, can affect the world around it. Those atoms and their orbiting electrons, if collapsed, by removing the space between them, would allow an entire solar system to fit into an expanse the size of a sugar cube.*

Sage addressed the entire Tribunal. *Every being, large, small, brilliant, or foolish, depends on the contribution of all others. Therefore, where is the wisdom if intelligence is not used in the service of compassion?*

Stillness fell on the assemblage.

Thunder roared as if a giant foot had stomped and shaken every iota of the Empyrean and Firmament. Then, silence filled the amphitheater. The brilliance that was the Artisan glowed steadily overhead.

Then the booming rumble of the Artisan's voice filled the space. *My trillionist,* ▲▼178♦✿, *has made errors; yet, it can learn and grow from this experience.*

Sage's heart sank.

Young spirit, you have great courage to speak. Even an Artisan can learn from a lowly spirit.

What?

I have come to my ruling.

Sage wished he could reach out a hand and grip Tamara's palm.

The people of Tidon will have their solar system returned to them. I will stretch out my hand and remove their threat. ▲▼178♦✿ — *one day — you might make a fine assistant — perhaps even junior Artisan. But from this visitation you will learn patience, forethought, and humility. For one recycle of the Recycliun Inner Universe — fifteen billion years — you will make visitations only to the non-sentient species, beginning with the lowliest, that you may learn their value in the Artisan's plan.*

With a bellow, ▲▼178♦✿ exploded into a rain of black shards, compressed, then popped into nothing.

I have spoken! The Artisan's booming thought erased all sensation, all movement.

Chapter 27

SAGE GASPED. His lungs balked, an immense weight crushing his chest—

Then there was relief. He gulped air, panting to refill them with oxygen.

The cloth of his bed felt real against his face. He was back on Tidon, inside Cos-Ob, lying on his cot, face-planted into the mattress. He pushed himself to his knees. The room was dim, hot. He was alive. Whole and real.

He reached back inside himself... but could not touch the mosaic.

Tamara lay motionless next to him. For a moment his racing heart skipped a beat— she looked so pale, crumpled on the bed. Was she even—

He pressed his ear to her chest. No heartbeat. She was warm, but no exhalation tickled his cheek.

Artisan, no!

He lifted her chin, pressed his palm to her forehead, pinched her nose and put his mouth to hers. He sent his breaths into her. Listened. For long seconds. Nothing.

Tamara! Perhaps her spirit had stayed in the Firmament and not come back down its tether?

He filled his own lungs to capacity before forcing air harder and deeper into her lungs.

Her chest rose. Air escaped her mouth. Her eyes opened. Blank.

Sage bit his lip, staring into her dark irises.

Then with a blink, she focused and smiled faintly at him.

Joy flooded Sage.

"Trying to kiss me while I was away? I saw you from above," she whispered. "Glad no one else was here. They might think it morbid, your kissing a corpse."

He bent over her, into a deep, truly passionate kiss. Tamara reached her arms around his body and kissed him back.

They moved apart, holding each other with their eyes, and Sage breathed. "I was pretty sure our bodies would be dead when we finally came back down. It seemed we were in the Empyrean a long time."

"Not in a Tidonese measurement," she said answering his query. "Time is a feature created solely for this inner universe, for Recycliun. And although going up and down the tether seemed lengthy, it was mere moments here."

"I imagined coming back to a Tidon that was normal, not still hot and burning." He faltered. "Perhaps the Artisan..."

Her head moved slightly in the negative. "Patience, my sweet Sage."

"Sliding down the tether," said Sage, "I fantasized that Tidon had grown colder." He smiled, remembering a scene from behind one of the white doors; of a winter wonderland filled with skiing, hockey, and a game played on ice where very large stones were smashed against each other above a painted pattern of concentric circles. "Then I awoke here to— heat."

"Let's see." Tamara grinned at him and pulled herself to a sitting position. Then, standing slowly, she held out her hand.

Sage took it — the sweetest hand in all of Tidon — and followed her to the back of Cos-Ob. She opened the door and they walked out onto the loading dock, looking downward to BYSA at the bottom of the hill, and then far upward.

The sky was flooded with the red light of a desert dawn. A harsh streak of light poured from the sun, disappearing into one dense, black point. The dark matter was still devouring Sintosy.

"Look." Unbelieving, Sage pointed up towards the black gap in the sky.

The stream from Sintosy suddenly faltered. Tamara stilled in his arms, and they watched as the searing brilliance grew thinner and wispier until it was cut off and extinguished entirely.

"It's over," she breathed.

"Yes," Sage said, "It will be thousands upon thousands of years before Sintosy goes Supernova."

"Exactly." She nodded, "We bought some time." She laughed, rose on her toes, and kissed him again. "The next fifteen billion year cycle has to come sooner or later."

"I feel like I've learned so much; grown. But, there's so much more to know." He felt so small next to her. A thought struck him. "Tamara, you really *didn't* want to go to the Firmament or the Empyrean. Why?"

Tamara nodded guiltily. "You're right. I didn't want to take this issue to the Artisan."

"You were worried that the Artisan might rule against us?"

She shrugged. "Although it seemed a given that ▲▼178♦✿ was in the wrong, I've been around enough to know that the Empyrean has a bigger view than just one planet. And," she continued slowly, "I broke my contract. I was supposed to watch. Not intervene. I was afraid the Empyrean wouldn't understand why I disobeyed the purpose I was given."

"But they did understand in the end, right?"

Tamara smiled; her attention full on him. "Yes," she whispered, "Something you said made the difference."

"What?"

"'Do we close our doors to differing views.'"

Sage, captivated, looked intently at Tamara. "Tamara..."

She tilted her head and looked at him quizzically.

"All these years..." He searched for the words. "The shadow made me keep my distance from you; keeping me focused on its work. And all that time you were hiding your identity, watching."

She peered into his face.

"And you've always found it easier to shove me away," he said.

"Maybe that's still my plan?" she teased.

"Would you..." Suddenly, his throat dried. The words wouldn't come. "Would you... consider going out with me?"

"You mean a date?" She grinned as though enjoying his discomfiture.

He nodded awkwardly, his heart sinking. She was so far above him—

She shrugged. "I guess we could start over. It would be refreshing to park our spirit advantages for a while. Sort of begin from scratch and pretend our minds are born again, like new spirits cleansed of past memories from previous lives."

Happy but uncertain, Sage replied. "The Library. The mosaic, the white doors— they're all gone. It's just me flying solo. Feels

good. Different." He swallowed back on his fear. "Tamara —
without the shadow — I might not be as smart..."

"Hush!" She pushed him back to look into his downcast face,
chiding. "You're everything you were before. Everything!"

"But... without the shadow... I can't do all the things, all the—"

"What it did to the people of Bella Yareo — through you —
was unnatural. It was wrong."

"People will expect—"

"Forget 'people'! You've given them a lifetime-full of achievements." She shook her head. "It's time to live for you. Don't
forget, you're now the sole heir to Bristol Industries. You'll have
your hands full. Remember, Duggin Bristol never buffered the
effects of exponential growth by investing in environmental and
social programs. There were costs to what ▲▼178♦✿ brought
to this planet."

He frowned, released her and leaned against Cos-Ob's outer
wall. "That's true. The cheapskate wouldn't spend the money.
I urged him to initiate land reclamation projects, clean up the
sewage that went into the canals, put scrubbers on his smoke
stacks."

She lifted his head. "Technological advancement is only wisdom
when used in service of compassion. In service of *all* Tidonese."

Suddenly, startling them both, the quiet around them was
broken by the ring of Tamara's phone. She searched for it. "Hello,
Tamara here." She put the call on speakerphone.

"Beya, Tamara. This is Director Brantford. I tried Sage but he
didn't pick up, so you were next. Great news; the dark matter
has disappeared, as if it never existed."

"We've seen it," she replied, grinning up at Sage.

"Bella Yareo, Tidon, Sintosy, the solar system— they're all
saved! People are dancing in the streets," Brantford cried. "It's
miraculous."

"Sage did it." She held back her laugh, playfully winking
at him.

"Then I suspect the press is going to have a field day." Brantford
cleared his throat, "Hey, for what it's worth," his tone softened, "I
want to say, from me — and from everyone at BYSA, the palace,
and the government — thanks. Can you tell him that for me?"

Tears sprang into Tamara's eyes and she blinked up at Sage
as she spoke. "I'll tell him."

"And, let him know his mom's awake. As near as we can tell right now, she seems fine."

Tamara gripped Sage's hand fiercely. "He'll want to go to Porturn right away. Can you arrange for a helicopter?"

"Expect it in a few minutes, at Cos-Ob."

She disconnected the call.

Sage was already scanning his bedside table and desk for keys, wallet, and phone. "Let's go," he yelled out to her.

"She's your mother." Tamara demurred. "I'd only be in the way."

He turned and gripped her hand. "I— I want you there."

She looked at him questioningly.

"I want you with me." He knew this more deeply than he had ever known anything in his life. "I want you by my side. At Bristol Industries. With my family—"

She melted into him. "You really want that?"

"Yes! We have our whole lives—"

"Hush!" She put a finger on his lips. "I— I've already checked with the Empyrean. They said I could stay a short time—"

"Short! How short?"

She shrugged. "A hundred years. More, if needed."

He stared at her in disbelief, until she laughed. "You mean it?"

"Absolutely." She nodded, eyes shining. "Your Sage spirit — twentyish; my ✛✛**63**✣✣ spirit — billions of years older — quite the contrast. As opposite ends of the spectrum, it's no wonder we attract."

They heard and then saw a helicopter approaching the landing pad.

"You're going to have to invent an amazing story for the media," she shouted above the noise of the helicopter. "They're going to want to know how you saved the world."

"I'm not worried," said Sage. "I've got the best PR genius on Bella Yareo to help me get it right."

www.trillionist.com